THE DIVA

BY
ANNA MIONE

authorHOUSE™

1663 LIBERTY DRIVE, SUITE 200
BLOOMINGTON, INDIANA 47403
(800) 839-8640
WWW.AUTHORHOUSE.COM

First published by AuthorHouse 2/22/2006

ISBN: 1-4208-8051-9 (sc)

Printed in the United States of America
Bloomington, Indiana

This book is printed on acid-free paper.

Special thanks to the Metropolitan Opera House archives division for the cover picture.

FOREWORD

The earliest opera house in New York was the Park Theater on Park Row in lower Manahattan, followed by the Academy of Music on fourteenth street and Irving Place.

In 1883, the first Metropolitan Opera house on Broadway and thirty ninth street was built. It was inadequate. Seven hundred seats had obstructed views. There was room on stage for one production only, therefore when it was used for a performance or dress rehearsal in the afternoon, the evening sets sat on seventh avenue and 39th street outside the building in all kinds of weather, protected only by a thin canvas. This became a quarter of a million dollars a year expenditure, which covered transportation of the sets, as well as constant repairs of the sets. Yet, eighty three years later, when the opera company quit the old theater, there were many who protested vehemently.

On May 14th 1959, President Eisenhower turned the first spade of earth in a ground breaking ceremony initiating the building of Lincoln Center, the new home of the Metropolitan Opera Company and the New York Philharmonic.

The opera house had it's own quarters, but with the condemnation of Carnegie Hall the Philharmonic had no home of its own. They were looking for abandoned theaters and arenas used for prize fighting to give concerts. Ultimately, Carnegie Hall was saved from demolition, and refurbished as one of the great concert halls in the city. Since the

Philharmonic had no home, the first theater built was for the New York Philharmonic, now known as Avery Fisher hall.

With the Kennedys in the White house, the "cultural explosion" began a new and exciting period to house the arts in New York City.

Chapter One

1926 The Hidden Agenda

Gemma Liguori, a young woman blessed with looks, talent and success, had a love she adored and a devoted set of parents. Yet there was a desperation she exuded as she ran across the giant piazza in front of the opera house.

The Catholic church provided her with the guidelines for entry into heaven after death, and here she was, wishing for death, and even more frightened of God's wrath if she took her own life. She called out to Him to whisk her away like the wind which ripped objects from people, who ran under the galleria around the piazza. Umbrellas, having been torn from the secure grip of their owners, created an eerie scene in flight as they were swept upwards, then, caught in a downwind, came crashing down. Like the wailing sound of a bagpipe the wind howled like frightening screams.

Never had Gemma wished for eternity as she did that March day, and as she clung to her wrap-around coat, she shut her eyes and walked with a fierce determination into the funnel of the brutal wind. As she approached the buildings, voices came flying through the air in a wireless energy so that she could hear the hysteria of the Milanese running into the stores for refuge. Almost as a frightful dare, she asked God to take her now. But, He didn't seem to answer her plea; instead a beam of sunlight shone before her, an oasis in the storm, and she stopped and looked up visoring her eyes from the blinding sun. She

1

shook as the shroud of light touched her, creating a sense of peace in the midst of the furious wind.

Every eye in the surrounding shops stared at this incredible young woman, mesmerized by the calm surrounding her in the midst of nature's frenzy. Suddenly she dashed into the coffee shop. Her tousled blonde hair was unkempt and several hairs clung to her lips. Two people got up from the small table to give her a seat. She nodded gratefully and sank into the seat. The waiter asked her if she wanted café espresso or cappuccino, and she nodded, so he brought her both.

A strong hand touched her shoulder, and she looked up into the eyes of Santo Averso, mayor of Mugenta.

"Signorina Liguori, are you alright?" he asked in a half-whisper.

"Yes," she said. "Now I am."

He had known her every move for months now. Six months ago, he attended a piano concert and fell in love with her.

"Let's go to my restaurant just a few doors down from here. Are you up to it?" She sipped the cappucino and realized that everyone was staring at her. Italian people stare openly. It was an art form in Italy, never casual, but deliberate.

Santo put his arm around her and held her close to his large frame. He smelled rich--French cologne, had elegant clothes and was a handsome imposing figure of a man. He looked like royalty. In fact, Santo Averso was a Count, from the lineage of his father, Basilio Giacomo Averso. Santo dated many women in his own class but could not get close to anyone because his mother found fault with every woman he brought to her. Her comments were always the same. *The woman was an opportunist looking for security, or the Countess would have heart palpitations and asked him to wait until she died, for death was imminent.* Santo revered his mother and wouldn't defy her for fear that it would kill her. Her emotional blackmail served her well. Santo was now fifty years old, facing old age, and solitude. He cried himself to sleep many nights wanting a wife and a family. Even his father confessor told him that he had to honor his mother's wishes.

He had, until he saw Gemma Liguori at a concert. Unlike other pianists, she'd come forward to the edge of the stage and shared anecdotes about the composer's life. Years before this approach would be acceptable to serious music lovers, Gemma had tried it. Because of her beauty and charm, she'd gotten away with it. Gemma's informal "chats" had been suggested by an admirer, Alberto Ciecco who was the music critic of the newspaper.

Alberto had met Gemma at a reception after one of her performances, and he'd suggested that she change her format on the concert stage. He'd appeared at every concert and wooed her. Because he was handsome, capricious and sensuous, Gemma succumbed to his charms. She'd had a brief affair with him, and when Maurizio suspected another love interest, she'd broken it off after a few weeks. However, he continued to write about her in his column.

Santo brought her to his private dining room in the back of the restaurant. She felt shabby in the posh environment.

"You are a brave young lady," he said as he helped her off with her coat; his hand lingering on her body and the waiter took their coats away.

"You seem distressed," he said, and she laughed sardonically.

"That's because I am. How did you see me? Were you in the coffee shop?" The waiter brought a bottle of the best frascati white wine and hot antipasto.

"Half of Milano saw you on that piazza. We also saw the beam of sunlight guiding you, and no wind blew on that lit path. It was miraculous, Gemma. I was in my restaurant waiting for you to come to this side of the piazza. Your bus stop is on this side of the piazza, isn't it?" Her back stiffened up and she gave him a sidelong glare. "You know where my bus stop is? Count, were you waiting for me?"

"Honestly? Yes." His blue gray eyes stared into hers, and she squirmed away. She could hear his breath quicken.

The waiter brought a hot minestra soup with sliced chicken in it. Gemma wasn't hungry, but the aroma of the hot soup whetted her appetite.

"Thank you. It smells great." She sipped her soup as he stared. "Count Averso, you're staring. I look awful, don't I?" she asked as she pulled her long tresses away from her face. He took her hand and kissed it. "You are so beautiful, that I can't get enough of you."

A man of power, he expected she'd succumb to him. She was frozen, not sure what to do. He grew closer, and his tongue licked her ear as he murmured terms of endearment. His hot hand rested on her

3

knee, and she gasped as his hand crept up her leg. She pushed him away and eased out of the circular seat, towards the coat room, then grabbed her coat and ran out.

He ran after her and intercepted her flight into the storm. She almost made it out the door but he was fast, and he pulled her back and into the cloak room, dismissed the attendant, and held her firmly.

"Gemma, I did not mean to offend you. I'm in love with you. I want you. Marry me! I can give you everything you need. Look at me!" She glared at him and wasn't afraid any more.

"I'm involved with another man. You know that. You know too much about me and it bothers me. You live in Mugenta. Why are you in Milano?"

"Gemma, I own this restaurant. Please, let's go back to the private dining room. I swear I won't touch you. We must talk." He offered his hand, and after seeing him back off, she put her hand in his. He realized at that point that she could not be pursued the same way he had pursued other women. This woman was different. Her fiancee, Maurizio Brescia was out of town. Time was of the essence. Santo's strategy depended on getting rid of Maurizio.

They went back, and this time he asked her if he could help her with her coat. She laughed. Well, that was a good sign, he thought. At least she wasn't distancing herself.

"This time, don't touch my body the way you did. You will never do that again, do you understand?" Nothing subtle about her. He smiled to himself. "I understand," he said as he helped her off with her coat. His exaggerated moves to take extreme precaution of not touching her amused her. She laughed. "You're used to getting your way with women, aren't you?"

"Yes," he said softly. "I apologize again."

"You don't have to apologize. When I want a man, I let him know." He was stunned. Now he was even more excited over her, but he had to tread carefully.

"Gemma, I have a box at La Scala. There's a marvelous soprano from Sweden. I want to take you. Will you come?" She arched her eyebrows.

"What's the opera?"

"Traviata. Do you like Verdi?" He already knew that she would. He knew all of her likes and dislikes.

"Yes, very much so, but not his Traviata. His later operas were better written, but I'll come." He was impressed with her critique, though he didn't agree.

"Let me take you home. My limo's on the side street. I'm going home to Mugenta, and you will not be taking me out of my way." She agreed, and people stared at the older man walking with the beautiful young woman; they arched their eyebrows in the knowing looks of men who envied the Count's new conquest.

As the temperature dropped rapidly, Gemma grew chilled, and she shivered. He asked her if she would sit closer to him, but she declined.

They were caught in traffic, and to the right was an elegant fur shop. Santo pointed out that his mother bought all her furs there. Gemma looked at the shop then turned away disinterested.

"Do you own a fur coat, Gemma? This cold weather cuts right through the woolen coat." He was trying to hear her thoughts on the subject.

"I'm a concert pianist, Count Averso. I have a very elegant wardrobe."

"I'm sorry, I meant no offense." He looked out the window. The traffic was moving again. He found himself annoyed that every other remark ended up by an apology from him. How could someone from her station in life rattle him so? She was not going to be an easy conquest.

Gemma spoke to Davide the chauffeur and told him to go two more blocks then make a right on to her street. She told him to stop the limo in front of her building, and Santo Averso got out of the car, helped Gemma out, and walked her to the vestibule. The wind had abated for a short while, and she took her key out of her bag and opened the inside door to the building.

"I'll call you. The opera is at 8:00. Would you like to have dinner first?"

"I'll let you know," she said. She stood on her toes and kissed him on either side of his face as Italians do, and he gasped at the impromptu sign of warmth from her, and he cautiously and gently caressed her face.

"Beautiful Gemma, I'll call you."

"You're a good person, Count Averso. I'm looking forward to the opera. Thank you for dropping me off." She ran upstairs, her heart beating like a drum. Jenny Liguori opened it and wanted to know how she got to get a ride home from the Mayor of Mugenta. Gemma told her mother that he was interested in her.

"Good, a sign from God," Jenny said. "So what did the doctor say?"

"The baby should be here in October."

"When Maurizio gets back, tell him. Don't be a fool. He's depressed, and you're pregnant. He's got to know. I don't care a fig about his damned depression."

Jenny poured herself a cup of demi tasse coffee and one for her daughter. Gemma declined, saying that she had had coffee a little while ago and recalled Dr. Gambone's words that wine and coffee would not be permitted if she wanted a healthy baby. Gemma's attention from then on was to watch her intake of food and beverages and think only of her child when she ate and drank.

Gemma told her mother that the Count had asked her to go to the opera with her. Jenny was pleased, for if Maurizio reneged on his responsibility, Santo Averso might step in and legitimize the child by marrying Gemma. A baby born out of wedlock would be a marked child. The fact that Santo was old enough to be her father didn't matter at all to Jenny.

Chapter Two
THE DATE

The next day, just before Gemma's piano student was to arrive at 2:00, the doorbell rang and Gemma's father opened the door, and saw two men with garment bags in the hallway. They said they had a delivery for Signorina Liguori. Luigi let them in.

Luigi asked, "What is this?"

"Fur coats, for her to choose, compliments of Count Santo Averso."

Luigi told them to wait outside the door as he stormed into the apartment. Gemma came into the kitchen and Luigi spoke.

"There are two men carrying fur coats out there, and I was told you are to make a choice. What did you have to do for it?"

Gemma grew pale, "nothing, Poppa, I'm speechless." Jenny Liguori overheard them talking, "what happened?" she asked, thimble in hand and her sewing needle poised midair.

"Ask your daughter why is Count Averso rewarding her, is he the highest bidder?" he croaked.

"How about only bidder," Jenny retorted angrily. "In seven months, it'll be born, and it'll have bastardo on its birth certificate. We're doomed, Luigi, no one will come to your store again, Gemma will get no offers, for what Italian man wants a woman who's second hand goods?"

Luigi grew sullen, his wife was right, and Gemma wanted to die.

"I'll dismiss the furriers. Please don't argue, I'll go away to a convent, have my child, give it up for adoption and no one need ever know."

The furriers were told that there was a mistake, and Gemma dismissed them, "but, signorina," one gentleman said, "Count Averso gave us specific instructions to show you the furs, and ….." Gemma was firm. Already they got the drift of the situation, and they admired the young woman who could not be bought. Working men disliked the ruling class, and especially when an old Count was trying to get a beautiful young woman to compromise herself for the luxury of his largesse.

As she walked back into the apartment, she heard the gut wrenching sobs of her father who had collapsed in his bed sobbing. Gemma kneeled by his bedside and held his hand, "perdonami, poppa," (forgive me father.) His hand was inert, he could not respond to his daughter's pleas.

Finally, Luigi fell asleep, and Gemma covered him with the small blanket at the foot of the bed. She washed her face and came into the kitchen. Jenny was hand stitching the hems on the grempiulini (school smocks) of her neighbor Carla's twin sons. She did not look up.

"Momma, I have to leave. I'm killing my father."

Jenny put her sewing down deliberately and looked at her daughter directly.

"You solve nothing by leaving, can't you see that Count Averso has been sent to you by God? Sleep with him, tell him you're pregnant, he'll marry you. Act quickly."

Gemma was shocked. She hadn't thought of consequences when Maurizio had made love to her right before the La Scala audition, so sure that he was going to be hired, and they would marry right away. That night no contraceptives were used, and Gemma didn't care if she conceived. It had been foolish to precipitate a favorable outcome. Yet, the audition had gone well, and Maurizio was sure that they'd offer him a contract. When he got notification that someone else was hired, he fell into a state of inertia, and couldn't function.

Gemma was devastated, and in a week, she had received a call from Anna Brescia, Maurizio's mother that Maurizio had gone to Switzerland to recuperate. Gemma checked on all the mental institutions in the environs of Milano. Maurizio wasn't registered any where, so Gemma assumed that he simply wanted to get away. When she realized that she was pregnant, she was frantic and for the first time in her life, she did not know where to turn.

* * *

That evening, Santo Averso called Gemma at 9:00 p.m. He had received a call from the fur shop. Miss Liguori had refused the offer.

The phone rang. Gemma expected his call.

"Gemma, I understand you wouldn't even look at the coats."

"Exactly," Gemma answered.

"Why?" There was an edge to his voice.

"My father assumed that I earned the fur coat."

The count was shaken by the implication, only because he did have an ulterior motive. He weakly argued, "how could an act of generosity be so misconstrued?"

"We come from different classes in society, your generosity appeared to be an act of arrogance. I must go." She hung up the phone abruptly.

All evening periodically, the phone rang, but no one picked it up. Luigi had begun to calm down after "the sleep of the dead" as he put it.

Meanwhile, Santo was half crazed with anguish. He could hardly function and he found it difficult to deal with his mother who had listened at his bedroom door when he made the call to Gemma. The drama unfolded even more so in the Averso household. The Countess was relentless in her query about the phone call. She banged on his bedroom door demanding that he let her in. Santo was weeping. All the feelings of the punishments and mind games his mother had played on him seemed to well up in his psyche and he wanted none of it. However, he couldn't bear the banging on the door. He finally opened it, and she was shocked to see her son in such a horrendous state. He had been weeping, and his face was swollen with anguish.

"I told you that you don't need a woman. This puttana you're chasing is setting you up, she wants your money, and your name, are you too stupid to see it?" She dug her crooked arthritic finger into his chest as she preached to him.

"Momma, she doesn't want my money, my gifts, nor me."

"Really? then do me a favor, try this, don't call her, let her call you."

"She won't," he said sadly, "mark my words," the countess said smugly, "when she calls you, you'll know that it's a trap, to get you to propose, and then run the hell away from her."

"My God, Momma, how can you think like that?" he demanded.

"That's how I got your father," she said smugly. Santo grimaced.

And so the Lord's Prayer was on the lips of Contessa Genoveffa on a daily basis, especially in his presence. He had been subjected to her predictable script for years. He was going to have his way, but she would throw everything at him. Santo was determined to snare Gemma, he had invested so much to that end.

He had paid off Donato D'Andrea, impressario at La Scala, to reject Brescia from the position. All of Gemma's moves were under surveillance; even the obstetrician was on his payroll. His plan to ensnare the beauty was methodical and deliberate. In fact, her pregnancy was the key to marriage, for she'd need legitimacy for her unborn child.

He fell into a fitful sleep and dreamt of running after Gemma, who was running away from him. He tossed and turned all night, and finally the dream manifested itself into a figure with a hawk nose and a giant fork and the figure prevented him from chasing her. He screamed as he saw the figure's face, because it looked like his mother. He called out Gemma's name, and woke up from a dreadful nightmare.

The next day was a difficult day for Santo Averso. Here he was a man from a titled family, related to King Vittorio Emmanuele, now dethroned to make way for the fascist regime. Yet, all of his energies were focused on the woman of his dreams. At 9:00, he called Gemma.

"Hello?" she said, and the minute she heard his voice, she hung up. Santo could not bear it any more. He called his chauffer and told his mother that he was going to meet a senator in Milano The Contessa admonished her son, "don't call on that woman." He shrugged, he wouldn't dare tell her that he had disobeyed her request. "I won't, momma, but would you take a message if the telephone rings?" Countess Averso felt in control again, and she squinted her eyes, and felt empowered. Her son was under her thumb, she controlled the money, and therefore, his life. Santo loved his creature comforts, his weekly subscription to a box in La Scala, a chauffer to drive him around, and fur lined coats for the winter.

He looked like a prince when he dressed, because she made sure that he had the best sarto in town to make his clothes. What they didn't know, was that the best sarto in town was Vittorio Brescia, Maurizio's father.

Santo went into town, met some friends for lunch at his restaurant and was deeply engaged in politics over the mushrooming political cloud of the fascist regime.

"But the trains finally run on time," his friend Enrico argued.

"And what about the highways he's building? Mussolini is putting Italy in the twentieth century, impossible under the regime of King Vittorio Emmanuele."

Santo grew pale at the mention of the King's name, and Claudio realized that he had said too much, "Oh, pardonami, Santo, I forgot that he's your cousin."

Santo grew sullen, and Enrico kicked Claudio under the table, which he responded to immediately.

He changed the subject to the opera, and how very lovely Santo's love interest was. With the mention of Gemma, Santo sighed and seemed more spirited.

"Have you scored with her?" Claudio asked, "No," answered Santo, "she's not for sale, tried getting her a fur coat,…she refused and won't take my calls."

Claudio burst out laughing, "I wasn't born yesterday, Santo, there isn't a woman born who can't be bought, discover her price, and you'll score." he retorted caustically. Santo proudly said, "this one can't."

"I'll wager you twenty thousand lire, do what I say, she'll be in your bed within two weeks, let her think she's lost you."

Santo's heart started to beat faster. Just the thought of a conquest excited him, "but how?" he asked Claudio.

"No verbal contact, write and say that she has to resolve her personal situation before you can see her again. Tell her to call you only if she needs you, and make sure you add: as a friend."

"And this is how I'm supposed to seduce this woman?" Santo was perplexed. Claudio was unrelenting, "you want her? Do what I say."

Enrico was enthralled. It made sense to him. He agreed with Claudio's strategy, and Santo truly marveled because Claudio had in effect said the same thing as his mother had said.

The men parted, and Santo went back home by limo. He was faced with a choice, one which cerebrally made sense, but emotionally was tearing him up. He had the box at La Scala on Saturday nights for the season. Gemma would enjoy the performances. Now he had to change his strategy and it was terrible for him.

Enrico and Claudio went to a bar for a cup of espresso and a pastry. Both were upper class Italians who's families had made their fortune in auto sales. Enrico was mulling over the conversations between his friends and though most of it made sense, Enrico wondered how Claudio could be so sure of the outcome of such a strategy. He asked Claudio who responded simply, "I happen to go to Maurizio's father for my custom made suits, and though men don't talk frequently about family matters, Vittorio was very perturbed over the orchestra's rejection to hire his son after an outstanding audition, he said, "my son will lose everything, his fiancee' and his career. My wife and I are devastated, where does he go from here?"

It wasn't until Gemma received Santo's note that she realized the severity of her situation. Maurizio was gone, he'd never come back, and Gemma took to bed, and didn't get up for days.

The mood in the Liguori household was bleak indeed. The only activity in the house was Carla the neighbor tearing into the house for whatever she needed. Both Luigi and Jenny welcomed her singular source of levity in their home.

Gemma refused to eat. She wanted to die, and hoped that the earth would swallow her up. She dismissed all her students, and it was then that Jenny and Luigi took a hold of the situation. Luigi had no recourse but to present a solid front with their daughter.

Jenny made the plan, and Luigi executed it. On the fourth day of the week, Thursday, Luigi told Carla not to come into their home for a few hours, and Jenny had to be pulled off the bed, and washed, and dressed and joined her parents.

"Do we put you away in an asylum?" Luigi asked. Jenny was stunned. They had a plan and she must listen to it. She was to call Count Santo Averso and ask if he still wanted to take her to the opera.

"Gemma," Luigi said with a quivering lip, hoping his daughter hadn't snapped entirely, "you have my blessings to pursue Count Santo Averso, and if you have to entice him, get him to propose to you. There is no other way here. Please, if you don't care about yourself or us, think about the baby."

Gemma seemed very sanguine to the idea. She sighed deeply almost from the pit of her soul, and smiled wanly, "I can do that," she said, "good," Luigi answered.

Luigi was shocked. It had worked, and to celebrate, he invited his wife and daughter out to dinner at a restaurant called "Il Milanese" which served only food from the chefs of Milan. But first, Gemma called the count.

He wasn't home, and when the Contessa answered, Gemma hung up. They went out to dinner, and finally after enjoying a meal, and half a bottle of wine, Gemma felt as though she could climb mountains. She went into the living room at 10: 30 p.m. and called the Count again. The phone rang several times, and Gemma was about to hang up after the fifth ring, and then Santo picked up.

"Count Averso, it is I, Gemma Liguori." He could not breathe, my God, they were right, and he couldn't talk. Gemma plodded onward, she heard nothing, perhaps she was speaking to his mother, and she grew anxious, "I'm sorry, I must have the wrong number," she said and hung up. Her face was hot, Jenny came in and gave Gemma a glass of well water which Carla had delivered to them earlier in the day. The phone rang again, this time Gemma let it ring up to four rings, finally, she picked up. It was Santo. He sounded nasal as though he had a cold.

"Gemma? I'm sorry I was working on some papers, dropped the phone, and didn't answer you, sorry," it seemed casual, "how can I help you?"

"I received your note, Count thank you."

"Not at all, do you need anything Signorina?" he asked, putting his fist to his heart which was pounding furiously.

"Only if your offer for the opera is still open, I'd like to come."

"My friends are anxious to hear this Swedish soprano. Several seats in my box have been reserved for them. I'll call you tomorrow?"

"Very well, ciao," what happened to his feelings about me? Did they get turned off like a faucet? she thought.

Gemma was shaken. She conveyed the conversation to her parents, who were surprised, as Luigi said, "and you said he was crazy about her?" and Jenny blushed, "that's what Gemma said," Gemma skulked away to the living room and slumped back into the couch. She fell asleep, and her mother covered her with a blanket.

Meanwhile, Santo was a man on a mission he called Claudio, and asked him to invite a beautiful model, tall statuesque, dressed to kill, and bring her to the opera. She was to sit next to Santo and Gemma was to sit in the back of the box by herself. This had to be staged like a major battle.

The next day when Gemma went out shopping for hot bread, Santo called. Jenny answered the call, "tell your daughter that my limo driver Davide shall call for her at 5:00 p.m. for dinner . I shall not be able to pick her up. Grazie, Signora Liguori."

Gemma got dressed in her most elegant black dress. She knew that she was going to be with Santo's friends, a posh elegant classy crowd. She had second thoughts, but the persistent plea of her father drove her to do that which was distasteful. She was compromising herself.

When Davide came to pick her up, Gemma decided to keep one shred of dignity, she declined the dinner invitation and told Davide that she would be at the box office fifteen minutes before curtain time. Davide was stunned. "Signorina, the Count shall be furious. How can I go back and tell you that you couldn't make it?" Gemma gave him a good excuse, there had been a medical moment in the household. Davide was satisfied, and Gemma delayed her toilette, and took her time to get to the theater. Jenny Lind was the rage, and Gemma really wanted to hear her. She took a cab to the theater, and got there just as the curtain was going up. Santo had not seen her slip into the box. Grateful for the last seat, she checked out how close she was to the ante room and the door to leave. Good, she would have the upper hand.

The overture began and Gemma sat back, grateful for the dark, the anonymity and the lack of contact with the Count who was flanked by two beauties, Gemma stifled a laugh, this is better than the opera she thought to herself, maybe I'll stage an intermission drama.

Truly Jenny Lind had a stupendous high range, and she was breathtaking to listen to. Gemma had to stand up in order to see the singer, but no one saw her.

Each time Santo made an attempt to look behind him, Gemma bent down as though she had dropped something. He had no idea when and if she had arrived. And so the cat and mouse game continued during the first act. He was perfectly miserable, and his body language showed it, deep sighs, distractions, fidgeting, constantly looking back, and finally Claudio saw the game Gemma was playing. He leaned forward to Santo and whispered, "e arrivata," (she's arrived). Santo sighed deeply, and relaxed. Gemma was not visible to him, and he promised himself never again to engage in these sinister plots to disarm or mortify the woman he loved. Basta! (enough!) he thought to himself.

In the final scene of the first act, Gemma slipped out of the box. She ran towards the ladies room and then to a phone. She described the scene in the box to her mother, and Jenny was perplexed. "Where is his fervor? Why didn't he save a seat for you next to him?" she asked her daughter, "to mortify me," Gemma replied, "I'm not going back, I'm taking a cab, and for heaven's sake momma, make me a plate of pasta with butter. I'm starving."

After Gemma left, Santo tore out of the box leaving everyone wondering, and he searched for Gemma, she was no where to be found. He had no idea what she was wearing, how to describe her, because he hadn't seen her at all. Claudio followed him, "What is going on?" he demanded, "you tell me. She wasn't here tonight, you pulled a stunt on me, what the hell are you thinking when you take my emotions and trample them like grapes?"

Santo was distraught. He had no recourse except to call up the Liguori household. Jenny answered in one ring. She was shocked to hear his voice. "Signora Liguori, forgive me for calling, but did Gemma come to the theater tonight? I never saw her in the box, and I'm frantic." Jenny was perplexed. However, she did not want to discourage this man, so she said, "Count, my daughter called and said she was sitting in the back of the box, and couldn't see a thing. She felt badly that you had invited her and left the back seat for her. She's on her way home, and she asked me to make her a plate of pasta with butter. She was so agitated that she hadn't had supper. So that's where we're at, Count Averso."

"Okay, would you set an extra plate? I didn't dine either." Jenny grinned widely, "of course. White wine or red wine?" she asked, "I don't care, I'll take whatever you serve."

Gemma came home, stormed into her bedroom, and changed into her father's shirt, and a skirt. She pulled the pins out of her chignon and tied her long blonde hair with a rubber band. Jenny couldn't wipe the smile off her face. Luigi was apprised of what had happened, and he sat in the living room in his chair reading the newspaper tranquilly, waiting. Whatever had happened had been for the best, the count was coming and that was wonderful.

As Gemma stormed into the kitchen barefooted, there was a knock on the door, and Jenny told Gemma to answer it. Gemma pulled open the door, and was shocked to see the Count standing there.

"Well, aren't you going to ask me in?" he asked,

"Is this a joke? Weren't you at the opera house?" she asked,

"Weren't you?" she retorted, "come in, I don't know what happened, but I'm glad you're here. are you hungry?" he slipped his overcoat off and Gemma took it to her bedroom, as Santo walked into the living room to greet the Liguoris. Luigi poured him a glass of wine and they sat down opposite each other and talked. Gemma was thrilled. Jenny ran into the kitchen and put the pasta into the boiling pot. She had farm whipped butter, and fresh parsley and basil from her garden on the window sill.

The conversation was casual at first, and then Santo cut right in to his intentions. In a few words, he had won over Gemma's parents. "Signor Liguori I'm in love with your daughter, and I want her to be my wife, that is if she'll have me, I'd like your permission and your blessing." Luigi stood up and shook hands with Santo, then they embraced and kissed each other on either side of their faces, as was the custom. Gemma over heard it as did Jenny, she strolled in barefooted, pushed her straggly hair away from her face and was relieved. Santo looked at her with the adoration he'd have towards a saint, "Gemma, will you marry me?" she smiled and said, "Santo, maybe." Luigi paled. How could she continue to play her games? Was she crazy? He glared at his daughter and told her to get him a glass of water. She obeyed, and knew that her father was angry.

They dined in the kitchen by the open window which showed the line for drying clothes outside. Santo kissed Jenny's hand and thanked her for the pasta. Jenny joined her husband in the living room. Santo prayed aloud, "Lord help us to build a life of love, hope and joy for our future baby, whom I shall love as my own, Amen." Gemma burst into tears, and Santo put his arms around her, "you know?" she cried, and he said, "yes Gemma."

Chapter Three

THE MUSICIAN COMES HOME

The Liguori family was at peace over their daughter's plight. Santo wasted no time in getting Gemma a ring. On Monday they shopped for one, and Gemma was ecstatic. He was so attentive, that a warm response to him was easy. For months she had felt like low life, and now, she was coming out of the dark corridors of uncertainty to the light of an honorable outcome. She'd be able to keep her baby.

Santo announced his engagement to Gemma to his friends. There were celebrations all around as the only bachelor in the elitist group was finally entering marriage, with one of the most talented beautiful women in Milano. Claudio insisted on being best man, and Santo agreed. However in Italy, more than one best man could officiate, so Santo chose Enrico and five other male friends to be witnesses to the wedding. Seven in all, in Italy, a lucky number. Meanwhile Contessa Genoveffa Averso divided her time between saying the rosary and cursing Gemma. Sometimes the curses and the prayers were intertwined. Santo laughed at his mother's inventiveness in reciting the litany of puttana and prayer; his frustration was that he couldn't share this laugh with anyone.

Gemma felt that the situation for her was made in heaven. However, she hadn't met the Contessa yet.

Santo took his seven friends out, and told them that there would be a wedding by the end of the month. Surprise was expressed by such a short engagement, but Santo smirked, and said, "we have no time to lose." Suddenly they simultaneously lifted their glasses of Asti Spumanti in a toast, as Claudio stood up, "here's to our Count Santo Averso, and his prowess in bed, the sly dog who said Gemma had no price, she was unattainable, instead he had scored big time by offering her marriage. Bravo Santo! Why did you avoid it all these years? Let's tell him gentlemen, you don't have to give up your comare on the side just because you're married." They laughed, clinked their glasses with his and in unison said, "Saluti!"

"When is the baby due?" Claudio asked and everyone laughed. Santo smiled slyly "in October, I think," he said. Enrico, Santo's best friend whispered, "when did you score with her?" Santo replied, "many times." Enrico persisted, "does your mother know?' and Santo's face dropped, "yes, and you know my mother well, I hope she doesn't frighten Gemma away." Enrico responded, "She's pregnant, you've got her captive, was that why you didn't take precautions?" Santo loved Enrico, though his questions were personal, there was no hidden agenda. "Precisely," Santo answered, "Gemma has not met my mother. If she had, there'd be no marriage. I don't intend to introduce her until the wedding day, and I'm going to have a friend keep her away from my bride."

"Oh my God, Santo, good luck. I hope you give your mother separate quarters in the mansion." Santo muttered, "that'll be a most hellish day for me, but if my wife is to have peace I must do that."

The waiters came and brought each an antipasto of anchovies, artichokes and roasted peppers with slices of fresh mozzarella. The food came and they ate and talked and sipped the scintillating wine.

Santo and Gemma's weekly dates increased to 3 a week, then 5 a week. He took her out to the best restaurants every night and once a week even invited her parents along. When Jenny inquired about the Contessa Averso, Santo gave an excuse that she never went out during the week. He had to delay their meeting until the wedding date. His level of anxiety grew every time the Liguoris spoke about meeting the Contessa.

The Liguoris discussed the mystery mother's inaccessability, and Luigi Liguori smelled a rat. "He has no mother, he's making it up," he said one day after breakfast. Each day, he'd start the day with another conjecture about the countess. "She's mad and he locks her in the cantina when he leaves the house, maybe he leaves her bread and water in a pan."

One morning, he added, "she's worried that she'll have to share her money with another woman."

One evening after dinner at 9:00, Maurizio called. Gemma was shaking. "Oh my God!" Gemma cried. He had just come back from Switzerland and was coming over. Santo was at the house, and Gemma asked him to leave. Intuitively he knew who it was. Gemma seemed so excited yet agitated that it was time to step out of the equation. In a half an hour, Maurizio bounded up the stairs and knocked. From the rapid rhythm of the knock, Gemma knew that Maurizio was in a good mood. He walked in, the Liguoris greeted him coldly, and then he held Gemma in his arms, murmuring how much he loved her.

They went to a hotel in town and took a room. Pent up emotions, hurt feelings, fear, beginnings and endings in each of them drowned in the unity of their bodies in the act of love. She wondered what could have elevated Maurizio's usual somber mood? He seemed so happy.

Excitedly he explained that he had met a Sicilian young man who had a run in with Mussolini's Blackshirts in Naples. After a skirmish, they'd been killed. Salvatore Leone had escaped to Switzerland and was anxious to go to America where his uncle Charlie Cascio lived. An apartment would be waiting for him as well as a job in a restaurant. Maurizio's only hope was New York, and the Metropolitan Opera House. As he talked, she interrupted him to ask simply, "when do we marry? When do we begin to have a family? I am 28 years old."

He jumped out of bed outraged and said, "we had an agreement. We marry when I am successfully employed by an operatic orchestra. I shall send for you. I'm leaving within the month."

Gemma had hoped for a more favorable outcome, but Maurizio was self-engrossed, certainly he wouldn't welcome news like her pregnancy at all. He'd walk out on her in disgust. She had to save her pride. Even if Santo Averso was not in the equation, she'd walk out.

"We used to want the same thing." she commented sadly.

"Give me time. My dreams and hopes will be realized in America. Salvatore's uncle has connections. As soon as I get established, I'll send for you." She slipped out of the bed, dressed in a hurry, and he was stunned at her reaction..

"Really? I have other plans." She walked out on Maurizio sobbing as she ran home. She sobbed as she ran down the street to her home.

Maurizio called every night, but Gemma was no longer available. He left for Naples, joined Salvatore Leone, then left for America.

Gemma was waiting for Maurizio to break down their door and pursue her, but he didn't. After he left for America, she married Santo in a ceremony in Mugenta, surrounded by people of the upper class. It was an auspicious event, with a constant flow of Asti Spumanti and other prestigious expensive wines. The food was magnificent, and the reception was held in the sala of the mansion which held at least two hundred people, none of whom were friends of Gemma's. Gemma invited none of her friends. She wanted to keep her former alliance secret to protect her honor as well as her husband's.

Gemma vowed that she would be a good wife to the Count. After all, he had saved her reputation, and her child would not have bastard written on its birth certificate.

The Liguoris were shocked at the appearance of Contessa Averso. She had beady eyes and a hook nose, which were frightening to anyone who saw her for the first time. She was introduced the day of the wedding. Her response to meeting them was to glare at them and give a small nod of acknowledgement, then she walked away.

Luigi whispered to his wife, "I told you she was mad. He should've kept her hidden in the cantina."

"I hope she doesn't live with them, dear God, how frightening that has to be."

"Now I know why the Count never married. By the way, I'm paying Vittorio Brescia a visit tomorrow before this hits the newspapers."

"Why?" Jenny asked deeply concerned.

"For two months they kept Gemma hanging without word about their son. I want to rub it in his face that Gemma has married into a lineage of royalty, can't wait for that satisfaction."

Contessa muttered "puttana" as they left the chapel. When the Liguori's heard it their eyes widened.

* * *

After the wedding, Jenny and Luigi went home, and Luigi sat down and wrote a speech which he'd make to Vittorio Brescia in his store, to his face. Jenny didn't approve, but he was determined.

Vittorio Brescia opened his tailor shop on Monday and as he perused his daily calendar of jobs, the door bell rang. It wasn't store hours, so he ignored it, but then he came out of the back and recognized Luigi Liguori. The level of stress went up as Vittorio walked slowly to the door, to unlock it.

They greeted each other perfunctorily and Vittorio offered Luigi a seat as well as a cup of espresso coffee which he had just made. They sat in the back, and Luigi revealed what had happened the day before, in great detail. Vittorio was stunned, "my God," he said, "Signor Liguori, congratulations are in order, but I'm contrite over the turn of events. Our children had an agreement, what happened to it? Why couldn't she wait? I'm devastated."

"Wait? For how long, 8 years, 20 years? How long?" Luigi sipped the coffee, and the sincerity of Vittorio's regrets melted his antagonism towards the Brescias.

Vittorio wept, "my only son has chosen a most difficult career. He was outstanding in the audition, Gemma heard it too, from the hallway. They came home so ecstatic that day, and they went out to celebrate, all day long like two carefree children. A few days later, Maurizio got a letter of rejection. He collapsed in bed, and medication was the only thing that got him up. He didn't want to see Gemma, not in that state. We respected his wishes, then the doctor suggested Switzerland. I closed my shop and accompanied him there, so afraid in his condition to get there by himself. I'm sorry we didn't get in touch, but we too were embarrassed, Signor Liguori, yes I feel for you, for Gemma, and for our loss of your beautiful, beloved daughter whom we loved as our own. I hope that she didn't marry in haste only to regret it for the rest of her life. For Maurizio there was always only one woman, and that was Gemma." By the time Vittorio got through, Luigi was crying too. They hugged and kissed many times, and promised that they would keep in touch, but of course it was over.

On September 3rd, Anna Averso was born, prematurely. Santo was the happiest of men as he held his eight pound baby girl in his arms.

Anna was dark like her father, Maurizio. She had his large black eyes, long lashes and curly hair.

The old Contessa continued her barrage of puttana, and Gemma had two choices: one to kill her, or secondly, to ignore her. She chose the latter. She wanted to retaliate, but Santo did not deserve to hear contention.

* * *

The political climate in Italy was volatile. Mussolini declared war on helpless nations just to flex his muscles. Towards the north, the Nazi machine grew, and between Mussolini and Hitler, a world war of such epic proportions would erupt to destroy human life and destroy nations.

Santo owned a large food export company, and his Italian manager Gino Derisi headed the New York office. Santo had only to finish his business, sell off the restaurants he owned, take the assets, and transfer them to the American bank through Derisi. He belonged to the Socialist Democratic Party and the status quo was deteriorating rapidly. He didn't share this plan with his wife, but at some point, they'd have to leave Italy for good.

* * *

Santo hired a professional baby nurse for his daughter, Anna, and Gemma was free to be at his disposal for whatever diplomatic and social interaction she had to perform. She read the paper daily, cut out political articles, and made a scrapbook for her husband. He studied the articles, and it was clear that soon fascism would be the singular political voice in Italy.

One day, as Luigi Liguori went to his tailor shop, a riot developed across the street in one of his friend's shops. His friend Marco belonged to the Socialist Party, and because Marco had given out leaflets at the piazza in Milano, he had been photographed by the black shirts, and was targeted to be the object of elimination.

In Marco's shop, a fire bomb exploded, sending a human fireball into the cobblestone street. Luigi Liguori ran out of his shop with a coat to put out the fire. As he did, two black shirts appeared and beat Luigi

Liguori bloody. His beaten body remained in the middle of the road as the authorities were called to take him away. When the blackshirts realized that Luigi was not dead, they put him in a sack, drove away to the outskirts, and buried him alive.

That evening, Luigi Liguori did not come home. Jenny called her daughter in Mugenta. Santo utilized his underground network to find out what had happened to his father-in-law. They found him in a sack in a freshly and poorly dug grave. His face was unrecognizable. Jenny wanted to have her husband cremated so that she could have his ashes. Santo obliged his mother in law's request.

* * *

After the death of her father, Gemma closed down her mother's apartment and had her move into her own quarters in the villa.

Gemma named her daughter after Maurizio's mother, Anna Brescia. It was the Italian custom to name the first child after the father's side of the family. Santo was upset over her choice of name for the baby, but he said nothing. He wanted Gemma to look up to him and to be loyal to his wishes. He had woven the web of submission in this beautiful independent woman. She wasn't even aware of it.

When he asked Gemma if she would have a child of his, her response was negative. Her rationale? Times were too perilous to bring another baby into the world. With daily incidents of growing violence against those who bucked fascism, it made sense to Santo.

Their early relationship had been fun. But now? Fantasy had turned to grim reality. His mother's daily litany of curses, Luigi's murder, and Jenny's move into the volatile household. His only solace nightly was to sleep with the woman he loved.

As little Anna evolved from crawler, runner, and a destruction machine, Santo indulged the child more and more. His energies turned towards his daughter, which was the best distraction. Anna grew up privileged, and she knew it.

Santo called her "Regina", (queen). She adored him and did what she willed to him. She combed his thinning hair to one side and got so frustrated that a long strand slipped in another direction, that she took the small sofa pillow and put it on his head. "Wear a hat, Poppa," she said with disgust as she got off his lap. The family screamed with laughter and Anna enjoyed this reaction.

She provided levity after dinner, when her mother performed on the piano. The Contessa came up from her quarters downstairs by invitation only and sat next to her son; holding his hand like any doting mother.

One evening, during Gemma's musicale, Anna got up and sang. She astounded the family with the piercing quality of her voice. Gemma accompanied her and was enthralled as was Santo. Anna had talent, and every time her child revealed another facet of her precocious musical behavior, Gemma thought of Maurizio. She thought of him every time she looked at her daughter, and it saddened her to know that Anna would never know her biological father.

* * *

After Anna's 5th birthday in Mugenta, on September 3rd, 1932, Santo conferred with his family, revealing that he had transferred his funds to New York. It was time to leave Italy.

Gemma asked what they could take with them, and he said only important papers.

She went to the basement. He had told her to pack only files and leave his law books behind. As she picked up a fallen law book, out of it slipped a note, almost yellow, and obviously old. In the dimness of the cellar's small electric bulb, she opened the note. "Count," it read, "I have notified our young musician that he didn't get the position. Too bad. He gave a great audition and is a fantastic sight reader. I thank you for the gift. You were too generous. Gratefully, D. D'Andrea."

Gemma shook uncontrollably as she reddened; a vein stood out on her forehead. Santo had paid off the impresario to block Maurizio from getting the position at La Scala. She felt as though she were going to die. After fifteen minutes, she heard footsteps. She took the note, folded it, and put it in her bra.

"Gemma?" her mother called out. Gemma showed her the note. Jenny read it twice. She could hardly believe what she was reading.

"Oh my God." Jenny exclaimed. "Poor Maurizio. I hated him so much. Oh my God, Gemma, don't do anything. Wait 'til we get to America. Too much is going on. Don't react. I beg you." Jenny held

Gemma to steady her swaying body. Her skin was clammy and she felt ill.

"I want to kill him, Momma. He took my life away. He took the only man I've ever loved and methodically tried to destroy him. My little girl doesn't even know her own father. This old bastard has wormed himself into my daughter's heart. I hope he goes to hell."

She couldn't confront him, not now on the eve of escaping Italy to America. She gave the note to her mother for safe-keeping. Jenny saved it in a place no one would ever find, the urn with her husband's ashes.

"I hope to use it against him, Momma."

"I'll save the note you'll need it some day," Jenny whispered.

"Divorce is too good for him." Gemma was hanging on to the banister. "I hate him. Some day, I'll get back at him."

"Gemma, focus on escape, okay? Maybe you'll find Maurizio in America."

"Oh, Momma," Gemma cried, "he's probably married." They went upstairs, and terminated all talk of the note and it's impact on their lives. The note changed forever the loving marriage she had enjoyed with Santo.

Chapter Four

CROSSROADS 1932

The Aversos arrived in New York's harbor on May 13, 1932. Because of The Depression, immigration from Italy that year was at its lowest quota. The government simply wouldn't take in more people with the economic floor of the country having dropped out.

The family was apprehensive about the situation, but Santo assured his wife that they were in a financially good position.

"Look Poppa, a big doll!" Anna screeched as the ship came into New York Harbor. "The statue of liberty!" Santo said in awe. "Beautiful! At least the French did one good thing."

Gino Derisi met them and accompanied them to their new home, the Ansonia Hotel.

Santo had asked Gino for a very large apartment with a separate wing for his mother. The Aversos moved into a seven room suite in one of the most exquisite architectural hotel/residences in the city.

Truly its residents were the likes of Enrico Caruso until his death, conductors, singers, and people prominent in the arts. Studios at the Ansonia provided the professional operatic singers lessons in coaching, voice, and diction.

Gemma was thrilled. She planned on the resumption of her musical career, and the Ansonia was a wonderful place to be in the early part of the 1930's.

Gino and his wife Letizia obtained basic furnishings of chairs, beds and kitchen furniture adequate for a beginning. It was a touch of the best of European villas.

They were exhausted from the trip, so Gino told Santo he'd see him in the morning, then left to go home. Many things had to be gone over, and Santo wanted information about the extent of the economic depression as well as how they could continue to do business. These were hard times, and not the America they had dreamed of.

A telephone was installed in the center of the apartment for easy accessibility. Gemma took Anna to her room. Jenny also retired for the night. Contessa Genoveffa Averso went to her rooms and complained bitterly to her son, accusing him of giving her the maid's quarters, which he'd done. Tonight she was just too tired to fall into her usual aggressive patterns.

So this was America, she thought, noisy, dirty, and no gold in the streets. They'd lied. She would miss Italy and now with a new language, she'd never talk to anyone again.

The whole household was filled with enemies, and she couldn't converse with them. She unpacked her only bag and went to bed lulled by the rhythm of the city.

Santo made a list of household furniture, items they needed badly.

The following evening, the Derisis came with trays of prepared food and wine. Letizia and Gemma became instant friends. Pino, their twelve-year-old son came too. He was tall and slender and very affable. La contessa Averso was normal for a change, and Letizia had no idea of the extent of Santo's mother's quirks.

Letizia thought Anna was adopted, because she looked nothing like her parents. It was obvious that the child was the center of Santo's universe. She sat close to her father instead of her mother.

The wine flowed, and even Anna was given wine with some water. Letizia asked each about their impressions of New York. Gemma was impressed with Letizia's social graces.

Following Letizia's style, Gemma asked Pino what his favorite subject in school was. He told her, music. "The oboe is the most important voice in the orchestra since it establishes the pitch for the orchestra to tune to." Gemma's heart skipped a beat, "then you must have a good music teacher," and Pino answered, "yes, he's with the Metropolitan Opera orchestra."

What were the odds that it was Maurizio? Gemma was tempted to ask, then decided not to, but the possibility lingered, and gave her reason to hope.

Santo and Gino talked business at the end of the table. They discussed the needs of the populace in such a depressed economy. Gino's connections with distribution of foods were with large companies, and, so far, even though they were hurting, sales still continued. People had to eat.

At eleven p.m., Jenny, little Anna, and the Contessa had gone off to their bedrooms Pino was sleeping on Santo's and Gemma's bed and the ladies were preparing coffee in the kitchen with the new demi tasse pot Letizia had brought that night, with a pound of black coffee.

Gemma needed furniture and private English lessons. She made a date with Letizia to go shopping. Letizia's friend Kay from Ossining would possibly do it as a special favor to Letizia after school. "We'll pay her well," Gemma said, and Letizia called the next day to set up private lessons. Kay taught English to foreign born students, and added the Averso family to her schedule.

Santo was tutored by himself since he had to learn as quickly as possible. His lessons lasted an hour. He found the charming petite 35 year old English teacher very attractive.

Within a few months, ornate Italian style furnishings filled the large apartment with an aura of old world elegance.

Anna was enrolled into a small exclusive school for kindergarten children. Within weeks she was speaking the language, and became the center of attention since she sang in perfect pitch and played the piano.

The family's daily routine was established, a quick Italian breakfast which was a cup of black coffee, and fresh fruit for the adults, and toast and milk for Anna. Santo left for the office downtown near the bowery, and Gemma and Jenny walked Anna to kindergarten school. With everyone out of the way, the Contessa Averso then would come into the kitchen and make her own breakfast. She avoided contact with the family, which was of mutual benefit for all.

A new Steinway piano was delivered for Gemma who practiced four hours a day, after she returned from dropping her daughter off to school. Jenny then continued her long walks, exploring the city by foot. She stopped in at a church, and prayed daily for the repose of her husband Luigi's soul. The memory of his murder, was a constant pain in her heart.

The Contessa's only human interaction was with her son. She kept out of everyone's way, and never spoke to anyone. Gemma locked her door when she practiced, because she felt uneasy about her mother in law's fragile mental condition. She was fearful that some day she might verbally attack her.

The Contessa had made her sentiments known after the birth of Anna. She made no secret of it either. She had said, "this dark haired child belongs to another man." The mortification had been devastating to Gemma, Jenny and in particular, Santo.

Yet, the contessa did not stop there. She even caught the ear of Santo's friends. One by one, she told them that her son had been cuckolded and had been led to believe that he was the father of la puttana's baby.

Santo, in order not to be publicly ridiculed, lied about having had a Moorish grandfather in his lineage. No one believed it, and as Santo grew aware of his humiliation, he isolated himself. When he left Italy, he said good bye only to his best friend Enrico..

Gemma was aware of everything, and she realized that Santo had indeed paid a big price in his marriage to her. She had grown to love him deeply until she discovered his personal papers indicating that he had set out to destroy Maurizio's career because he wanted her. It destroyed any modicum of love which Gemma had for Santo.

Yet, Gemma felt sorry for her husband. His mother was a negative presence in their lives, even though she isolated herself in her quarters when the family was home. Supper was difficult. The Countess refused to eat with La puttana and the family. In order to keep the peace, after supper Santo would bring in the tray of food to his mother, and sipped his demi tasse coffee while she ate and talked to him about her miserable life. That was the daily routine in the Averso household. Santo had indeed paid dearly in his pursuit of Gemma Liguori. His happiness was sporadic, yet, the one great joy in his life was the daughter who wasn't his. His moments of complete happiness were spent with her. After his mother's meal, he'd take the tray into the kitchen, then take over the bedtime story to Anna. This ritual was the best event in his day. Then he was completely happy.

* * *

In November as the weather got cold in New York and occasional snow flakes fell, Letizia asked Gemma if she would accompany her son at his oboe recital. Gemma said yes. Pino gave her the piano score one afternoon, and she sight read it then accompanied Pino. It was a wonderful piece by Schubert, the great melodist of the German school.

* * *

The concert was on a Sunday afternoon at Letizia's Fifth Avenue penthouse apartment facing Central Park. It was a collection of young people who would perform one selection.

Letizia offered a buffet after the concert, something which had to be explained to Gemma. Italians did not entertain informally, so for her it was a novelty.

Jenny took Anna to the Museum of Natural History, and Santo and Gino worked at the office, near the Battery.

Gemma was delighted to be involved in performing again. She chose a pale lavender lace dress for the concert. Her long blonde hair was pulled on top of her head in a chignon and she wore a lavender ribbon through her hair. She looked like a high fashion model.

Letizia welcomed the young musicians to her home. The large living room was set up like a theater, and the accompanists sat in the back of the group while teachers stood in the area behind the last row.

Pino Derisi was announced by his mother. Gemma stood, and walked to the piano holding her musical score. She sat at the piano, opened her score, and waited for a signal from Pino. He nodded, and she played the first chord. The performance went well, and Gemma was in her element. Pino bowed deeply, then gallantly kissed Gemma's hand. She bowed and returned to her seat at the back of the living room.

As the last child, a fourteen-year-old virtuoso played the violin, Letizia slipped away to the dining room and Gemma got up and followed her friend to help set up the food. She passed in front of Pino and his oboe teacher and handed Pino the piano score.

Letizia and Gemma carried the huge tray of finger sandwiches to the dining room table. Nothing required dishes or forks, and, not used to the informal American way of dining buffet style, Gemma was amazed. Cheese was served in small cubes with toothpicks, and olives, celery, and carrots were finger food.

After the last performer, people got up and milled around the marvelous display of sandwiches, and shortly they were all consumed.

The teachers, most of whom were from the Metropolitan Opera Orchestra or the Philharmonic Orchestra, talked about their students proudly pointing out individual talents. Maurizio Brescia was in shock. Gemma was filling the cups with punch and setting them on the tray.

Gemma still hadn't looked up. Maurizio waited until the rush of people went back to their seats with their food. He approached the table.

"May I have a refill?" he asked. She looked up and thought for a moment that she was hallucinating. She swayed, and felt faint. Maurizio ran around the table and caught her before she collapsed.

"O Dio!" she cried, and he led her quickly away from the table to Letizia's study. She sat down, and he sat facing her.

"I can't believe it," she said.

"When did you emigrate?" he asked.

"In May," her voice was raspy.

"I thought I saw you get into a cab."

"Probably," she said softly.

"Where do you live?"

"At the Ansonia," she said.

"I live two blocks away from you. I work at the Met."

She smiled. "Your dreams came true, Maurizio."

"Did they?" he mumbled.

"Did you marry?" she asked.

"No. But I keep getting engaged." He laughed thinking of three sopranos who had jilted him. Gemma translated that to "not available."

"Is he good to you, Gemma?"

He continued to caress her hand, then her arm.

"Very."

She felt her loss acutely and didn't want this moment to end.

They exchanged news of their parents, and Maurizio's empathy towards her father's tragic death touched her deeply. My darling, why are we living apart?

He told her that his work extended to a music school in East Harlem, Manhattan School of Music on East 105th Street. He suggested that she contact them and mention his name if she wanted to teach piano there. She told him that she was interested. Letizia walked in and realized that she had come upon a very private moment. Maurizio stood up. Gemma seemed shaken. Letizia had no idea what had transpired, but as a writer of romance novels, she was used to hatching plots. This one loomed very clearly in her mind's eye.

Maurizio and Gemma left, and since they lived on the West Side of Central Park, they shared a cab. They got into the cab, and, as the cabbie drove to the crosstown artery on 79th Street, Maurizio took her in his arms and kissed her. They clung to each other and the years of separation melted in the moment. Then Gemma pulled away begging him to stop. Shaken and deeply moved, Maurizio realized he had to or he'd arrive at the apex of passion in a way he wouldn't want to. He asked to see her again. She said, "Maurizio, my situation is not easy." Gemma was reticent about further information. "Gemma, I understand, but here take this." He gave her his business card and she took it. "Call me or meet me," he said. "We must talk; I won't live without you. I've tried, God knows I've tried, but I'm no good without you, everyone seems like a mannequin, you? You were the last of the great goddesses of the renaissance, my love, I can't eradicate you from my heart."

He walked her into the lobby of the Ansonia, kissed her, and told her he'd wait for her call. He paid the cab driver and walked home, a puzzled look on his face.

Gemma went up totally drained. The impact of seeing him, and then hearing him say that nothing had changed, shook her world. That evening, after Anna was put to bed, Santo joined his mother in the sitting room of her quarters. Gemma went to her mother's room and told her that she'd seen Maurizio again.

"I knew that you'd find him" Jenny said, "did you tell him he has a daughter?" Gemma was torn by conflicting emotions.

"He's engaged, Momma. It's too late. I'll never love like that again." Gemma described his joy at seeing her, and didn't hold back his sentiments. Her mother was thrilled, for Jenny there were no choices for her daughter, and she said so. She told her daughter that, although her life with Santo was comfortable, the Countess was like the cross of Jesus Christ.

"You have a way out. You're cheating him, you know."

Gemma precluded any further discourse as she said: "Momma, our time has passed." She said sadly, "when he came back from Switzerland, I never told him that I was pregnant."

Jenny Liguori was shocked. "What? How was he to know? Oh, my God, Gemma, what were you thinking?"

"Thinking? Momma, he had made up his mind that he was going to America. He said he would send for me. Had he married me because he had to--he would have resented me. That would have killed me. It's too late, too late." Gemma burst into tears, and her mother's heart broke to see her daughter so torn up.

Jenny said, "Too late? Only when death enters the picture, it's too late. Think about that, my daughter."

Gemma composed herself to return to her husband's bed. Her mother's last words resounded in her head like a series of echoes. The seed had been planted.

Chapter Five
AFTERMATH

After the concert, Maurizio went home and collapsed on the couch staring at the ornate squared ceiling in the 35-foot living room. Momma Anna heard him come in, but he didn't come into the kitchen. She wiped her hands and found her son on the couch. His arms were crossed over his eyes, and he was on his back. "Figlio mio," she cried, "what's wrong? Didn't the concert go well for Pino?"

Maurizio patted the sofa, gesturing for his mom to sit down. "Fantastic! Beautiful tone, excellent technique and exquisite phrasing."

"Why are you in such a state? What happened?"

"His accompanist, Momma." He put his arms down and sat up slightly leaning on his elbow. "She breathed with him, the phrasing synchronized, the single thread of musicianship binding them, and I knew in my heart who she was."

Anna's eyes opened wide and chills overcame her. Dear God, dare I ask. She put her hand over her mouth and moaned. "Oh Dio! Maurizio!" she cried.

"My soul companion," she put her arms around him. "How? When?" she asked. Vittorio, who sat at his desk in the far end of the living room, reading costume magazines and sketching revisions on a separate pad, put down his glasses on the desk, then walked to the couch to find out what had transpired. They were so engrossed that they didn't look his way.

Maurizio described the concert in minute detail. He also mentioned that he saw her getting into a cab two weeks earlier. At that time, he'd thought he must be going mad, for often he'd see a woman on the street who looked like Gemma and pursue her. It had never been Gemma.

"Momma, I asked her for a refill, and dear God, when she looked up, and saw me, she almost fainted and I ran around the table and caught her. She was pale, cold and in shock. I took her into Letizia's study and finally color came back into her face. We talked. They live at the Ansonia. No wonder I saw her. Not every encounter was my imagination. It was she."

Anna was stunned. She told her son to talk to his father; she was going to make a cup of cappucino, to celebrate the occasion. Maurizio looked pensive, worried. Vittorio looked confused. Maurizio told his father that he asked to see her again, but she seemed reticent. He gave her his phone number, but he didn't expect her to use it. His mind was racing in huge sweeps of emotion between hope and despair. In essence, he felt a deep sense of loss.

"I'm in a dark place, Poppa. I have everything and nothing. What do I do? I acted desperate. I think I frightened her."

"Son," Vittorio said, "let her know you love her and want her."

Maurizio told him that she knew that. She didn't seem anxious to change her circumstances, and perhaps their time had come and gone, and he was to suffer for the rest of life, having her live so near and yet she was unattainable. "A just punishment," he said to his father.

"Ask for another chance." Vittorio was not surprised at Maurizio's insecurity.

"Don't you understand, Poppa? I was too direct."

"In America, everybody is direct."

"Maybe she is happily married," Maurizio said sadly.

"Maybe she's not. In America, divorce is possible. You don't have the Church sending you to hell for eternity. Maurizio, if you are faint of heart now, how will you deal with real problems in life when they come up? Be resolute."

Maurizio didn't know what the playing field was ahead, but his father interjected. "You didn't know the playing field in music did you?

Yet your career is where you want it to be." Vittorio, impassioned, raised his voice. His son was on the emotional pit of quicksand. Vittorio looked concerned.

His mother rushed in. Anna was furious. She reprimanded her husband to be quiet and to get back to his costumes at the desk. She was sending him to his corner as if he were an errant child. Had she thrown something at him, it would have been easier to take. He went back to his corner in the living room, put on his glasses, and stared at the magazine before him as he sank into the black hole of anonymity. Anna called out "are you interested in a cup of cappuccino?" as she passed his desk.

"No," he replied.

Vittorio's talk with his son was well-timed. Maurizio, infused with his father's urging, decided to stop second-guessing what Gemma's life was like, and be single-minded about what he wanted. Maurizio had discovered that he couldn't have a deep relationship with any other woman. The missing ingredients were simple: eight years of a history together. She knew every phase of his life, including his soul. Without her, his existence was in limbo. He had to see her again.

It was almost 6:00 o'clock at night when Maurizio left and headed for the Ansonia Hotel. He wore his Italian borsolino cap as a cover. In the lobby, he pulled his cap over his eyes, sat on a sofa chair and perused the tenants and guests entering and leaving behind an opened newspaper he wasn't reading.

Suddenly a child, arguing in Italian, threatened not to walk another step. Obviously she had the upper hand. Maurizio was amused to see this little girl exasperate her caretaker. The elevator door opened, and the child ran to her mother. It was Gemma! "Momma, Momma, Grandma made me walk all over the city," the child wailed.

Gemma whispered in her child's ear, and without another word, they walked into the elevator, and as the doors shut, he ran out of the lobby feeling wretched.

No wonder Gemma was reticent. How could he break up a family? "Mia Culpa," he said to God as he walked home. At home, he told his parents what he had seen.

"Then it's over," Anna said sadly.

"And so it is," added Vittorio.

Gemma took Anna directly to the bathroom to supervise her bath time. The child was exhausted. Gemma knelt on the tiled floor and helped to expedite the removal of New York's dust from her body.

The next day on Monday, Letizia called Gemma to tell her that she belonged to the Metropolitan Opera guild, and since she was a financial supporter of the opera house, she had access to rehearsals--and would Gemma like to come. Gemma begged off. She was overwhelmed with the previous day's events and needed time to think. She didn't need Letizia's intrusive nature to reveal her own confusion.

Gemma confided in her mother about Letizia's offer and asked her what she thought.

"Why are you avoiding doing this? You don't have to see Maurizio, nor do you have to mention him to her. Enjoy the day. By the way, Gemma, you got a call from a Mrs. Whitford from Manhattan School of Music. I think they'd like to interview you. Call them."

Gemma was ecstatic. What a wonderful teaching career this would be! She called, and her interview was scheduled for Wednesday morning. Her mother urged her to go to the opera rehearsal. "Enjoy before you get involved once more in your own career. I wouldn't exactly throw Maurizio away." Gemma retorted, "Momma, my daughter is insane for her poppa. How do I justify breaking her heart?"

"How do you justify living as though you're walking on eggs with the madwoman of Mugenta in there? Do you know what I think of? Her hate of you is so strong that one day, she'll take a kitchen knife and plunge it into your heart while you're sleeping, and that old bastard will swear that she was only sleep-walking."

* * *

Maurizio had difficulty sleeping. He broke his engagement with the soprano Loretta Franciosa, and was consumed with thoughts of Gemma. He grew distracted, and tore around the apartment losing everything and anything he needed to function: his eyeglasses, his oboe, his reeds, his black bow tie. His mother ran more than usual in the apartment, begging him to put anything not attached to his body, on the grand piano.

* * *

Three months later, Letizia finally made a date with Gemma. Gemma avoided her, but agreed to a luncheon. Gemma told Letizia that her teaching schedule was full. Socializing was impossible now. Suddenly, without thinking, Letizia said that Anna looked like Maurizio, and just as she uttered his name, Gemma ran out, and hailed a cab. Letizia was heartbroken and guilty over her lack of sensitivity and her stupidity. She called every day, left messages which were ignored, and finally wrote her a letter:

"Gemma: I apologize for being so stupid. It's ended our friendship and I've lost a treasured friend. I never meant to hurt you. Some day I hope you can forgive me. Humbly, Letizia."

Snow fell in great quantities in New York City, and in 1933, since city schools rarely closed, private schools did. Gemma got a call from Manhattan School that lessons had been canceled. Miss Sartime, her daughter's teacher, asked Gemma if she would chaperone the children to the Metropolitan Opera house the next day. One more parent was needed. Gemma inquired how this came about, and Miss Sartime told her that it was Mrs. Derisi from the opera guild.

Gemma's anger towards Letizia was like a rock in Gemma's stomach, her unforgiving attitude hurt her deeply. Santo was also upset over the termination of their friendship. It was time to end it. She called Letizia on the telephone, and without alluding to past hurts, told her she was going to chaperone the trip to the theater. Letizia almost cried when she heard her voice, and did after Gemma hung up.

The next day, Gemma, dressed casually in blue slacks, a blue shirt, boots, and a full length mink coat. They took a small bus and drove the two miles to the opera house. Letizia, as promised, was there waiting at the backstage entrance. There were two other mothers with the group as well as Miss Sartime, the teacher.

Letizia was delegated to escort small school children's groups through the theater. They would see the make-believe world of props. The stage manager as well as the stage director, was present with Letizia, to show, explain, and answer questions.

The orchestra was not a part of their itinerary for that day; however, a few members strolled into the theater as they saw the five year old children sitting, wide eyed, and in awe.

Maurizio once more had forgotten his case of oboe reeds in the orchestra pit, under his chair. The director saw him, and asked him to come out of the pit. Maurizio apologized for the intrusion. However, the director asked him to participate, and he cheerfully did. He showed them the parts of the oboe, then played the mouthpiece by itself. The children laughed at the high-pitched sound.

Gemma's heart was racing. He was so wonderful with the children, and she could see that they took to him. He had no idea that she was sitting at the end of the small group, watching him in the darkened theater. He covered his eyes, because he couldn't see with the lights shining on stage.

"Any questions, children?" he asked. One little girl with dark curly hair raised her hand without hesitation.

"When you hit the high notes on your hobo, does it scare you?" she asked. She felt foolish because her classmates laughed.

"Yes, it scares me sometimes," he answered her, ignoring the laughter, and the children thought that it must be a good question.

"Sometimes," Maurizio continued, "certain instruments are made to scare people. That's their job. The bagpipe is like that. Ever hear of a bagpipe?" The entire class raised their hands. He was impressed.

"What can you tell me about the bagpipe?" he asked. Hands went up and one little boy jumped up.

"I know, I know," he said, and Maurizio acknowledged him.

"A man came to our school. He played it. We covered our ears. It was scary." Everyone agreed.

"You children are very intelligent. Where is that first little girl? What is your name?" he asked, and she stood up.

"Anna," she said.

"Anna?" he repeated. "Really? That's my mother's name." She smiled, pleased that he was giving her all that attention.

There were other children who wanted to be acknowledged and it was fun hearing themselves in such a large theater. Maurizio was quite good as he engaged the children in guessing games with scales. He played a scale and asked them to point in the direction it was going. As he ascended, they pointed up, and when he descended the scale, they pointed down.

At the end of a half hour, Maurizio was asked to end the impromptu lesson, and the children spontaneously applauded him. Letizia caught his attention by thanking him personally, and he came off stage to join her. A table of refreshments was waiting for the children backstage. Gemma put her shawl on her head. There was nowhere to hide. Gemma tried to get her daughter's attention, but Anna was off, holding the hand of the "hobo player."

They went to the reception room, and Maurizio set his instrument down on a chair, then helped serve the punch and small sandwiches to the children. Letizia told him to entertain his young admirer-- and that she'd take over the serving of the refreshments.

Anna's eyes were compelling. Maurizio pulled up two chairs, and handed her a plate with food. He was amazed at how easily she conversed with an adult. She wanted to know more about music, obviously enthralled with the theater.

"Tell me, Anna, you like music?" he asked.

"Oh yes! I'm a singer," she said, and he laughed amused at the exact statement of one so little.

"How do you know?" he asked.

"I'm good at it." Again he laughed.

"So much for modesty. Do you play an instrument?"

"My mother does. She's teaching me the piano."

He felt a chill come over him. His look darted to the group of young women at the other end of the table, one faced towards the door, but her linear figure was unmistakable. Suddenly the pieces of the giant puzzle came together.

"Is that your mother?" he asked, and she nodded. "Tell her to come here, Anna, okay?"

She was pleased that the "hobo player" was giving her so much attention. She took her mother's hand and brought her to Maurizio. He stood up, and bowed politely.

"When were you going to tell me?" he whispered in her ear.

"I wasn't," she said, her eyes downcast.

Maurizio put his arm around Gemma, led her backstage to a narrow dressing room, and shut the door.

"I looked at her, and I saw myself," he whispered.

"I didn't want to disrupt your life, Maurizio," she said.

"Disrupt? Do you want to know what it is to disrupt? My daughter being brought up by another man. My God, Gemma, why didn't you tell me?"

"Remember you said we had an agreement to wait," she reminded him, "I wanted to die, you weren't there for me."

"I wasn't there for myself, Gemma," he put her fur coat on a chair and faced her, "God's given us a second chance, we must take it."

"I know," she said softly. Maurizio was still in a daze over the events, "when she said her name, I knew that the child is mine."

Maurizio asked Gemma to come to his apartment the next morning for breakfast to see his parents. He told her that they knew only that Gemma had a child. Wait until they found out that it was their grandchild.

The lovers parted until the next morning, and soon the final cadence of their reunion would fill the emptiness they had borne all these years.

Chapter Six
THE REUNION

The following morning, Gemma paced her bedroom. She was not looking forward to the confrontation with her husband.

The day started like any other. Gemma dressed and came into the kitchen for breakfast. She cut up fruit, cheese, and bread, then set it on the table. Anna was told to have a small glass of juice because they were invited to breakfast.

Santo popped into the kitchen for his orange juice, kissed his wife, who didn't respond as she usually did. "What's wrong?" he asked, "nothing," Gemma answered.

"Really? you seem tense." Santo felt strange, as though a cold wind had permeated his soul. Could she possibly have met Maurizio again? She had said nothing, yet he felt the walls of his past transgressions closing in on his marriage.

Anna walked in rubbing her eyes, wearing one slipper and her flannel nightgown. Santo picked her up and nuzzled his face in her neck.

"You're eating too much pasta mia pupa! Soon I won't be able to do this." Anna snapped, "you eat too much, Poppa, I'm a growing child."

"A growing child?" he bellowed "soon you'll be as big as the Statue of Liberty" Anna retorted, "and everyone will have to salute me, even you!" He laughed and Gemma scolded him for letting her get away with such disrespectful talk. He retorted that she was only a baby.

The routine was broken this morning, and it was starkly evident to Santo. Anna who was usually nagged to hurry wasn't. Gemma avoided physical contact as well as eye contact.

"No school today?" he inquired as he looked at the kitchen clock.

"We're visiting friends for breakfast; I'm bringing her in late." She sipped her demi tasse coffee. Santo stopped shuffling papers, looked at his wife and frowned.

"Who are these friends?" he asked.

"People you don't know."

"From?" he persisted.

"Milano," she articulated clearly.

Soon after they'd arrived, Gino had bragged about his son's oboe teacher, Maurizio Brescia from the Metropolitan Opera. His scheming had caught up with him. They've met, Santo thought, there's a plot here, and I can't stop it.

"Oh," he answered weakly as his nerves got the best of him. He ran to the bathroom shaking at the prospect that life as he knew it was about to end.

Gemma dressed her daughter, and left without saying good bye. Jenny had gotten up early and left to have breakfast out before everyone was up. Santo grew physically ill, and remained in the bathroom until the Contessa grew concerned and banged on his door demanding he open it up. That moment, Santo realized how important his mother's concern was for him. He had lost his family.

As they walked, Gemma re iterated to her daughter that she was meeting new grandparents. Anna was puzzled. How did grandparents suddenly appear out of nowhere? Why was everything so mysterious this morning?

* * *

They took the elevator to the twelfth floor, and the door opened to a private foyer belonging only to that apartment. She rang the doorbell and Anna Brescia opened it. She and Vittorio embraced Gemma, then saw the child.

"This is Anna." Gemma said. The Brescias were shaken, the child looked exactly like her father. "She's ours, isn't she?" Anna Brescia cried, "Yes," Gemma answered. Vittorio wept openly, "you named her after my wife," it was a statement. Gemma said, "I respected our tradition."

"Gemma, welcome home," Vittorio Brescia whispered tearfully.

Grandma Anna led them into the magnificent large dining room, where the table was set with the best china.

As Anna served the food, Maurizio told his daughter that he was her daddy. He clarified his parents' roles. They were "Nonno and Nonna."

"Do you understand, Anna?" Maurizio seemed concerned, and rightfully so. His daughter looked from one to the other, her eyes wide. Looking upset she didn't speak unless she was spoken to directly. She was nervous and she swung her legs under the table back and forth and everyone noticed. After breakfast the adults each realized that this visit had to end soon. The child could hardly contain her nerves.

Vittorio and Anna showed Anna the apartment, careful not to mention anything about the pending move in front of the child.

The Brescias were happy about the reunion, but the visit was tarnished with apprehension at how perturbed their granddaughter was.

"The child is in shock," Vittorio said to his wife, "how could she not be?" Anna Brescia commented, "she's being told that she has a new father, and grandparents? Brace yourself Vittorio, I anticipate a rebellion here."

"Tesoro, I feel terrible for Anna, she can barely look at me," Maurizio whispered as they walked down the street. His hand was cold and clammy.

"My love, it'll be rough, but in time she'll understand."

That night, Gemma went into her bedroom. The Count looked like a lamb waiting to be slaughtered. His body was drooped, his eyes red from an entire day of weeping, and he had no energy left in him. Gemma galvanized every ounce of courage to confront him with his past deeds. She presented him with evidence about the bribe which had blocked Maurizio from La Scala. He was inert as he avoided looking at the letter. Gemma held it in front of his face, "Gemma, stop. I'm dying. I did it for love." Gemma winced, "it was your arrogance, which made you manipulate the lives of three people."

Gemma could not walk away from the emotional heap which Santo was. He hyperventilated, he wept, and she grew worried. What if he died of heartbreak? She did not want this on her conscience. Her manner swiftly changed to compassion. She got into bed with him and held him in her arms. He could not make love to her, even though he wanted to. Gemma knew that she had to lift his spirits, and she told him that she had always liked him, and found him to be attractive. When he offered to marry her despite her pregnancy of another man's child, she fell in love with him. Finally he said, "and I thought I could find happiness predicated on another man's ruin. There is retribution in this world, Gemma, and I can't even ask for forgiveness, I don't deserve it."

Gemma continued to try to lift his spirits, "Santo, don't beat yourself. You were passionate and tender with me, compassionate with my mother, and a stupendous father to my daughter. I'm not tearing you two apart. As a matter of fact," she giggled, "she loves you more than she loves me."

They talked for two hours. Gemma had managed to pull him out of the pit of despair, and as she continued to speak about the good things in their marriage, he was elevated to an emotional level of great intensity and he made love to his wife who returned his passion with equal fervor. At 3:00 a.m., Santo fell asleep with his arms around his wife. Exhausted from the tumultuous range of emotions he had experienced, he grew to love Gemma even more. The thought that she had cast aside her resentment and opened her body and soul to him, penetrated his psyche so deeply. His last words as they finished their final act of love, were: "I've never known such love as you have given me, if it's not good, come back to me." Gemma held him close and said, "Santo, I'm not turning my back on you, we'll see each other. I'm not cutting you out of Anna's life, nor mine."

* * *

On Saturday, with the help of professional movers, Gemma and her family moved to the Brescias. Contessa Genoveffa Averso sat in the living room gleefully watching the movers, fingering her rosary beads and talking to herself.

Santo came out, and tousled Anna's hair, and she put her arms around his legs, but instead of picking her up, he told her to let go. This morning, he pushed her away and pretended he was going back into his bedroom; then he ran around the kitchen and slipped out of the apartment.

Suddenly, Anna ran from room to room looking for him, thinking that he was playing hide and seek. She opened and shut doors and called, "Poppa, where are you? Answer me, Poppa!" She continued the frenzy of her search for him.

Gemma told her that Poppa had to leave. Anna cried in heart wrenching sobs: "No, Momma, he's hiding." She ran to the Countessa's suite, opened the door, and commanded, "Poppa! Come out, now!"

The Contessa shuffled after Anna screaming, "Figlia di puttana!" For the first time in her married life, Gemma reacted to her mother-in- law.

"The only puttana here is you! Strega!" she snarled and she walked away.

"Argh!" the Contessa shouted. She hobbled into the kitchen, got a carving knife and ran towards Gemma to plunge it into her back. Luckily the moving man walked in and pulled Gemma away so that the Contessa's aim was thwarted. Jenny ran towards her daughter and cried in horror. "I knew she'd try to kill you."

The moving man told Gemma she should call the cops. Gemma refused, and she and her mother left and escaped to the Brescias. The three of them were shocked at the final attempt of murder. The child was traumatized, for she had witnessed the act of wanton hatred against her mother. Defiance and anger were replaced with relief that they had left her Poppa's house. Anna was only five years old, yet the impact of that moment changed the way she would look at her real father, Maurizio Brescia.

* * *

Santo went to the only refuge he knew, the Derisis. He couldn't stay too long because his confused old mother might snap. They told him to go home, put his mother to bed, and they'd be over in a little while with some fruit and refreshments.

Letizia already had plans for Santo. She told her husband that Santo had commented on the attractiveness of the American English teacher, Kay Semanci. "That's it. He needs to have a woman."

When Santo got home, he found his mother overwrought and fingering her rosary beads Ave Maria was followed by a litany of "puttana Gemma, puttana la momma, puttana la figlia," followed by Ave Maria. Suddenly his own anguish dissipated, and he picked up his frail hunchbacked mother and carried her to her bed. The poor little thing had been traumatized by the confusion of their move during the day. He helped to undress her, gave her a shot of whiskey and put her to sleep.

The Derisis came over and Letizia listened, as did Gino, to the turn of events which had initiated in their house and wiped out the existence of his family. Letizia felt guilty, and Gino was furious, because he didn't want to see his mentor, the man he admired so, in such a pitiful state of desperation.

The following weekend, Letizia invited Kay, the English teacher to Santo's house for dinner. The Contessa made an appearance, but Santo got a prescription for sleeping pills so she'd remain in bed and out of the way.

Eventually the casual dining excluded the Derisis, and Santo hired a nurse for his mother so that he could pursue this young woman without impediment.

His mother then transferred her litany to Kay. When Kay inquired about what his mother was saying to her, Santo explained that she was speaking in Latin and had a nervous speech tic. Santo proposed within weeks, and Kay accepted. She was the only Contessa in all of Ossining, and got teased relentlessly by all her friends. After a few weeks of marriage, her husband asked her to quit her job and help him socially and in his business.

What seemed like an impossible set of barriers worked out for both couples in the most peaceful way. Gemma had not spoken about the incident to anyone, until at one point, when Santo confronted her about it.

It took Anna years to "get over" something she never could get over, the loss of a beloved father. She was disappointed in him for not being there when the Contessa attacked her mommy. After the divorce, Maurizio adopted his real daughter and gave her his name. The idea of adopting his own daughter drove him crazy, but Gemma knew how to calm him down.

Chapter Seven

NEW FAMILY DYNAMICS

The changes in the Averso as well as the Brescia household created a new dynamic. The moment Santo came home to the blasting silence of his day with no child to run and jump in his arms was the saddest moment. The ritual of sitting in the living room with Anna bouncing on the couch and describing her day at school was the highest point of his day. No one walked in to the living room while Anna had her evening tete a tete with her father. Even the Contessa hid away from the scene. It was, as he said, his private time with his daughter. Anna had an uncanny gift of imitating her fellow students. When she imitated Pietro, the child of an ambassador from Italy, she spoke English with his thick Italian accent, which was a little more pronounced than hers. Santo marveled at the fact that her ear was so uncanny that she could sound like someone else. After she had enacted her day in school, she would cross her arms as he did, constantly studying his every move, and say to him, "and how did your day go, Poppa?" and this would break him up into gales of laughter, because she sounded just like him. Those moments were now gone forever, and he would come home, sit on the couch now, and shut his eyes and play the whole familiar scene through the projector of his imagination.

A month after Gemma's move, Santo called her to meet for coffee. He asked how the baby was adjusting to her new family, and Gemma told him that Anna wanted to know why Poppa Santo had run away from them. His jaw dropped open, "is this what the child's been told, when it was you who ran away from me?" She explained that the trauma of seeing the contessa lunge at her with a kitchen knife had shut Anna down for weeks, crying "where was poppa? why did he run away from me?" She had nightmares, and whimpered often while she slept. "You weren't there to intercede, and she assumed that you had run away, and I told her that you had left for work, so she thought about it, and now she's ready to see you."

"Have you made arrangements for us to meet?"

"Santo, be patient, I have to convince Maurizio."

Santo was furious. He walked away from Gemma afraid that he'd threaten her, with contesting the divorce, with fighting for Anna's custody, and suing Maurizio for breaking up his family. He had the money, he had enough anger, and having dealt with Italian politics, and being in an enviable social position as a member of the royal family of Italy, he knew how to retaliate.

"Gemma, I have enough anger to kill, right now. Perhaps we should just part right now. I cannot deal with such a humiliating situation where you and I, can't even come to an agreement. I have loved you more than anyone has. I have manipulated, paid off, and bribed everyone who kept me from you. No woman has ever been so worshipped. Yet, you stand there and have the audacity to humiliate me with this snip of an arrogant oboe player, to keep me away from my child. Yes, she's mine. No court in the United States will keep me from her. If the court awards me the custody of my child, my mother will be housed in separate quarters with a twenty four hour nurse. I am prepared to do this. I give you two weeks to settle this with the musician..after that, I'll get the best lawyer in New York, and I shall hit you with everything I can."

Gemma was shocked. "Santo, retaliation is not necessary, work with me, for the sake of our baby. Can we do this amicably?"

He put his arms around her, and he saw how gentle she had been in her answer to his threats. A woman he would never eradicate from his heart. "I'll try," he said as his facial expression softened up. She thanked him and he pulled her into his arms and kissed the nape of her neck, "How," he said gruffly, "am I going to live without you?" Gemma held him closely, "Santo, I still love you," he answered, "I know, what I felt in you, could not be faked."

* * *

Letizia and Gino finished dinner at 8:30, and as they listened to their son practice the oboe, they sipped their espresso coffee on the small balcony facing Central Park.

"Letizia, what has Gemma told you?" Gino asked.

"She doesn't trust Santo. He's vindictive, and arrogant. People are pawns in his dealings, like a chess game, to be disposed of, or moved from here to there." Gino shot her a look of disapproval, and she shrugged, "well, haven't you said the same thing? Come Gino, you don't have to be protective of him with me. He's been good to us, but he's not a friend. You told me yourself that when you're at an impasse with him, he pulls rank..and out oozes his royal persona."

They continued to make observations, but the telephone rang and it was Gemma. Letizia was anxious to learn about her meeting with Santo, and Gemma simply said, 'he waved his verbal armor at me, and I met it with a disarming point of view. I told him that I was caught in the middle. Suddenly he became a knight in shining armor, and said he'd be more compliant."

Letizia shrieked with excitement. "What do you do, Gemma? Even Maurizio mentioned that you have a way with him which calms him. He is never as happy or secure as when he's with you. You must teach me how to do that. My husband and I lock horns frequently. I have no diplomacy in my nature, as you witnessed when I blurted out that Anna didn't look like Santo's daughter. How can I learn not to be so blunt and to disarm people as you do."

Gemma told Letizia that being so close to a musician one third of her life, she learned how to deal with his extreme emotions. Letizia asked, "and what about your extreme emotions?" Gemma laughed, "I've learned to convince my man to believe that he is in charge, lessons my mother taught me, so in answer to your question how do I deal with extreme emotions? Privately, with no audience, Maurizio needs an audience, I don't."

* * *

Maurizio came home from dress rehearsal of Madame Butterfly, and his wife ran a bath for him, he put on his robe, and got into the tub.

Whenever Gemma was home, she'd scrub his back, even though he had a long handled scrub brush to do it himself. Those private moments sometimes were the only ones they had to speak privately. Maurizio wanted to know what had transpired between her and the Count, as he called him.

"He wants to see Anna once a week," she said as she rubbed her fingers in his hair, Maurizio groaned, which he did any time Gemma referred to the Count.

"Who does he think he is to make such demands?" he bellowed, "her father," Gemma answered softly. Maurizio didn't react.

She rubbed his back in the tub, and he moaned with pleasure. "that spot on the right shoulder blade, I think I got a draft from the open door in the pit." Gemma pressed her strong fingers hard into the muscle and Maurizio cried out that it hurt. Gemma said, "I assume that you're okay with it."

"I'm not," he replied, "but Anna wants to see him, and my God, how can I deny our child? It's killing me. She had his name, she loves him, and I'm the outsider who has disrupted her life. I have no choice."

"Then it's settled," Gemma said as she poured water onto Maurizio's head to wash out the soap. She dried her hands, and left the bathroom. Maurizio yelled out, "come back, Gemma," she walked out and went to her mother's room. Jenny asked her daughter if they could take a walk. Gemma ran in the kitchen to tell Anna Brescia that she and her mom were going to the store. Young Anna was busy mixing the dough for cookies.

Gemma related her meeting with Santo to her mother, and stated that she would never want him as her adversary. Jenny said, "so he's out of your life, why do you have to deal with him?" Gemma answered, "he rescued me, has given my daughter legitimacy, has protected me from being a social outcast, need I go on?" Jenny agreed.

They went to the diner, ordered coffee and fruit and Jenny spoke to her daughter about how very unwelcome she feels in the Brescia home. Much as the madwoman of Mugenta was a thorn in their existence at the Ansonia Hotel, this was worst. "I have to move out get my own room, even a small room with a tiny kitchen." Gemma sighed, "Momma, that will create questions, turmoil, guilt, accusations, and the list could go on. I want you to stay put, for now, but avoid having any contact with my mother in law. Join the family for dinner, and do what you did at Santo's house, remember, you were never home."

Jenny agreed. The dynamics had changed in each household, and the adjustment was stressful for each member of the household. However, Maurizio was protected from knowing how the members of the housefold felt. His father was like a mute, no one ever heard his voice. When he did speak, he was ignored, or ridiculed by his wife, so the sound of his voice was rare. In the few times he tried to engage Jenny Liguori in conversation at the table, Anna Brescia would glare at him, and he'd be quiet again, sipping his soup and mentally escaping his life.

Santo sought help for his mother. He hired a woman to take his mother on outings. She went to the zoo, and under great protest, attended lectures at the Metropolitan Museum of Art--which she didn't understand and dined in the most prestigious restaurants of New York with her paid companion. Now she had someone to talk to, to make her feel as though she were being attended to and not ignored. In time, her anger diminished somewhat, but old habits were difficult to break.

When the Contessa woke up in the morning, her first thought was to criticize someone. She liked her paid companion Marta, who spoke fluid Italian. In order for her to interact with Marta, Santo asked her to lie about her station in life. He explained that his mother would respect her only if she was a titled person. So Marta became Duchess Marta. Contessa was thrilled. At least the riff-raff were out of the house, and she could take her rightful place in the home. She moved into Jenny Liguori's old room but still resented her son for having put her in the maid's quarters.

After he explained that he did that so that she would be closer to him, she reluctantly forgave him. Things balanced out and improved as Contessa Genoveffa Averso stepped in center stage in her son's life.

However, since old habits were difficult to break, Contessa had to recite her litany of curses, and did that daily for five minutes after she got up, right after the rosary. Luckily she had graduated to compartmentalizing the ritual by doing the rosary first, without interruption, and cursing secondly after the last Our Father. She improved in her demeanor and behavior after indulging herself in her "sfuocare"--letting out fury, only behind her own closed doors.

* * *

Maurizio's life was exactly what he had envisioned it to be. Unaware of the backstage business in his household, for him, finding Gemma, his daughter Anna, and Jenny was the best event of his life. He did not take Gemma for granted, seeing how very much she had been loved by a count who moved an opera house impressario to ensnare her.

His daughter and he grew close. He spent time with her in music, bike riding, concerts and the Central Park Zoo, their favorite place. Maurizio enjoyed the monkeys and told his daughter that his first oboe teacher looked like one of them. Anna laughed heartily and enjoyed her father's exaggerated sense of humor. The only thorn in his side was that Santo Averso commanded half an hour a week from the two females in his life, his wife and daughter.

He readily told everyone that he and Gemma were married. It took a year to get the divorce, and then marriage was performed by a justice of the peace, which infuriated Maurizio. He had wanted a Catholic marriage ceremony, but since her first one to Santo was in a Catholic chapel, she could not be permitted to receive the Catholic church's sacrament of marriage. Gemma, as always, calmed him down, and he insisted that she wear a wedding ring and tell everyone that she was Mrs. Maurizio Brescia. Gemma did. A year later, when Anna was six years old, the immediate families gathered for a ceremony at City Hall and a wedding dinner at the Plaza Hotel. Maurizio wanted a honeymoon but career constraints and schedules didn't permit one. He toasted his wife, "at last I am complete."

* * *

Anna was now in the first grade, and she was a brilliant student, as well as a talented music student. She practiced piano for over an hour a day.

Her mother was her teacher, but Gemma was looking for another colleague to teach her daughter since it was difficult to do so, both emotionally and musically.

Anna had perfect pitch. She loved singing and did it all the time. She loved doing scales and vocalises with her mother matching notes almost simultaneously. These were her games. This was her childhood.

Her parents had made a good decision to allow her to see Poppa Santo once a week with Gemma present. Anna adored him, and often Gemma would go sit at another table and read a book, so they could interact freely.

As Gemma predicted, Anna grew to love her real father with a great deal of zeal. She was flesh of his flesh and her soul was akin to his. Her likes and dislikes and even her temperament, displaying impatience with things if they didn't go her way, were just like her father's. Gemma kept a close watch on her daughter and tried to tone down her arrogance. However, she couldn't, because ultimately it was life that taught her that lesson.

* * *

Vittorio Brescia was enthralled with the addition of Jenny Liguori and his son's family to the household. He'd always liked Jenny. She was kind, had a great sense of humor and, like he, adored her offspring as he adored his. He was pleased that his wife whose life was one of hard work and solitude, finally had a female companion, their son's mother-in-law living with them. They had so much in common. They had one child, talented and beautiful, one magnificent precocious granddaughter in common, and they'd come from Milano. Yet Vittorio ignored what he knew in his heart that his wife Anna resented Jenny Liguori. She was jealous when her husband spoke to her at the table. After enough dirty looks, he grew silent even in that.

Since Vittorio was in the costume department at the Metropolitan Opera house, he worked long hours, longer than the musicians. After each performance, they had to collect the costumes and put them back in their places. Every costume belonged to a different opera. Every operatic role involved more than one costume, and that one costume had to be duplicated in different sizes to suit the singers' bodies. Alterations were a constant, and Vittorio worked hard. Often he got home at 3:00 in the morning, and only Jenny heard it because her room was near the elevator, and she could hear him come in.

It took a few months for Vittorio to see that his wife and Jenny barely spoke or tolerated each other. The apartment was huge. Two rooms and a small study belonged to the senior Brescias. Jenny had one small bedroom, young Anna the larger one, and Maurizio and Gemma the largest and most elegant master bedroom tucked in the far end of the apartment. There were four bathrooms, a luxury one didn't find in Milano.

Vittorio felt that his wife was on edge all the time, and after having his feelings ruffled once too often by her snappy retorts, or by making him feel invisible, he did just that. He decided to become invisible, and having any interaction with a woman on any level was delegated to women outside the household. And so, the invisible Vittorio Brescia lived in a house with revolving faces, all looking the other way in order to not have their space invaded. The happiest of the entire household, was rightfully so Maurizio, his bride, and young Anna.

Much as paradise had not been achieved in the family dynamic, it was sometimes good, or sometimes intolerable. Yet, it was never lonely. Anna the beautiful spunky bright grandchild, provided the tendons which connected the three families to each other.

* * *

Gemma, too, had the best life in the household. She had found a man who communed with her in every way. They were beautiful and handsome young people, they had a bond of classical music sustaining their souls. They had an absolutely outstanding child in Anna. They needed to be involved with their music, and more and more, Gemma's career blossomed. European trained musicians were looked at with greater prestige, from the opera singer to the instrumentalist.

Gemma enjoyed friendships at school, and because she was so sensuous and gentile, men adored her and sought her attention. She entered into this marriage with the full knowledge of her beloved Maurizio's fragile ego and short temper. She tempered his outbursts, and he looked to her as his angel. What they meant to each other and how they interacted was the affirmation of truly two soul-mates.

Gemma knew that she was happy, but--because of superstition that if you say something, someone would give it the evil eye--she never articulated it to a soul. "Are you happy," was a question she never answered, not even to her husband. In this regard, and only in this, she thought like a Sicilian, secretive and silent about what she was feeling.

Chapter Eight
JENNY BREAKS AWAY

A year into their new life, Anna was registered for the Catholic elementary school of the Sacred Heart, which was a short walk from their home. Jenny was chosen as Anna's caretaker to and from school, and Jenny welcomed the opportunity to meet other people outside of the Brescia compound. The school was on 71st Street between Broadway and Columbus Avenues.

Rosa Cipolla was in her thirties, but she looked older. She spoke only Sicilian, and came from Corleone, the town in Sicily that had a bad reputation. After they dropped off the children, they went to a diner up the block, and Rosa took her home baked hot rolls out of her pocket and shared them with Jenny. They ate on the sneak because bringing food in the diner was not permitted. Jenny was mortified, but Rosa loved the "game" of sneaking and said, "It's more fun this way. Relax!"

Rosa took private English sessions in exchange for cleaning a woman's apartment. She had to do this "on the sneak" or her husband would beat her.

Jenny was appalled. She asked Rosa if she loved her husband. Rosa replied, "I saw him twice before we married. We're poor peasants; my family paid a thousand lire for my dowry to get me a husband. We sleep together. Is that love? I don't know. I live with our dog, too. Sometimes we eat together. Is that love? I don't know." Jenny learned that not everyone in Italy lives well.

The first half of the year, Anna was in Class 1A. After Christmas, she was moved to Class 1B. When Anna was in Class 1B, Jenny noticed that her friend Rosa Cipolla wasn't around. A week later, Jenny learned that Luchino Cipolla had died of lung congestion.

The following Monday, Rosa Cipolla appeared dressed in black. Jenny was truly sad about Rosa's loss; it brought back her husband's death.

"Oh, Rosa, I'm so sorry," Jenny said as she embraced her. "What happened?"

"He had coal dust in his lungs. He died."

"What are you going to do?" she asked.

"Work hard, learn to speak Americano, and get married." Jenny thought she was joking, but on the other hand, Rosa never joked, she had no sense of humor, "what are you saying?" she asked with a smirk.

"My brother in law is marrying me. He has to. I'm his brother's widow with his brother's son, and it's understood." She didn't realize that other people didn't necessarily follow that tradition.

"Oh Dio!" Jenny said in awe. Had they had a flirtation? An affair? Had this been going on for a long time? How could they just get married?

"When you're poor, and there's no hope for you, no money, no home, family takes care of you. A man and a woman can't be in a room by themselves without a marriage. So that's what we're doing."

Jenny persisted, "Is he in love with you?"

Rosa laughed. "Again, that word. He needs a cook, a clean house and I need a home, and a father for my son. One hand washes the other. Jenny, what's wrong?"

"Nothing, it's just different." She didn't wish to sound critical.

They went for coffee and talked about the stark differences in their traditions from Milano to Sicily. The Sicilians had a culture, an ethic native to that island. It all was tied in to economics and thousands of years of being invaded by the Normans, the Saracens, the Greeks, the French, the Turks, and others. The hands of the clock moved slowly in a land where change was a threat to the people.

Surely, two weeks later, Rosa met Jenny outside the school as they left off the children, went for coffee at the diner, and, instead of taking out the hot rolls from her pocket, Jenny took out little triangular fig pastries.

"My wedding pastry," she said as she handed a small bag to Jenny.

"Congratulations!" Jenny was overcome with happiness for her friend, but soon her joyful tears dried up, because Rosa thought she was a little crazy to take such pleasure in her plight.

"What for?" she asked.

"You just got married," Jenny answered incredulously.

"A marriage of convenience, Jenny. We're moving to South Beach, Staten Island. Bernardo Cipolla has a home out there. He's a fisherman, and he sells fish wholesale at the Fulton market. We have paesani out there from Corleone, the Cascios, the Leones, the Scalisis, and others. It'll be like Sicily again. I want you to visit me." Jenny had mixed emotions about the news. She didn't want to lose this friend; she was envious that she had gotten married so soon after her husband died; she thought about the Sicilian rituals and how protective they were of family. It was to say the least, a comfort.

Gemma always spent a half hour with her mother after the evening activities and family obligations had been met. She was astounded by her mother's narrative about Rosa Cipolla. Gemma's opinion about Rosa's second marriage to her brother-in-law was that it was medieval and insane.

She never had heard any woman say she didn't know about love. What kind of a prehistoric life did they lead in Sicily? Gemma's opinion of Sicilians, always low, always prejudiced, now hit bottom. "Barbaric!" she said. "Momma, absolutely a civilization behind the times. Oh, Dio. I hope you don't envy her."

"How did you guess? The body isn't even cold in the grave, and she's got a husband. I'm jealous, Gemma. Living with the Brescias? Not for me! I have to go. Anna Brescia and the Contessa are miserable women. One cuts you with the tongue and the other with a tongue and a knife. For me? They're the same!"

Gemma was saddened that her mother felt like an outsider. Surely after Jenny lived with her own in-laws for fifteen years of her marriage, then fifteen years with Luigi and Gemma, this Brescia compound made her feel homeless.

"Momma, I'm making money at school. Maurizio is doing well, and I would like to see you get your own place. I think now is a good time. God knows a year has passed, it might not be noticed as a rejection of them, that's my only concern, but I'll smoothen it out. Let me talk with my husband. Why not?"

Jenny protested, "let me find a job, I have to pay my own rent; I can't depend on you both. That's not right."

However, there was hope now. Gemma embraced her mother, then went to bed and waited up for her husband as usual.

Gemma and Maurizio talked about Jenny's plan. Her mother wanted her own place, and Gemma thought that it would be a great idea. Maurizio was upset. Surely how could anyone want to leave this wonderful situation where they all lived together, separately but under the same roof.

Maurizio tried to improve the situation for Jenny, by offering her the practice room where their daughter had her piano, as her own sitting room to be used for her guests. He took it as a personal affront that his mother-in- law had to leave because he had not fulfilled his family responsibility towards her.

"But Momma Jenny," he argued, "you were able to live with the Aversos and that mad woman for five years, what is happening in this house that is making you so unhappy?"

She blushed furiously and sipped some water as she thought of how she could possibly answer that without offending anyone. Surely this was not going to be a moment of truth. He looked so perturbed, and she was deeply touched by his love and concern.

"Maurizio," she began, "I used to have my own home. My husband died, and I'm homeless. At the Aversos, I felt like a prisoner, and the hostage was my daughter. I prayed she'd find you. Look around you. There are two couples here, your parents, and you two. I'm alone. It's nice to see good marriages here, but it hurts, and I have to find a husband of my own."

His brow was furrowed with concern. He held her hands, and kissed them. "I love you, Momma Jenny. I want you to be happy. I want you to have your own place but it has to be close by. Don't worry about money; Gemma and I are doing well."

She embraced him and told him that she had money she could furnish her own small place with, but she needed a job so that she could be independent. In accord with her wish, he told her that if she wanted to come back, her room would always be there. In fact, he asked if she would sleep over several nights a week so that he could see her.

"He's a prince!" Jenny said to her daughter that night. She asked the principal at the school of the Sacred Heart for a job, a vacancy in the kitchen came up, and they offered the job as food server to Jenny.

Within the month, she hunted for a small apartment and found one across the street from her daughter's building. It was a one-bedroom with a small eat-in kitchen, and a postage stamp living room large enough for two small upholstered chairs and a coffee table. The rent was eight dollars a month, and Jenny earned twenty dollars a month, and had enough to live on. She was ecstatic over her "palace" and decorated it with plants, paintings, and lights. It was her home. It was perfect.

Jenny left early, picked up her granddaughter, took her to school, then reported to the school's kitchen to work. It was such a made-to-order job.

Finally, she had found a spot in the city of New York to call her own. However, after her job and family duties, Jenny went to school. She took up English as a second language and read voraciously. She worked on her appearance and modernized her look to appear more American. A vibrant, fifty-two year old, she started to draw attention to herself. As she acquired the layers of goals she had set for herself, she grew in self esteem. She had joy. Fair haired, blue eyed, tall and slender, Jenny Liguori came into her own. Her Italian accent was a charming asset and shortly she became articulate and knowledgeable.

Rosa Cipolla grew at her own pace, and she and Jenny talked frequently. Once a month these two unlikely friends met. They shared an insatiable desire to grow and improve.

In the spring, when Jenny Liguori visited Rosa Cipolla, she met the contingent of Sicilians who lived in South Beach. She learned that the Cascios had welcomed Maurizio when he came to America. The entire weekend was spent in talking of their experiences and why they emigrated.

The climate was right, because Rosa Cipolla let it be known that her friend was looking for a husband. This was met with surprise because they couldn't imagine such a beautiful woman would have to look for a man.

Charlie Cascio, who was the world's problem-solver for friends families and strangers, went on a mission. He inquired with all of his paesani, "are there any good men out there?" It happened within the month. Jenny Liguori was introduced to Arcangelo Pallone, a church-going, widower without children. His family were back in Castellamare del Golfo. He was alone in this country and was ready to go back, find a good Sicilian woman, and marry her; he was tired of doing his own laundry, mending and cooking. Therefore, when he met Charlie Cascio through his best friend "compare Massimo," he was ready.

Arcangelo was fifty eight years old. He owned a wholesale fruit market, was prosperous and extremely handsome. Unusual for a Sicilian; he was tall. His dark curly hair was filled with independent curls, each one going in its own direction. His mouth was petulant, and his brow always crinkled in a worried look. It made him look mysterious. Though deeply attractive, Sicilian women were intimidated by his height of 6'3".

Jenny and Arcangelo were terrified to meet. When he heard that she was a woman from Milano, he felt as though he were going out with royalty. He too had his stereotype ideas of a woman from Milano. He had heard that they were snobs, highly educated, and part of the upper class. Arcangelo was incredibly nervous. This was worst than his first date as a young man in Castellamare, which looked like a parade with forty people following them up the dirt road as they walked not daring to hold hands or touch. Arcangelo was shy. Looking into the eyes of a woman embarrassed him. He knew that he was going to make a fool of himself. For the date, he went to Manhattan and had a linen suit custom made. He looked sensational, like a movie star.

Jenny felt foolish. The entire Sicilian neighborhood in South Beach were commanded to find Jenny a tall, handsome, and rich Sicilian, preferably one who had a good suit of clothes instead of work pants. If this came off, her big concern was Gemma's censure. Her daughter disliked Sicilians, as did many people from the mainland, but Jenny couldn't be a chooser in this quest for a husband. She had become acquainted with a Sicilian woman first, then the rest of the Sicilian friends warm, loving and cordial. They were so different than the superior Anna Brescia. The Cascios had volunteered to come along God bless them, she thought. Good, good people.

The first date was orchestrated by the Cascios. Jenny was staying at Rosa Cipolla's house on Foch Avenue. It was late spring, and it was warm. Maria asked Jenny if they could all go to an opera so that they wouldn't have to stare at each other, enjoy the music and steal a glance now and then. Jenny agreed.

They went to the Metropolitan Opera house and they saw a performance of Aida. Maria's plan was perfect. They met Arcangelo at their house, then picked up Jenny at the Cipollas. It was obvious that these two people had an immediate attraction towards each other. Jenny wore a blue dress which matched her eyes, and a hand-made navy blue shawl. Arcangelo, tall dark and handsome wore a gray linen suit and black and white patent leather shoes. He looked like a handsome Mafioso.

Charlie chose a good Italian restaurant and, as they sat next to each other, Charlie was pleased to see Arcangelo turning his body so that he could look at Jenny. He was obviously smitten. His face was flushed, and he seemed as excited as a young boy. Charlie mentioned that Jenny's son in law was at the Met. Arcangelo's eyes opened wide. He was with a princess. Dear God, he thought, he had wanted to cancel every day for the past two weeks when the date was made. Early on, they realized that there was compatibility in their tastes, as well as a strong physical attraction. Arcangelo held Jenny's hand between his. She was jumping out of her skin because she was afraid to even think that she could fall in love so quickly. He felt it, too.

"We done good!" Charlie Cascio whispered to his wife during the intermission, and she squeezed his hand.

"Thank God, Charlie, or you'd turn Staten Island upside down until you found somebody for her."

"You know it, Maria."

The wedding took place at the church of the Sacred Heart in November. Jenny was ecstatic, the groom adored her, and everyone in the circle of family and friends was happy for her. Jenny caught the disdainful look of the senior Anna Brescia, and she shuddered.

"I'm proud of you, Momma," Gemma whispered.

"You're my heroine," Maurizio said to Jenny. She glowed.

Arcangelo felt blessed by the gods. Not only was he madly in love with her, but her other attributes added prestige to his life.

They went to Niagara Falls for their honeymoon. Arcangelo, had always felt like a second class citizen because he was Sicilian. With Jenny, his feelings of self worth grew. Like an expert potter, Jenny molded his self image very diplomatically, and taught him the niceties of social protocol. Arcangelo was an avid student, and he learned to not only feel good about himself, but to adore his teacher. As a second marriage, this one was a winner. Conversely, Jenny's own self worth accelerated with every loving act of her new husband. He made no secret of his love for her, and treated her as though she were a queen. The euphoria of a young couple in love gradually diminishes, as they go through the growing pains of their union as a couple.

But the older couple has lived through that ritual of change, and their meshing becomes a more solid relationship, taking nothing or each other for granted.

Italian women did not defy traditions easily without censure, but she had. Jenny had broken away and found her dolce vita with a forbidden species: A Sicilian man.

Chapter Nine

175 WEST 72ND STREET

Katy Cascio Leone, divorced her husband, and decided to take her twin sons and move to the city, at 175 West 72nd street. "What? her father Charlie Cascio bellowed, "you can't move without us," Charlie's eldest daughter Paula was friendly with an opera diva who lived there with her operatic coach husband, and called Paula to tell her that there were three apartments available in her building. They lost no time. Charlie, his wife and daughters visited the building, and put a deposit down for three apartments. They closed up their houses in Staten Island and made one massive move.

"Poppa," Paula had said to her father, "this is the city, not East Harlem okay? The kids have to have constant supervision, to and from school, can you handle it?" Charlie was insulted, "since when does a daughter question her father's ability to do anything? Hah? Don't question me again, you hear?" Paula heard, but she got her point across.

Paula thought about East Harlem which seemed like another country rather than New York, because Sicilian was spoken in the neighborhood and on occasion, broken English. Often another language erupted, bastardized English. "Pighia la begga e metterci l'isi screama" take the bag and put the ice cream in it. (Begga was bag, and isi screama was ice cream, in the melded language.)

107th street had tenement houses, of eight and ten family railroad apartments. Every stoop had a grandmother sitting on it with a metal chair, shelling peas for the evening meal. Every stoop had a bunch of kids playing stoop ball, and running out in the street to get it. The cars played dodge ball by avoiding hitting the kids. Anybody who came on the block belonged there. Often some of the racketeers would stand by the curb observing the cars as they went through the block, "get the hell out of here, you don't belong here," one would say. Cops cars didn't pass by too often, they had been given the word not to. Past history had changed their privilege of driving on 107th street.

On the rooftops of the tenement houses, there was another species flying around, pigeons. There were homing pigeons, and regular pigeons, some cost a fortune, but they were intelligent and were trained by the young boys on the roof.

Every back yard, had fig trees as well as tomato plants and swiss chard growing. Some creative landlords, dared to grow flowers, frowned upon by the average Sicilian, who said, "what good is it if you can't eat it?" Some flowers you could eat, like the zucchini flowers which were a delicacy. They were washed, and then put into an egg and milk batter and fried with hot oil.

City people had clothes dryers, but Harlemites had the line-o pole in the back yard where no matter what the weather was like, clothes were put out to dry. Sometimes the pigeons did a number on the billowing sheets on the line, and the woman of the house would yell, "schifosi disgraziati" from her window.

Rituals like the Sunday pranzo were very important. Before everyone went to Mass, the meatballs were made, fried and put in the sauce. Roasts and chickens were prepared and put in the oven until they came home from Mass; then the oven was turned on. At 2:00 in the afternoon, across the Italian sections of the city, the ritual of the pranzo began with the call, "put on the Pot" One could always smell where the Italians lived on a Sunday, just by sniffing in the hallway.

The early 30's was a time for interaction with peripheral family members, grandparents, uncles, aunts, and even godparents. The children were "king," and whatever it took to help the young couples, the family did.

After the divorce, Katy married a senator from Washington D.C. On her honeymoon with Tom, Bruno Leone her ex husband, found out that Katy had gotten married, and kidnapped his twin sons and took them, his parents, grandmother to Naples, Florida.

When Katy returned from her honeymoon, she discovered that her boys were missing as well as Bruno and the family. The F.B.I. was informed, and her husband, Senator Tom Porter used his influence to intensify the search through all the states.

Charlie Cascio did too. He had a couple of favors owed him by some of the "boys" on 107th street. They got on it right away. Eventually it was the "boys" who found the Leone twins in Florida, and brought them back home, but it took a month and some strong arm methods with members of the Leone family to get that done.

* * *

Meanwhile, Katy's apartment was now vacant, and once more Eileen shared the news with Jenny Liguori Pallone. They immediately rented it and moved back to 175 West 72nd Street, in Katy's old apartment. Jenny didn't realize that Katy was a Cascio, and that it was Charlie's efforts to find Jenny a husband which precipitated the blind date with Arcangelo Pallone. After the marriage, the casual friends went their separate ways, they thought, when all the while, they lived in the same building.

* * *

As the second year of elementary school began for Anna, she met and befriended Carli Mulligan, the Cascio grandchild, and began a lifelong friendship.

Anna was picked up daily by Grandma Jenny outside the school, and enthusiastically spoke about her new friend, Carli Mulligan. "She sings on pitch, Grandma. We sang 'The Star Spangled Banner' this morning, and both of us were the only ones you could hear. It was so wonderful, Grandma; she loves music. I liked her right away." Jenny thought that her granddaughter had been brought up in Santo Averso's world of "class" distinction something that wouldn't work in America. No one ever had told Anna that when her natural father adopted her, that she'd lost the title of "Contessa." Jenny was very uncomfortable with this. Anna's arrogance was a trait of the royal class.

Anna bragged about being a Contessa and told Carli about it. That afternoon, when Charlie Cascio picked up Carli from school, she told him that she had met a real live Countess.

"Let me tell you something, principessa, all grandparents give their grandchildren royal titles in Sicily, and yeah, even in Italy. It's a common thing to call a kid 'Regina,' or 'Principessa.' Carli got frustrated when her grandfather didn't believe her. She insisted that Anna was an Italian Countess. "Look, Principessa, don't I call the twins, 'General One' and 'General Two?' They've never been in the army. They're only six years old. Grandparents do this. She wasn't born a Contessa. Why the heck do you believe everything people tell you? She's a kid. What does she know?"

Carli was angry. However, after they went to the ice cream parlor for their afternoon ice cream sundae and Carli noticed the sad expression on Grandpa's face, something he had tried to hide by a too wide and too ready a smile, the royalty issue seemed so unimportant.

Grandpa Charlie tried hard to amuse her. She too was traumatized for she missed her twin cousins so. Every afternoon after school, they'd go to the ice cream parlor, and while they had their snack, Grandpa told the children stories of how they used to make wine in Corleone. Now he had few stories to tell. He was preoccupied with moving heaven and earth to find them. He was in constant contact with the "boys" from 107th street, three of the meanest looking thugs he'd ever seen. It was a terrible time in the lives of the whole family.

* * *

The city streets were not filled with children playing, unlike east Harlem, where ring-a-leerio and hide-and-seek and patsy games and pick-up jacks were played on the stoops of the tenement houses. On 72nd Street, another wide thoroughfare, children were seen only as they came home from school with a chaperone.

Anna and Carli parted at school and went with their respective grandparents. Carli to the ice cream parlor, and Anna directly to her home, where grandma Anna prepared a feast of fruit for her granddaughter.

Ironically Charlie Cascio waited on the corner while Jenny Liguori Pallone waited in front of the school. They never saw each other in the crowded sidewalk as nannies and grandparents picked up the children.

Grandma Jenny dropped Anna Brescia off in the Brescia apartment. Anna Brescia changed out of her school uniform and got into cotton pajamas and started her study routine. She had no time to play or "hang out," like other children. She practiced scales, arpeggios and technical exercises for an hour, followed by her piano pieces on her own piano, in her own study. The room was white, had plants, and white lace curtains on the windows, and a small loveseat sofa. Anna loved her music room the best. She did her homework, then read and had to cover several pages of reading aloud in Italian to Grandma Anna in the kitchen while Grandma cooked. At 6:00 p.m. or sometimes later, young Anna had completed her music and homework. She, her grandmother, and her mom ate dinner together because her father and grandfather were working at the Metropolitan Opera house on 39th street..

Maurizio always got up early to spend time with his young daughter. He asked her about school, and she asked him about the opera house. Maurizio related the mishaps on stage which amused Anna. As she took her schoolbag and jacket to go off to school with Grandma Jenny, Maurizio hugged and kissed her on the forehead, then exclaimed, "Oh Dio, Anna, I've swallowed one of your curls." Anna laughed heartily and Maurizio made that dialogue his daily ritual just to hear her laugh. After she left, he crawled back in bed until almost noon.

175 West 72nd Street was a "city" dwelling. The building was posh, had a doorman, and an elevator. It was occupied by tenants who were professionals. They did not fraternize, nor did they want to. New York City residents walk with blank stares, they try not to look at people, nor at what's going on around them, mind their own business, don't interfere in any incident on the street, and act as though they've been brought up Sicilian. Their homes are places to retreat to, from the hub of the city.

* * *

As the first semester drew to a close, right before Thanksgiving, Sister Philippa ordered a nativity play involving the first five grades of the school. It was pulled off in one month, and it was brilliant. The play was divided up among the grades. They had after-school rehearsals every day and two dress rehearsals for Christmas week. The entire class of second graders did the vocal music of traditional Christmas songs, accompanied by Anna Brescia and her mother on piano, in a four-handed arrangement written by Gemma.

Brian Mulligan and Charlie Cascio worked on Saturdays at the school to build the sets, the creche of Baby Jesus, and the other props. Maria sewed the costumes for the main characters, and other parents contributed their talents. Jenny Liguori Pallone was in charge of the refreshment committee, and she volunteered her husband Arcangelo Pallone to help build the sets, and that's where he and Charlie found each other again and exclaimed, "what a small world," Charlie Cascio uttered, "not in New York City," Arcangelo observed, "we've probably passed each other on the sidewalk a dozen times, yet we never knew." The biggest shock was that they all lived in the same building, and had never met before. But there were more surprises for the city dwellers, who can live a lifetime in a tall building and never know their next door neighbor.

One Saturday morning. Maurizio Brescia showed up with his wife Gemma to rehearse a piano accompaniment and an oboe obligato for Anna's solo. It was there that Charlie and Brian were stunned to see the Milanese musician as part of the parents group of participants.

Maurizio had met Charlie Cascio, when he came to this country with Charlie's nephew Salvatore Leone. Paula Cascio Mulligan had taught him English. Once more the cross threads of human contact were uncovered. "A small world" Maurizio commented, as he affectionately embraced Charlie Cascio.

The night of the show, young Anna Brescia sang "Oh Holy Night" with her mother and father accompanying her. Anna's high melodious voice, accompanied by the pure sound of the oboe obligato, filled the auditorium. Charlie whispered in Maria's ear, "our principessa was right. The kid's a real Contessa!"

After the Christmas pageant and show, Sister Philippa invited everyone to the reception planned and executed by Anna's grandmother, Jenny Liguori Pallone.

When the Cascios and Mulligans got home that night, they speculated about Maurizio's wife. "Don't you remember he said that his Italian sweetheart was a pianist?" Charlie reminded Paula. "She's not only beautiful," Paula commented, "but talented. It has to be the great love he left behind." Charlie recalled, "but don't you remember how heartbroken he was when his mother wrote him and told him that his sweetheart had married someone else? We had to practically pick up the pieces of his heart, don't you remember Paula?" Paula smirked, "I know I know, but Gemma has to be the woman he left behind, I swear to you, Poppa, they found a way to be together..I'd bet on it." Charlie said, "kids talk, Anna'll probably tell our Carli."

A day later, Carli begged her parents for piano lessons with Mrs. Brescia, and the Mulligans acquiesced. Carli flourished under Gemma's tutelage, and luckily she took her piano lesson upstairs in Gemma's studio.

Other conveniences fell into place, which was of mutual benefit for Carli and Anna. When the families renewed their friendships, Anna and Carli were encouraged to develop theirs.

175 West 72nd Street was the building which attracted theater arts people because of its close proximity to the theater district. It also brought two young girls with talent and ambition together to share in parallel paths in the field of music, as well as a lifelong friendship.

Chapter Ten

THE IMMIGRANTS REFLECT ON LIFE

Rosa Cipolla was limited in her vision of life until she met Jenny Liguori. Through Jenny she learned about love, about the value of education, and about self-improvement. Rosa was an avid student, and she hung on to Jenny Liguori's every word.

Rose's only son, Antonio spoke about Anna Brescia particularly on assembly day. Only eight, yet, his heart had been touched at the beauty of this child's voice. One day, he came home from school and shyly said to his mother as he gazed at the crucifix over his mother's bed.

"Momma, some day I'm going to marry Anna Brescia." Rosa was stunned. "Why do you say this?" "I'll love her forever, Momma."

Love? Even her son felt this emotion. She was deeply touched at her son's declaration and wondered what that feeling was like.

She had seen it when Jenny Liguori met Arcangelo Pallone for the first time in her South Beach home. They looked at each other and seemed to drown in each other's gaze. Was it that? The chemistry? The electricity?

She would never know it. How could electricity happen when Cipolla never looked at her? She had to pour his wine. She ate her food cold because something was always forgotten on the stove. What was it, this thing called love? Would she ever find out? she wondered.

* * *

The Brescias were very concerned that their progeny was too serious for her age. She needed more socialization in her life, and her parents decided to orchestrate activities to balance her life.

As if in answer to their need, Brian asked Maurizio if Anna could join Carli in the Cascio Saturday morning ritual of breakfast by two great chefs. Maurizio's curiosity was aroused, and he told his wife about it.

Gemma laughed. "Much as I hate to admit it, I like that Sicilian family, especially Carli. Any fraternization with her is very amenable to me. Would you take her, though? I have make up piano lessons at the school." On Saturday morning, Anna carried a small basket of home-made cookies Grandma Anna had baked and brought them to the Cascios. Maurizio knocked on the door, as Charlie opened the kitchen door, appearing in a high chef's hat and a white apron, followed by Brian with his. Maurizio laughed heartily, and asked if he could watch them in action. Sicilian music was played on the victrola, and Charlie moved to the beat of the music, and occasionally grabbed Brian's arm and they danced a complete turn. The girls covered their mouths trying to stifle their giggles. "Maurizio, this is our show. It's a little different than the one you're used to."

What an incredible spirit Charlie had. He was his own show. He didn't have to go anywhere for entertainment; he did it himself. No wonder Brian hung around Charlie. Brian, who was so conservative, became a kid when he was with his Sicilian father-in-law.

Charlie came out singing the drinking song from Traviata to the lyrics of "la la la la la" because he didn't know the words. Maurizio couldn't stop laughing. They were a team, but Brian was definitely the straight man. Charlie set the tray on the table with the three choices of coffee. Each coffee needed a different size cup, and all the sizes were lined up in the middle of the table like a ceramic army of soldiers. Italians took plenty of sugar with their coffee, so the sugar was put in the deep soup bowl.

Maurizio chose espresso and watched with glee as Charlie and Brian danced around each other making the breakfast for "la Principessa e la Contessa."

Therefore Maurizio became a frequent breakfast buddy in the Cascio household. When he told his wife and mother about it, he said,

"Charlie Cascio might not have class, Gemma, but he has something more important, a noble soul, and his Saturday production of food, music and antics is an act of love for his family."

Gemma realized that her prejudice against Sicilians should not be a blanket attitude, for there were good people from that island, and her husband had encountered the best. Ironically, Charlie Cascio had not only harbored and nurtured Maurizio when he came from Italy, but had also found a good husband for her mother, who's transformation after she met Arcangelo Pallone was miraculous. Yes, this was all due to Charlie Cascio's love for people. Her mindset against the Sicilians was changing, one Sicilian at a time.

However, Gemma immediately took to Carli Mulligan. The child was open, enthusiastic and musical. She learned fast and practiced diligently but wasn't so rigid that she wouldn't give up a practice day to go to a party or to another event.

Carli enjoyed watching her grandparents and making observations about who really was in charge in that household. Grandpa felt strongly about everything and everyone. People were either good or bad, life was either black or white, and what tempered his strong opinions was his wife. Maria arched her right eyebrow, right after Charlie announced a directive set in cement, and Charlie would gesticulate in a desperate gesture and shout, "What? What? Why are you looking at me like that? Talk! Damn it! What's wrong?"

* * *

"Charlie, it won't work," she'd say, and he'd reply in a sentence beginning with a conjunction, "and now you gotta tell me?" Charlie often started a sentence with a conjunction. Carli "hung around" just to eavesdrop, and Charlie would use her as his sounding board.

"You see your grandmother? She knows everything. Don't ask me what time it is, ask her. Without a watch, she could tell you. She sees the shadows fall on the floor and she knows what time it is. And she doesn't even have to get up from the chair to look. If she loses something she calls St. Anthony, and if he's out of town, she calls St. Jude, and then it pops up. You know why it pops up? Because even the saints know that she knows everything--you hear Principessa? What do I know, right? but your grandmother she knows, you know

79

why? because she knows everything, just ask her." Carli would giggle, "Grandma, is it true you know everything?" she'd shrug and totally unaffected by his drama, would say, "Carli, ask him, he knows nothing about nothing but he knows about me." With this, Charlie would go storming out. The dialogue never changed, it was always the same, and though it was predictable, Carli never missed any of these soap operas her grandparents created, and would commit them to memory, so that some day she might tell her children the way it was.

* * *

One of the important social issues for the Brescias, was seeing to it that Anna rubbed elbows with well-to-do, or professional people's children.

Maurizio had many friends in the wind section of the orchestra. Most of them were married with children. Once a month, they'd entertain the wind section of the orchestra with their wives and children if they were close to Anna's age. On Sunday evening, Maurizio invited them for dinner. The children indulged in games in the smaller parlor, and enjoyed activities such as painting and sculpturing.

It saddened Maurizio that the Derisis were no longer invited to their musical soires. Gemma's rationale was stated succinctly, "with her glib tongue, she'd probably give Santo news about them." Maurizio felt strongly about keeping Santo out of his life in any way possible. Therefore the interaction between the Derisis and Brescias was terminated, however Maurizio continued to teach Pino, in his own home on Fifth Avenue.

One Saturday afternoon, Maurizio went to the Derisi home for Pino's oboe lesson. Santo Averso was working in the study with Gino. Letizia had gone shopping. Maurizio rang the doorbell and was admitted into the apartment by the maid. He knew his way into the music room, and went in, set up his oboe, and the hand-written double oboe arrangement of a Bach Two Part Invention. Pino was thrilled. Maurizio transcribed the piano pieces.

"You did it, Maestro!" he said gleefully. "Oh my God, I want to play this at the next concert." Maurizio was pleased. Surely the boy was capable or Maurizio wouldn't have arranged this music for Pino.

He did it between rehearsal schedules, and a few minutes before he went to bed at night.

They sight read it very slowly. Maurizio marked off phrases, in order to delineate where breathing should occur. Bach's baroque style of writing in one continuous line challenged the musicians and singers who needed their breath to execute the passages. Maurizio tried one phrase at a time to see how long he could sustain his breath. Pino would immediately play after him.

Meanwhile, Santo had strolled out of Letizia's study and was drawn to the beauty of the two exquisitely sounding instruments. He stared at Maurizio and realized what a magnificent young man he was. A twinge of jealousy tugged at his heart as he recalled that the five years Gemma had spent with him had been wiped out in an instant--when she'd seen her musical god again.

Had she ever been his? Had she been play acting when he made love to her? He felt the strength leave his body, and he slipped back into the study to pick up his spirits with a cup of espresso coffee, Gino noticed how pale Santo was, and said, "I forgot about the lesson, but, do you want to meet him?" Santo frowned, "no, Gino, I can't erase those years when she was mine and the most beautiful child in the world called me Poppa. I deserve what happened, I played God once too often in my life."

The afternoon went on, as Maurizio and Pino practiced the Bach transcription. Gino couldn't concentrate and neither did Santo who sat staring, just staring. The impact of Santo's loss was worst that Gino ever knew.

After the lesson, Maurizio went to the theater for a rehearsal, and when he went home and Gemma asked him how his lesson had gone, Maurizio enthusiastically commented, "Pino is incredible. Whatever I show him, he can do, the breathing is so difficult, and yet, he did it."

"Was Letizia there?" she asked, and Maurizio said, "why don't you call her and go have lunch somewhere? Why does the past have to permeate our lives like a poison? It would please me if you saw Letizia privately."

"Okay, I'll call her." Gemma said, and she did.

Chapter Eleven

THE 'TEEN YEARS

The United States was already involved in the European war long before Pearl Harbor. Americans were not complacent, but they did believe that Franklin Delano Roosevelt was sincere when he told the people in his radio fireside chats that their country would not get into a foreign war. Sicilians didn't believe it.

School children in New York were immersed in current events at school. The news in Europe was bleak, and desperate nations looked to America for aid. In 1940, America was still officially out of it. However, that was to change on December 7, 1941.

Anna and Carli attended the High School of Performing Arts, and on Saturdays at Manhattan School of Music on East 105th Street, for the study of music theory, keyboard harmony, sight singing and voice lessons. School now stretched into a six day week, leaving almost no time for recreation.

Carli complained. Anna knew no other lifestyle, so she worked, studied, and practiced as well as achieved the highest grades in her academic studies. Socialization came to a stand still, for, like a football player, she kept her eye on the goal.

Her grandfather Vittorio Brescia sometimes worked on repairing a brocade at home, and between seams, cutting, ripping and stitching, he sang.

Anna was amused by his voice. It was raspy and limited, but as he sang the arias, he turned red when he couldn't get the high notes. Anna stood behind the bedroom door and giggled uncontrollably. Sometimes he'd hear her, open the door slowly, and catch her in the act of eavesdropping.

"So where do you think you got your voice from?" and Anna laughed, wishing Carli would see her grandfather in action. This moment had to be shared. Carli, who studied her grandparents' routine like a hawk, would enjoy this one.

After she was caught, Anna called Carli on the telephone and shared the incident. Carli told Anna to take notes: "Memorable Moments, write them down. Too precious to forget. You can keep a log on stuff that happens so you can share these with your children some day."

"I doubt I'll ever have them. Who'll have time after I launch my career?"

"Don't discount it, Anna. You'd make a wonderful mother. No other kid in the world would get a lullaby sung to him quite that way."

"I suppose. I'd better get to this term paper." Anna hung up.

Carli lived one flight downstairs from her, but short visits were time consuming, so phone calls often numbered five or six a day.

* * *

Maurizio and Gemma's week extended into six days. Therefore, Maurizio's time with his daughter diminished.

Anna reconnected with Santo. She told her mother that she could not turn her back on a man who had been her father for the first five years of her life.

Anna grew rebellious, which threw Maurizio into a tizzy.

"Where does she get this nerve to defy us like this?" Maurizio said one night after he got home, in the nocturnal chats with his wife.

"My darling," Gemma said, "In America there is this unique phenomenon of the teen age years. In Italy one is a child, then an adult. In America, they add another stage, a teenager."

Maurizio moaned painfully.

"Sounds like a social disease," he said.

"It is." She snuggled up to him, and the topic was forgotten as they cast away all other concerns and made love.

Anna's time table was to make the Metropolitan Opera Company before the age of twenty-one. Her father was in awe of this incredible ambition. He didn't make it until he was thirty-two years old. However, as focused and single minded as he was, she was even more so. She seemed to be moving to the beat of her destiny, for nothing could distract her from her course. The adults in her life provided the climate to make this path smooth with little or no obstacles.

Another champion of Anna's destiny was Santo Averso. When he woke up to the dawn of a new day, his mind was filled with thoughts of her. Was she having breakfast, was she vocalizing, was she thinking of him?

He was ecstatic when he was able to spend quality time with Anna again. With both parents so involved in their careers, he was grateful that Anna was now available to him.

Santo and Kay met Anna on Friday afternoon at 5:00 for an early supper, so that they could share the daily events of her day with them. There was always a gift at the end of supper, and a cab ride to her door. Santo told Anna that whatever she did, she must have publicity. He would fund that by hiring the best in New York to report on her every move, operatic or otherwise.

"Poppa, I have no otherwise. I only have music in my life."

Undaunted, Santo responded, "you have no imagination. You must be in the public eye long before you step foot on stage. If you go to the zoo to feed the monkeys, a photographer will snap your picture with a caption that even opera singers take time off to visit the zoo. A good ad for the zoo. Get it? If people look at a newspaper and see your picture once a week, they'd get to know Anna Brescia. What does it matter if they hear you sing or not? They'd know you. Publicity is very important. It will provide your audiences."

He always had answers, Anna thought. A brilliant man! By sixteen Anna's voice had increased in agility and breath control. Her teacher Freidrich Schorr baritone of the Metropolitan Opera was thrilled with the possibilities and of course did everything he could to promote her career. She sang in the salons of the very rich; and she was becoming a household word in those social circles. Anna's recreation was strictly the theater. She and Carli attended together.

Carli loved those outings, in which she was included and treated like one of the family. Dress rehearsals at the Metropolitan opera, afternoon matinees. Santo, belonged to the Metropolitan Opera Guild, had access to rehearsals. They also went to Broadway and the ballet.

It was a wonderful time for the two musical friends. Every theater and every restaurant in New York was visited as a matter of course. Carli's expenses were willingly paid for by Santo Averso.

When Carli began these Saturday planned recreation days, her curiosity about the relationship of Santo Averso to Anna was aroused. Anna explained that Santo was her Italian father, and Maurizio was her American father. Carli asked, "Who's your biological father?"

Anna answered, "Maurizio!!"

Carli smiled. "And me? I'm my mother. My handsome, blonde, blue-eyed Irish father didn't pass on any of his gorgeous features to me."

"But your mother is exquisite, Carli. My father once had a crush on her when he first came to America. He told me."

Carli's eyes twinkled, "Really? Oh my God! We could have been sisters!" she said incredulously.

Anna's expression was pensive again. "Daddy has such a short fuse, Momma is his defuser. She's incredible with him. You know the three of them did that to themselves, and I don't understand why I'm guilty when I'm with my Poppa, but I am. I love Daddy. I adore him, but if I may borrow your grandmother's exact words, he's a pain in the ass sometimes." Carli opened her eyes wide and burst out laughing.

One Saturday afternoon, Anna told Santo that her teacher Freidrich Schorr suggested that she study German diction. Santo suggested that she take private German lessons.

"Poppa, just when am I going to fit them into my schedule?" she asked.

"When you decide that this is really what you want to do with your life, then you will fit them into your schedule," he said.

Carli was present when they had this conversation, and suddenly this very glamorous career of her dearest friend seemed to have the tentacles of a giant octopus. There was so much one had to learn.

Coaching of roles, diction in each of the languages of opera, drama, staging, memorization, and musicality; finally--and not the least-- the vocal production. Demanding and intense in terms of work, this was not the glamorous life Carli had always imagined. Carli realized how much pressure Anna was under.

There was nowhere this young lady could turn to for a calm oasis from the tentacles of this demanding career. Anna cried, and Santo felt terrible. He didn't want to take her home in such a sad state, or Gemma would not allow him to see her again.

"My darling child," Santo began as he put his arm around her "Why do you cry? You can just be a singer of songs and confine yourself to the salons and concert halls, without going into opera. You are a baby, and too young, and you do not have to do this. You can do it in ten years. Why are you pushing yourself before you're even twenty-one? Who told you this?"

"No one told me this, Poppa. I am not a baby. I've wanted this from the time I was little in Milano. I never wanted to be anything but an opera singer. I'll take private lessons in German. My father is struggling now, and I can't ask him to pay out more money for this additional expense. They work so hard, Poppa, that I feel terrible about asking him to foot another bill."

Santo reassured her that he would finance the lessons, and that he'd contact Professor Lutz Stutz from Columbia University to come to his place to give her lessons twice a week. Anna said she'd have to clear it with her parents. Santo said that it wasn't necessary to do so; what they didn't know wouldn't upset them. She insisted that it could only be with their approval, or indeed she'd be singing only in the salons of the very rich.

Carli listened to the two of them and realized that head games were being played. She was fascinated and didn't move as the two of them positioned themselves to win the battle through strategy and manipulation.

After their outing, Santo took them home. Nonna Anna was the only one at home.

Nonna served them cookies and milk as she had since Anna first came into their lives. They talked about the pleasant afternoon they had spent at the Brass Rail, and the Museum of Natural History, and then they went into the music room to talk.

"Anna, are you sure you want to do this? I'm upset seeing you cry like that." Carli kicked off her shoes and tucked her legs under the pillow of the couch in Anna's music room.

"Yes, I do. I don't know anything else. I'm sixteen now and I know what direction I'm going in, but every time I turn around, there's more that I have to do. Mr. Schorr says my German diction needs work."

"Then diction should be enough, shouldn't it?" Carli argued.

"Not really," Anna explained. "Enunciation is important, but if you don't know what you're saying, you're not convincing. The interpretation affects the credibility of your character, which comes only from knowing what the hell you're singing about."

Carli giggled. It was rare that Anna used profanity, and it was obvious that Anna was angry about that moment of weakness she had exposed herself to with her Poppa Santo.

"My darling, I'm going to kill you, la la la la la la la la," Anna mimicked in English what it would sound like if one didn't know the meaning of the words.

Carli burst out laughing and fell on the floor. "Oh, God, that's such a routine. Become a comedic opera singer. What a show!" Carli giggled and applauded.

"Poppa Santo would get a stroke over that one!" Then Anna really got into it as she imitated his memorized script with a thick Italian accent: "Remember you are a Contessa. You want to sing in parlors of the rich? Good! You will remain in the small salons of the wealthy and you, too, can be one of those who never made it to the opera house. The only way you get to the top is to do what I say. I'll pay the bills and you will be a diva."

Carli was hysterical. Anna was fabulous as an imitator of Santo, throwing her voice into a dark timbre in her gut.

Anna imitated her own parents next. She started with Maurizio. "Tesoro! He says to Momma as he paces the bedroom, 'I don't want that animal in my daughter's life. He stole five years of my life. She'll become a diva without him. She's the one with the voice, not that disgraziato!'"

At that point Anna transformed herself into a willowy sensuous, soft spoken Gemma. "Amore mio, Momma says to Daddy as she caresses his curly hair, 'I cannot possibly break our daughter's heart and tear her away from Santo. After all he was her father for five years.' Get that, Carli? She rubs it in all the time, that five years was his fault, anyway she continues to use the salve that soothes my father's ego, 'What can I do? Do you want a massage?' Now at this point, the innuendo is does he want to go to bed, an offer he never refuses, and she continues: 'tea? Anything amore mio, just calm down, don't get yourself into a froth." Carli was holding her sides, begging Anna to stop. She covered her face.

"Damn them all!" Anna screamed as she fell to the floor with Carli. Suddenly the door opened and Grandma Anna walked in, pale as a bedsheet, and stood there not knowing what to say and shocked at how her granddaughter had lost control of herself.

"What's going on?" Grandma Anna bellowed with her hands on her hips.

"Nonna Anna, please leave us alone. We are having a memorable moment here."

"With vulgarity?' Nonna said as she walked out and shut the door.

"How the hell does she know that word?" Anna asked, and once more the girls screamed and rolled on the floor.

"You know," Anna explained softly, "that she was listening at the door, because she never could have heard this from the kitchen." Anna was really frisky today.

Rare form, thought Carli, and she loved every minute of it. The vulgarity was the most hilarious, because Anna still had Sister Philippa's admonitions about sin categories in her head.

They crawled back on the couch, and groaned with exhaustion.

"Anna, don't sacrifice yourself for someone else's dream." Carli said.

"But it is my dream. It's just that they're all so involved. I remember my early years in Mugenta. I'd sit in the chair while Poppa sang with the recording of La Traviata. At the age of two-and-a-half, I knew one aria. He declared, 'you are a Diva.'

Carli realized that this dream of Anna's had been spawned so early in life. She knew nothing else, but the best thing was that she had the talent to go with the dream. Carli realized that Anna was on her way. There was no doubt that she would make it. Divine providence had blessed this young woman with this gift. Carli listened intently as Anna spoke about her childhood.

As the rebellious emotional battles of the teen-age years ended, a sigh of relief was breathed by the Mulligans and Brescias. A year later, in 1945, World War II would also come to an end.

Chapter Twelve

ANNA'S DEBUT

By 1945, World War II was nearing the end, and Anna Brescia now 19 , was realizing a life-long dream. She was auditioning on a Tuesday afternoon at 2:00 p.m. for the Metropolitan Opera Company.

It was not a morning like any other. She set the alarm for 7:00 a.m; got into the shower, and, as she washed, she began to vocalize. She sang small five-note-runs ascending and descending on successive notes. The voice needed time to "wake up," and she did this by small spurts of vocalises. She would not have lunch today, but she would have to have a sensible breakfast to keep her energy up.

She told her grandmother Anna, who dominated meal preparation and serving in the household, that she wanted two hard boiled eggs and some dry whole wheat toast that morning.

Anna was the only one up besides her grandmother. They had gotten up at the first glimmer of dawn and met in the kitchen. Nonna Anna opened her arms and embraced her granddaughter.

"There's an angel on your shoulder, my love, and he will be with you all day long. You will be magnificent." She kissed her cheek and made the sign of the cross on her throat.

"Thank you, Nonna," Anna said. Nonna was preparing fruit on a platter, and already the eggs were boiling in the water. Anna vocalized as she sauntered around the twenty-four-foot table. She was doing some sustained tones, then quick runs up and down the scale. The canary, whose cage was covered in the corner of the dining room, didn't know that dawn had come until his cover was taken off. Anna smiled as she heard his response to her voice. She pulled the cover off and put her finger in the cage, "there, now you can sing with me, Uccello." She stood in front of the cage and continued to vocalize softly near him. He was all a flutter, and responded with his own song.

Nonna came out of the kitchen with a platter of food for her granddaughter, and then went back for the coffee. They sat opposite each other and enjoyed breakfast. Anna ate her hard-boiled eggs, and took her coffee black with no milk. Milk created phlegm, and she avoided dairy products any time she had to sing.

After breakfast, Anna got dressed in slacks and a blouse with casual shoes and her grandfather Vittorio Brescia, had a sip of black coffee, dressed, and joined her in a walk around the block. It was early and the city was just beginning to wake up.

Maurizio and Gemma got up and found that Anna and Vittorio had gone out. He dressed and ran out to join them. He could see them halfway down the block just ready to turn the corner, and he picked up his pace.

He caught up and put his arm around her. Anna was startled. "Daddy, what are you doing here?" She was pleasantly surprised, and Vittorio could imagine the volcano of emotions his sensitive son was going through.

"I had to be with you," he said.

They talked of everything but the pending audition.

"Daddy, can we get another canary to keep Uccello company?" she asked.

"Anything you want my love. Where do we keep them?"

"Well, if we get a bigger cage, they can cohabitate. People are not the only ones who need people, canaries need canaries, too."

Was there something she was trying to tell him? No! Was there someone in her life? This thought added to the rest of the turmoil he was feeling. However Anna had no ulterior motive. She realized from her father's expression that he had concluded that she had a beau. She tried to reassure him.

"Daddy, I'm trying to make small talk. I can only handle this career right now. You feel better about that?"

He swallowed hard and didn't answer. Damn it! She read his mind just like his mother did. She put her arm around him, and he was trembling. After they walked around the block briskly, she said, "Daddy, I'll race you to the door." Vittorio was pleased to see how quickly Anna could change his son's mood. Just like her mother.

She ran and he, a runner, ran just behind her. They were in a jovial mood and waited for Vittorio then went upstairs.

Before Anna and Grandpa went for their walk, they stopped by Grandma Jenny's apartment on the eleventh floor. Grandma gave Anna the wedding ring Luigi Liguori had given her on their wedding day. Jenny was saving it for a special occasion before she gifted it to her granddaughter. Today was a special day. Today the soul of her husband Luigi would be praying for a successful audition outcome. Anna was deeply touched and put it on her gold chain, which she always wore.

The three of them came in laughing and breathless, and Gemma was delighted to see such merriment on a nerve-wracking day. Anna showed her mom the wedding ring, and Gemma held it in her hands, put it to her lips and kissed it. "Poppa, pray for her," she whispered.

Anna was invigorated by the run. She gave her father her coat to hang up and quickly put her arm around Gemma's waist.

"Momma, will you go through the vocalises with me on the piano?" "My distinct pleasure, darling," Gemma said. She urged Anna into the large studio/living room, with the two grand pianos back to back.

Anna vocalized intermittently, not using the full voice. She filled the apartment with exquisite vocalises. She started with a scale of sustained tones, then stretched the upper register by rapid scales. Uccello was singing a duet with her, and the rest of the family, sat and listened in awe to the human canary, and the real canary.

After the vocalises, Anna asked her mother to come into her bedroom. She had chosen a navy dress with a white linen collar for her audition. This dress had been custom-made for her as a gift from her parents. It was perfect. Gemma was pleased that she had chosen this dress. It was elegant but understated.

At noon, her teacher Mr. Schorr called to tell her he'd meet her in the Sherry Lounge off the mezzanine, for last minute coaching and a talk.

They met at the designated time, and he ran her through vocalises to prepare her for her audition at 2:00. She was in full voice now.

Anna had prepared the Queen of the Night aria from the second act of the Magic Flute, and Gilda's aria from Rigoletto, "Caro Nome."

At 2:00 Schorr, and Anna went down to the orchestra level of the theater and she went on stage where an assistant conductor waited to accompany her. No one was allowed to stay in the theater, except for her teacher. Maurizio and Gemma remained in the backstage waiting room, at Anna's request.

Edward Johnson, a former singer himself, was the general manager of the company. Next to him was Max Rudolph, conductor as well as music administrator in the company. Jan Behr, conductor of German repertoire was present, as well as Pietro Cimara, conductor of the Italian repertoire.

Mr. Johnson told her to begin when she was ready.

She opened her mouth, and though she was nervous, her voice was fluid and open. She sang with great agility and command. Her poise, as well as her ability to project the character through her interpretation and emotion was awesome.

Mr. Johnson leaned over to Freidrich Schorr, "she's 19 years old?"

"Yes, Mr. Johnson," Schorr responded.

The second aria, "Caro nome" began with a simulated musical sob of two notes. The character of Gilda was younger than Anna. Therefore Anna had to diminish herself physically through acting in order to portray Verdi's character. Her portrayal was poignant. Anna was escorted off stage.

The administration stood up and went towards the young singer.

Mr. Johnson told Schorr that he was pleased with the audition.

"Job well done," Johnson said. "I'll be happy to tell her that we are offering her a contract. As a singer, I enjoy watching a singer's reaction in these affairs." He was different than other impresarios. Because he too had had a singing career, he made it a point to visit each singer back stage before every performance. It was a rarity and it made for good interpersonal relations in the company with the singers.

"Miss Brescia, you have given a very impressive audition. I just want you to know that we are unanimous in our decision to make you an offer."

"Mr. Johnson, thank you," Anna lowered her head, put her hands together as in prayer and bowed slightly. Truly her breath was taken away with his declaration, and she felt as though she was floating on air.

"Do you have management yet?" he asked.

"No sir," she said.

"Let's go to my office." Johnson suggested. Much had to be done as quickly as possible.

Anna and Mr. Schorr followed the impressario to his office and passed through the backstage office. Her parents were anxiously waiting, and Anna walked behind Mr. Johnson, put her thumb up and smiled. Maurizio was very emotional. "Amore mio, this is a miracolo." Gemma said as she squeezed his hand.

Anna was offered a contract at 3:00 p.m, but details had to be worked out with a manager, which she promised would occur within days. Mr. Johnson asked her how many complete operas she knew, and Anna said she would make a list of them. "Magic Flute?" he asked. She answered, "Yes, sir. I know it."

He asked, "Staging?" She said, "No." He wrote on his pad as she spoke, and the calm Anna felt, was incredible to her as she observed her own emotional reactions. Strange! It was as though she had been born to be here.

Anna, and Gemma went home, while Maurizio remained in the theater for an orchestral rehearsal of Verdi's Nabucco.

When they came home, Nonna Anna embraced her granddaughter.

"Oh, bella bambina, I am so overwhelmed," Grandma Anna said proudly, "who ever knew that a desperate son those many years ago, would have a daughter who would surpass him?"

"Momma," Gemma said, "the saints are paying us back for the anguish we suffered in Milano twenty years ago. This is your son's reward. What a fitting tribute to him."

"And you, Gemma." Gemma hugged her gratefully.

They had a light dinner of chicken soup and tortellini, and they went to their own quarters. The phone rang, and it was Carli.

"Well?" she asked anxiously.

"I made it, Carli."

Carli screamed, "oh my God, you're on your way."

"So I am, Carli."

Anna began her coaching for the entire opera of "Magic Flute." She worked with Aldo Di Tullio. Aldo was well-versed in five languages, and helped her enormously with translations, and interpretation. His own wife Eileen Di Tullio was a Diva who was known in certain circles as a singer's singer.

Anna's last phone call of the evening which lasted over an hour was to Santo Averso. He was beside himself with joy and kept talking about La Scala, and a pending appearance there. Anna thought he had lost his mind, because he didn't make sense to her at all. He spoke with great enthusiasm over a debut there. He went on and on, and finally when he took a breath, she jumped in.

"Poppa, wait! Don't you know that the opera house has been demolished? Poppa, you're not making sense." She was worried about him. Was he losing his memory?

"You'll go, soon," he persisted.

"Poppa, listen to me," she implored. "I need management. Mr. Johnson asked me if I had anyone. What do I do?"

"I've already spoken to Sol Hurok. You're going to audition for him."

"Okay," how comforting it was to have Poppa Santo in her life.

"I'll call you tomorrow. Get some rest. I love you, bambina."

Anna hung up and smiled because her Italian father still called her a baby. Anna told her mother that Santo had already gotten in touch with Sol Hurok. Gemma was pleased.

Gemma did not object to Santo's part in her daughter's career. It would make everything smoother if he were behind the scenes. She knew that even in this country, as well as in Italy, money talked. However, Gemma had to tread carefully with her husband Maurizio, who seemed to be haunted for the rest of his days with the specter of Santo's intrigue always present. This time it was for their daughter, and he had to accept Santo's involvement.

Anna was on her way. The season was at its midway point, and much of the future casting had been set way back in October. A debut would not be scheduled until the next season. Anna did not expect to sing in a major role, so she learned many roles, and covered the established coloratura repertoire. Meanwhile, she learned the entire opera of the "Magic Flute" by working with Aldo every night for an hour. She was fiercely determined to be ready should the occasion present itself.

The opportunity came sooner than expected. In March, the scheduled coloratura from Argentina Creuza Diaz had a virus, and lost her voice. She wired the Metropolitan Opera Company. Frantically every cover to the part was either performing or indisposed. Mr. Johnson scurried for a replacement, one with some drawing power. Anna heard about it through her grandfather Vittorio, who got all the news before anyone else. He told her that if she was ready she was to go in to see Mr. Johnson personally. She did. Mr. Johnson looked at her incredulously. She seemed so self assured, and he laughed.

"Why not?" he said as he told her that intensive rehearsals had to go into effect and she was to cast aside other commitments. So Anna Brescia made her debut by default.

* * *

Quickly the machinery to thrust Anna Brescia into the public limelight shifted gears and went full speed ahead. The rotogravure section of the Sunday News featured a pictorial centerfold of the Brescia family. Every member of the Brescia household was photographed, and it was one of the most powerful human interest stories in the newspaper. It even superceded the peace accords in interest.

The night of the opera, the theater was filled to capacity. She had been propelled into the limelight and was ready.

Gemma stayed with her daughter backstage as she watched with amazement the costume department and the makeup department transform her daughter indeed into Mozart's queen.

Twenty minutes before the opera, a countdown of remaining minutes before curtain time came over the speakers backstage. Gemma hurried.

"Break a leg," Gemma said. (opera jargon for good luck)

"Pray for me, Momma," Anna said as she caressed her mother's pale face. Gemma was overwhelmed with nerves, and she showed it.

Gemma's box seated the two grandmothers, the Cascios, Arcangelo, Carli and her mother, Paula. The Di Tullio's sat in orchestra seats.

Anna sang in the first act, and it was flawless. Her notes spun like a golden spider weaving her web. The audience was enthusiastic.

During intermission, everyone ran to the bathroom. Gemma was alone. Letizia and Gino rushed to Gemma's box. Gemma gasped when she saw them. She opened her arms to Letizia. "Thank God, you're here!" she cried.

Letizia rushed in Gemma's arms crying, "I've missed you."

From the pit, Maurizio noticed and he made the sign of the cross.

The chimes rang for the second act, and the audience hurried to their seats. The most challenging for the coloratura soprano was the next one coming up, the Queen of the Night signature aria.

The audience was quiet as the second act began. Anna was thrilled. Working with a rapid flow of adrenaline, she felt that there was nothing she couldn't do on stage that night. Finally, her moment came again, and she sang the "big one," as she called it. Every nuance, every note, sung with a commanding demeanor, she filled the theater with the incredible sound of her voice singing rapid technical notes with facility. It was a spine-tingling performance and the audience was mesmerized by her. At the end of the aria, the bravas began and lasted for three minutes. Anna froze and waited until the applause subsided.

At the end of the opera, as the protagonists came out for their bows, the applause was thunderous. Anna came out for her solo bow, and the audience stood up for a four minute standing ovation. She bowed deeply, then looked up at the box, her hands folded as in prayer and slightly bowed to her mother, then turned and stepped forward towards the pit and bowed to her father. The audience found the personal salute to her parents to be touching.

After the curtain came down, the families went backstage and waited as costumes were removed, and makeup was creamed off. A half an hour of hurried undressing by Anna who was dying to see her family and friends.

Maurizio brought the entourage into Anna's dressing room. No one said anything; they were in awe of her. Anna sensed their feelings and thanked each one for coming. Aldo and Eileen popped in, and blew her a kiss. Anna was dying to hear what he had to say. "Tomorrow, Anna. Call me when you get up," Eileen said, "you were wonderful, ducky!"

Carli stood in the back of the dressing room dumbstruck. She nodded her head and looked at Anna as though she was seeing her for the first time.

"Carli! It's me. Aren't you going to say anything?" Anna was concerned at the wide-eyed look Carli gave her.

"I'm going to cry," Carli said, and she did as Anna embraced her.

Maurizio then asked everyone to leave because Anna still had part of her costume on under her robe, and lots of makeup to take off. Anna wanted Gemma and Carli to stay with her. Maurizio waited.

The next day the opera critics from each of the New York newspapers wrote about Anna Brescia's impromptu debut at the Met. The articles were cut out by Grandma Anna, who delegated herself to be the collector of newspaper clippings for Anna's scrapbook.

The next morning, Anna called Freidrich Schorr. "Leibchen, you were marvelous. Brilliant debut, Anna. We'll talk about it further."

Anna then called Aldo.

"Hello," his voice slid up to the upper range.

"It's me, Aldo. Well?" She smiled and knew that the special way he said hello was because he knew the call would be from her.

"Congratulations! You are a diva."

"Thank you for all you've done. The beginning was scary, and then I felt like I was skiing and the slope felt good, and I took off."

Aldo laughed, "You sure did. Now your father can sleep nights." Anna laughed. "Was he nervous, Aldo?"

"Darling, he was a wreck! He told me that he doubted whether he'd survive your debut."

"Great, Aldo! I'll paint it on a T shirt for him."

Aldo laughed, "Anna, we'll talk later; Lucia is here for a lesson."

She hung up then called Poppa.

"Poppa, it's me. Well? What did you think?"

"Every person in that audience breathed with you, my bambina."

"Don't say another word Poppa. I'm taking you out to lunch tomorrow. I'm paying. Choose an elegant hotel."

"You paying?" He laughed, "you?"

"Uh Huh, I'm a diva Poppa, you have to listen to me."

He was amused. "Okay."

The next day, he picked her up and took a cab to the Astor. The waiter knew Santo Averso and gave him a table in a secluded part of the dining room.

"Bambina mia, a long time ago, God gave you a gift. A golden voice. God said, 'My child, treasure this gift. Honor it and it will serve you well.' Last night, you honored it by an electrifying performance." Anna marveled at her Poppa. How could she have done it without him, or her family?

It was that concerted effort which had propelled her to realize her dream, and now she was indeed the Diva.

Chapter Thirteen
ANNA'S DELUSIONS

Anna Brescia was in a new world. She was the "mascot" of the opera company, envied by the women, and wanted and admired by the men. She was in the arena of a circus, applauded on all sides by enthusiastic face less people every time she sang. Slighted by many of her female colleagues in the company, and propositioned by the men, particularly the married ones, the delusion of what was and what she expected was polarized.

She was in an emotional house of distorted mirrors. No matter where she turned to look, realism turned to surrealism. There were no real people there for her. She left the safe protected cocoon of her existence, and was now in the arena of the make believe world of the arts, not what she expected. Every slight or dirty look or sarcasm from anyone became magnified, and she was not prepared. Hence, she reacted.

Anna had a recurring nightmare. It took place in a medieval castle of people in masks and costumes, reveling and dancing to the music, which sounded like two orchestras playing different music at the same time. She held her ears with the cacophony that their simultaneous playing created, and she ran through the crowds of couples dancing and kissing together. Everyone wore a mask except herself.

Without a mask, she felt naked and she panicked and ran towards the gates of the castle trying to escape. As the gates started to close with two masked costumed guards, she ran towards the small opening, only to have the gates slam shut before she escaped. She screamed for them to let her out, but she was trapped. The faceless public ridiculed her, and no matter how much she screamed, no one would let her out. The only way she could escape was to wake herself up.

She broke out into cold sweats night after night, and it got so that she couldn't go to sleep, afraid of where her subconscious mind would take her.

Gemma heard her cry out some nights and ran in to comfort her. When she awoke sobbing and sweating perspiration of terror, her parents listened to this detailed nocturnal dream, which never seemed to change. Fear swelled in their hearts; they were wondering if she was going mad, or if this was an omen of some disaster. Maurizio was afraid for her sanity.

"She's got to see a doctor. I'm terrified for my daughter." He paced up and down his bedroom.

Gemma took to sleeping with her daughter, so that Maurizio would get some rest. The grandparents were terrified, and the consensus in the family was to find someone who could help her with this repetitive nightmare. Maurizio asked his daughter to take time out from her work and go away with her mother to rest.

Anna did not want to walk away from the position she had been fortunate enough to have attained, but she knew that she needed help.

A psychiatrist, Dr. Gary Chumford, met once a month with Anna's parents. They discussed the discovery of past traumas, as well as her unrealistic expectations of the opera company. She had expected everyone to adore her, but instead there were plots and subplots against her. The women resented her enthusiasm, her beauty, and her talent.

Within months, she was able to face the reality of the dark side of human nature. She certainly was not prepared for the trauma of leaving the only father she ever knew, Santo Averso. When this childhood trauma was mentioned in group therapy, Maurizio felt terrible. He had never considered a little girl's feelings as she was "ripped away" from the only father she knew.

Maurizio backed off from any more directives concerning Anna's relationship with Santo. Maurizio felt that he was partially to blame. His beautiful talented daughter had never had a normal childhood. It was as though she had been on a single track, without the passages of an average American child. He felt terrible, and he and his wife discussed her every night until they gave in to exhaustion. Maurizio cried when he saw that he had created so much of her suffering. The recriminations of his as well as Gemma's roles in her life were the most painful.

Anna needed something outside of music which would give her joy. Gemma prayed for that to happen.

An event which would take her out of her own milieu to the real world was about to happen. When Carli went to Canada to perform in her gig with the jazz/classical trio the Classical Bridge, she came back with startling news. She was marrying the leader of the group, Chet Simon.

They had been seeing each other privately as well as professionally and had fallen deeply in love. Carli was pregnant, and when she told Chet, a marriage was quickly planned.

In February 1947, Anna Brescia was the happiest she had been in over a year, as she became maid of honor for Carli and Chet. Though Chet was Jewish, he deferred to Carli's request to marry in the same Catholic church her parents had married in, St. Ann's on 110th Street. Chet chose Al as his best man.

On a Friday night at 6:00 p.m., Anna took a cab to the church and met the bride and groom and the best man together with the priest. Al was more excited over being introduced to Anna than being best man. He had admired her from afar at the Manhattan School of Music when they passed each other in the hallway. Her incredible success at nineteen made her somewhat of an icon.   Introductions were made, and Carli and Chet looked at each other as Al's expression froze when they were introduced.

"You look familiar," Anna said as she met his penetrating gaze.

"So you noticed me? I'm flattered." Al answered with a hint of a smile. He offered his arm in a most gallant gesture, and she put her arm in his and they walked into church as the rehearsal began.

Al couldn't keep his eyes off Anna, and Chet couldn't keep his off the statues in the church. He saw the crucifix and grimaced. After rehearsals, the two couples went to Patsy's on 115th Street for an Italian dinner.

Al, who was always the talkative one, seemed to have lost his usual ease. However, after a glass of wine, he loosened up, and recaptured his usual persona. Finally everyone loosened up and Anna up close seemed so vulnerable. She was in a setting not normal for her. She was with young people her own age, and she looked from one to the other as though she was witnessing something new. Indeed, she was. Al became surer of himself as she talked with him. At eleven, no one had realized how late it was--then Anna looked at her watch. Chet took care of the bill, and the foursome found a cab to drive them home. The cab stopped at 175 West 72nd Street, and both couples got out, while the cab waited. Al kissed Anna's hand, then both sides of her face. He wanted to date her, but he thought it would be best to wait until after the wedding, so that if she refused, it wouldn't be awkward for them.

Anna went to bed and felt warm inside as she shut her eyes and pictured Al again. She was aware that Al's penetrating looks made her spine tingle. He excited her. The whole evening played in her memory from the first moment, and she realized that being together in a casual setting like that had never been part of her life. Her encounters with her peers had been limited to Carli and other events with her mother's planned dinner parties. All of this seemed so formal, and tonight she was pleased that she had experienced a casual social American scene.

The wedding day came the following Sunday; reception: at Mayer's Caterers in the Bronx on 233rd Street. Fellow musicians played at the wedding. The families meshed beautifully. Carli and Chet danced every dance; Al sat next to Anna on the dais, and asked her to dance.

"Al, I'm clumsy. I don't dance. I have to pass." She blushed, embarrassed that she couldn't dance. Al took her hand in his and traced the lines of her palm with his finger. She was curious, not knowing what he was up to. She loved the way he smelled, and she swayed towards him, then caught herself.

"This line tells me that you are a great musician. Following music is easy for you. See this line over here?"

She looked at the end of a long line on her hand, enthralled that Al was able to "read" her palm.

"This line ends off, which means that if you don't get up and dance with me now, you'll never learn."

She burst out laughing. "All of that in one line?" she said, and he pulled her to her feet and held her close as they swayed to the rhythm of the gentle fox trot. She stumbled a few times, but Al held her so that she could feel his body move and move with him. He counted the beats in her ear, like a metronome, and she laughed. The Brescias noticed. Maurizio said, "tesoro, I haven't seen her laugh in months," Maurizio whispered.

At the end of the dance, they went back to the dais, and Al took her hand again, and she giggled.

"Now, Anna, see this arch below the thumb?" She gave him a suspicious look. "Is it terrible?" Al got closer. "Now, don't breathe a word about this line to anyone." She promised not to.

"This line tells me that you're madly in love with me, only you don't know it yet."

She blushed and lowered her eyes. She was tingling to hear him articulate what she was indeed feeling. "You're playing games, Al." She pulled her hand away, and felt her breathing pace quicken.

"Anna, I have the same line. If you knew how to read palms, you'd see that I am madly in love with you. I have been for a long time. I couldn't approach you. You were a star--and me? A jazz musician. Baby, look at me. I swear I'm not playing games. I love you." He took her face in his hands and kissed her fully on the mouth. She was stunned at first then kissed him back.

"So our lines met," she said breathlessly. His eyes were teary, and she knew that he meant it.

Their relationship grew rapidly. He was her lover, her confidant, and her best friend. For Anna, this was her very first love affair, and for Al, who was smitten to the depths of his soul, it was a love which would haunt him for the rest of his life.

They became lovers, and Anna's indiscretions with a young man who had no ulterior designs on her except to love her, turned out to be the equalizer in her life. He left his parents' home in the Bronx and took an apartment in a cheap neighborhood on the east side, so that he and Anna could spend intimate time together.

Anna and Al often spent the weekend at his small one-bedroom apartment. He had to work on weekends, and sometimes Anna would go to the clubs in the village with him. After his club date, they'd go dancing, something she had never learned to do. He tried to teach her to cook Sicilian style, and she burnt the sauce. "I can't do this," she cried. He was so surprised that she wept at the failure. He realized why as he analyzed it. Anna had been a high achiever she could not tolerate imperfection. He embraced her and told her she didn't have to. He taught her how to speak Sicilian, and she laughed heartily when she couldn't pronounce the words correctly. Anna had studied German and French, and had perfect diction, but the guttural sounds of the Sicilian dialect eluded her.

Anna loved Al because with him she learned how to have fun. He had an incredible sense of humor, and she laughed all the time. She slept at home four nights a week, and the weekend was hers and Al's. He realized the more that he was with her that this would never last, and that it saddened him deeply. Yet, he kept their relationship light, and made no demands on her, because he loved her more than he loved himself. Anna was his one great love. His unconditional love was the balm that finally soothed the anguished soul of Anna Brescia. Years of therapy could not have done this for her.

Gemma had mixed feelings. She did not approve of Anna cavorting with someone out of her class, but Anna had come out of her depression. Al provided an essential emotional field for Anna. The serious little girl started to appreciate the simple things in life. She was introduced to jazz through recordings Al bought her. She felt good.

Keeping no secrets from her parents, she told them about Al.

Maurizio suffered enormously, particularly when Anna didn't come home to sleep. He'd toss and turn all night, and finally took hot milk and two aspirin to settle his nerves. Gemma wouldn't share with her husband the secret relief she felt about Anna and Al's love affair. She just told her daughter to do what she had to do, but suggested that she needn't feel obligated to marry this Sicilian musician just because she was sleeping with him. That would be a folly, because their worlds were so far apart. Anna's retort to her mother was that she wasn't ready for a marriage, but that if she were, she'd not think twice about marrying Al. Maurizio didn't want to engage his daughter in any dialogue concerning her lover. He couldn't cope. He learned to vent his disapproval exclusively with his wife, and his biggest anguish was that she was no longer a virgin.

What was it about Italian men who prized virginity so much?

Gemma knew that what drove Maurizio crazy every time Santo's name came up, was that he had made love to Gemma for five years. If only Maurizio knew about Gemma's other indiscretion, he would go crazy over it.

In Milano, when Gemma's talent was barely noticed by the newspapers despite her many brilliant performances, she had compromised herself for that career.

The married newspaper critic Alberto Ciecco propositioned her every time he saw her, telling her that a night in her arms would be rewarded by a glowing musical revue. They went for coffee, and she listened as he told her that she had to do something different than other performers, and he suggested the personal touch.

Alberto Ciecco had given her more support than her lover ever had. Much as she adored Maurizio throughout their lengthy relationship, his greatest concern was over his own career. It was as though hers didn't matter to him, and it probably didn't. Yet, she loved him and wanted him anyway.

Alberto had given her the greatest ego trip in her life by writing about her talents so eloquently. Ironically, though no one knew about her affair with him, and Gemma was afraid that Maurizio would find out, so she eased out of the relationship, which the critic regretted, but accepted.

Italy had rebuilt its opera house La Scala, exactly as it had been before the bombings, which practically leveled it. The plans of the original structure were found and copied. The war ended in 1945, and the opera house was opened in 1946. The Italians needed their art form of opera putting behind them the world of war and madness.

Hurok made overtures to La Scala for Anna Brescia. The company had heard of her glowing debut in 1945, and because of the human interest story of the family from Milano, the offer to hire her was even more intense. Italian newspapers were already singing the praises of the young soprano, already a seasoned singer of one year. "A Milanese, Anna Brescia, youngest star of Metropolitan soon to sing at La Scala."

The newspapers went wild, as the publicity of music, drama, nostalgia for one of their compatriots' great success, was on the lips of the populace. They were so sick of death, destruction, and poverty, that she was their "Cinderella story".

What began with Anna Brescia continued in Italy over the decades. Italians loved everything American. The women adored the American woman's independence, which had come about when men went to war and women took their place in the work force. This was also the first time that women were allowed in the armed services of the United States.

The story of Maurizio Brescia was featured in all the Italian newspapers as a young struggling musician who was educated at the conservatory of Milan and auditioned for La Scala opera company. Since he wasn't offered a contract, and left for America, speculation over the possibilities of his life were fodder for arguments among the Italians.

Italians discuss ad infinitum. They love arguing different points of view, and this story whetted their appetite for this sort of activity.

An old concert review of one of Gemma Liguori's piano concerts was printed on the third page of the weekend edition, with the caption that Gemma was Anna Brescia's mother. Interest grew, and the Italians clamored for an invitation to be extended to Anna. Further articles and letters to the editor printed points of view, and interest.

Santo Averso got a call from Sol Hurok stating that Italy was on bended knee asking for Anna's appearance. Santo explained to Hurok that as soon as she had time to spare, they'd make a date.

Santo was aware of Anna's emotional crisis. He and Gemma talked several times a week. He was also apprised of Anna's involvement with Al, a Sicilian jazz musician.

"Italy wants her," Santo said quietly.

"We don't know what to do. We're grateful that she's performing here. Why La Scala, Santo? Do you still have those connections?"

"Gemma, can't you forget the past? This isn't about us; it's about Anna. I yearn to see her. Will you tell her this?"

Gemma realized she had never forgiven him. "Yes, Santo, I shall."

"Thank you Gemma, goodnight," he said with resignation.

Santo was weary of spirit. He felt as though he had fallen into a chasm. Each one of the adults in this child's life had contributed to an unrealistic view of life for this child.

Santo felt deep personal regret at all the choices he had made. He felt responsible for Anna's mental health. All of it he had done in the name of love. Perhaps in the final cadence of his life, the Brescias would forgive him. Perhaps, then, he would find peace.

Chapter Fourteen

CONFLICTS BETWEEN THE LOVERS

Anna Brescia was double-dating for the first time in her life. Carli and Chet included them in many of their social and professional events. Although Carli was four months pregnant, she still sang with "The Classical Bridge" at the Village clubs. As the baby grew inside of her, she would have to take a leave from singing. Carli did not do throat singing, because she had taken voice lessons which taught her how to use the diaphragm in breathing and producing sound with proper breath support. At best, Carli had another four weeks left to perform, then she'd quit. Anna thought Carli's choice for the group's name was apropos. Each of the men started the show with a few phrases of a classic piece of music, then improvised that piece into a take off in the jazz style. Stunning and original, they had already gained a following from people "in the know." Audiences responded enthusiastically to their eclectic style.

Conversely, George played contemporary tunes as Bach, Mozart and Beethoven would have written them. The audience loved it. In nightclub situations, it was rare for people not to talk while musicians performed. When the Classical Bridge appeared, the audience listened. When George finished, they applauded, and they whistled.

At the end of George's interpretations at the keyboard, Al took the microphone.

"Ladies and gentlemen, it's so great performing our gigs here. You guys sure appreciate the big guns like Bach, Beethoven and Mozart as we do. Tonight I'd like to introduce you to another classic in the audience, my beautiful fiancee' Anna Brescia of the Metropolitan Opera company. Stand up Sweetheart." Anna got a tremendous ovation, with whistles and feet stamping and clinking of glasses. A few yelled, "Brava!" and others who didn't know, "Bravo!"

He smiled broadly and she stood up to acknowledge the audience's vigorous applause. Anna had had enough publicity so that even non opera aficionados had heard of her name. She bowed and blew the audience a kiss, then turned to the stage and blew one to Al, which he immediately returned.

The audience reacted with approval, and the Classical Bridge's appeal grew. Chet followed that by announcing that Anna Brescia was going to be the godmother of his and Carli's first baby.

Again, personal appeal and audience applause. Emotionally they were now bonded with the audience, and people crowded in for the performance. Unbeknownst to the group, a prominent columnist from the Daily News celebrating his second anniversary with his wife was so impressed with Anna Brescia's presence as well as the classy overtones of the group that he devoted the next day's column to her and her association with one of the members of the popular Classical Bridge.

During the breaks, Al and Anna talked, laughed and interacted with other people at the club. Carli confided in her husband that she never saw this side of her best friend.

"Honey, they are so perfect together," Carli said.

"I know. He blows my mind. He cooks for her, Carli. For a guy stuck in Sicilian traditions, he's ignored his." Chet laughed

"It's interesting to watch how this is developing. Talks about her all the time. You know how? He tells me how she loves his sauce. I mean, man, who the hell talks like that about a woman you're sleeping with? It's so out there that I can't figure. You'd think he just came off the boat."

Carli giggled. "Honey, food is a passion for Italian men. Dad and Grandpa cook together. The rituals of food preparation, what to make, how to cook it, is a nightly topic at my house and at Grandpa's. Wait! You'll find out."

She said smugly and he smiled, "I think I've heard your father talk about raped broccoli more than once." Carli smirked, "Raped broccoli? Honey, that's broccoli rape, pronounced rah pe." Chet laughed, "Oh yeah, I knew I screwed it up! Only the Italians put sex and food together."

Chet and Carli watched Anna "play the room," and Chet whispered to his wife, "Look how proud Al is. He's so nuts about her. Think they'll marry, Carli?"

She watched them too; took her time in answering.

"Nah! He's Sicilian. Gemma is prejudiced. They haven't got a chance. I think they're so perfect together."

Chet looked at his watch, a few more minutes until the next set. "Me too, Carli. Man, she's an opera singer, you know? I mean, I don't think they'll make it."

Anna obliged the patrons with her autograph at the bar while Al watched proudly.

Big Sam from Canada had called Carli and Chet asking them to come up for a gig whenever they had time. The group liked the reception they'd gotten last time, and they agreed after Carli's obstetrician gave his approval. Carli asked her mother if she could give Sam some recent photographs of her. He wanted to know how Paula looked after twenty years. In an intimate exchange between mother and daughter, Carli quoted Sam's parting words: "Your mother was the love of my life."

* * *

A week later, as plans were being firmed up by Carli, Al asked Anna to accompany him to Canada. She had a Rigoletto coming up at the Met, and was disappointed that she couldn't make it. It was the first time the lovers would be inaccessible to each other.

Al and Anna spent the last night together before he left for Canada. Al had made a Sicilian dish for Anna. He had melted anchovies in olive oil until they disintegrated, then put grated bread crumbs into the mixture and tossed it with a wooden spoon until they were toasty colored. Instead of the usual grated cheese, they used the sardine/crumb mixture to put on the pasta. Anna loved it and had two helpings.

"Just how am I going to survive without you, darling?" she asked as he served her the red wine.

"You'll get involved in your music and I in mine."

"Al, be serious. I'm missing you right now."

"Well, then, marry me," he said.

"Oh my God," she said softly, and sat down.

It was the wrong thing to say. The reality of the situation began to sink in. They came from two different worlds, and he knew in his heart that it was only a matter of time. Anna knew it, too. Yet there was a deep love between them.

She looked away sadly. Her shoulders drooped, and she clasped her hands in front of her, looking forlorn and vulnerable.

"I'm sorry, let's change the subject," he said with a bravado he did not feel.

She kissed him, but he didn't respond.

They finished dinner, and Al put on a recording of the Magic Flute. It was his way of touching her heart.

"When do you think of me?" he asked pitifully.

"I listen to jazz," she said quietly as they cleared the table and Al did the dishes.

"Our connection, isn't it?" he said with tears in his eyes. He hurried with the dishes, then shut the shades, and changed the music to the radio station with soft romantic selections.

This was the reality. He couldn't waste a moment discussing the impossible dream. She was there, she wanted him, and he wanted her. Projecting into the future only minimized the importance of the present.

"You are the most beautiful thing that will ever happen to me. I want to make love to you. I want to memorize you like a great composition."

He carried her to bed, and slowly took her clothes off, kissing every part of her as a preamble. Later they clung to each other in a sadness that was as bitter as it was sweet. Intuitively they knew that this was the beginning of the end of this euphonious "honeymoon" courtship, and they were afraid.

"Anna, I'll never love anyone like this again," he whispered.

"Neither will I. You saved me, you know." She lay very still, took his hand, and, with her index finger traced the lines in the palm of his hand.

"See this line? This is the line of eternity. Our love will go into that time frame, no matter what happens." He held her and stroked her back until she fell asleep, then he went into the bathroom took a towel and sobbed into it stifling his guttural cries. It was the beginning of the end, and they knew it.

Other forces pulling the lovers away from each other existed in the circle of their families' camps. The Brescias clearly refused to deal with Anna's romantic interlude. Yet, they couldn't verbalize their disapproval, because the love affair helped their daughter out of a pit of despair. The affair had served its purpose. Now their greatest concern was its termination.

Gemma expressed her concerns with Santo. He admonished her against verbalizing objections to Anna's current affair, until it died a natural death. She had to be kept busy. Without the propinquity young love required, it would end. Coming from Santo, the master manipulator, a viable rationale of inaction made sense. Santo suggested a fall debut at La Scala. Timing would be perfect.

The publicity machine of the Italian press had made way for this Italian debut. Enthralled with Americans to begin with, the Italians clamored to see her, since Anna had been born in Milano of Milanese parentage.

In America, ironically, Anna Brescia's Italian birth made her a foreigner--hence the fascination of her operatic appearances, even though she had totally been trained in America. America was self-conscious about being in the operatic arena, so doors were opened more readily, and large fees paid to Italian born stars.

Santo was in close touch with Sol Hurok and pushed for performances not only in America but at La Scala. The machinery was well-oiled for a major thrust in her career, as well as a fizzling out of a torrid love affair.

On the other side of the lover's adversaries, Al's parents, Biaggia and Beniamino, had gotten to Al through his close identity with the Sicilian code of suspicion towards outsiders. Milanese people were outsiders. On a daily basis, Biaggia talked to her son, who adored her, and dropped a word here and there about opening himself for a total disaster with Anna.

"They'll never accept you," she'd say when Al told her how well suited they were. "We're low class for them. You can't compete. The first few months would be fine, then you'd go down hill. You're also a jazz musician. How much do you think they'll be impressed with you? You'll get ignored, and some day you'll die in a chair in the corner of their house and they won't even notice. You won't count, my son." She pounded away at her daily litany of negatives, and like the repetitive dripping of a drop of water on a rock, an indentation into his mindset had been formulated.

She too went on an individual campaign to find a suitable young Sicilian/American girl for him. Al was 28 and it was time for him to marry and make his own nest.

Al listened. He didn't agree with what his mother was saying, but after hearing it on a daily basis for months and months, it started to sink in.

In Canada, he thought he'd concentrate on his music, but Carli told Sam about the wonderful relationship between Al and Anna Brescia. Instead of congratulations, Sam's arguments were verbatim those of Al's mother, Biaggia Russo.

Carli objected to Sam's list of why Al should walk away from Anna. It had nothing to do with the two of them but gave in to the pressures of regional hates in the Italian peninsula and in Sicily.

They returned to New York after a month-long gig, and Carli called Anna. Two days later, Anna returned the call and they talked about music, the performances at the opera house, and the performances at Sam's club. Anna talked excitedly about going to La Scala in October to do several performances of Rigoletto. She spoke about newspaper clippings which showed that she and her family were very prominent in the public eye.

"How were your performances?" Anna asked finally.

"Good. It was nice seeing Sam and Birdie again. It's almost like seeing family. Did Al call you yet?"

"Not to my knowledge," she said, and they had more small talk, then ended the conversation.

In September, when Adam Sidney Simon was born at Flower Fifth Avenue hospital, Anna and Al saw each other again as godparents to the beautiful ten-pound baby boy.

The baby was christened at St. Ann's Church after which the families converged at a restaurant in Riverdale. Because Al and Anna were godparents, they sat together at the main table with Carli and Chet. George Randolph and his fiancee Clarissa joined them. There was a reserve between Al and Anna noticed by all, and rather than be the object of stares and conjectures, Anna decided to be equally as charming to Al as she was to others.

He was obviously uncomfortable, and, when food wasn't being served, Al circulated among the fifty guests and went to the bar. Anna was hurt as he walked away from her. Al and Charlie were at the bar talking, and Anna approached them.

"Is this a private conversation?" she asked as she eased between their stools.

"Not any more," Al answered, and she backed away, as Charlie felt that something very private was going on between them. He took his drink and offered Anna his stool next to Al. She declined to take it and started to walk away when Al pulled her back.

"Sit. I don't want you to go." They got lost in each other's gaze, and the bartender asked if she wanted a drink. She ordered a ginger ale with a twist of lemon.

"I miss you," he said, and tears filled her eyes. "It's not over for you either, is it?"

She shook her head, no.

He put his arm around her and walked outside of the restaurant for privacy.

"Anna, any suggestions?" He was afraid to pressure her. He'd take whatever she was willing to offer.

"Friendship?" she said as she backed away from him.

He felt as though a knife had been plunged through him. It was over. Why the hell was he groveling? What was he looking for? His mother had been right. Big Sam had been right. He took a deep breath, and, as he expelled the breath, it came out unevenly sounding like little sobs without the voice.

"Just what I was thinking, too," he lied. He could act, too. He escorted her back inside, and as they walked to the table and sat down, the food was being served.

After the christening party, everyone left, and Al slipped out without another word to Anna Brescia. She went home with her mother and her grandparents, then went into her room. She laid down on her bed, and Gemma came in and sat at the edge of Anna's bed and saw her daughter's tears.

"Are you okay, Anna?" Gemma asked quietly.

"It's over. How do you stop?" She sat up, and propped her pillows behind her.

Gemma was puzzled at the question. "Stop what?"

"Loving him?" Anna asked.

"Time," Gemma said sadly. If only she could take away the pain from her child.

"Momma, he wanted to marry me," she said.

Gemma had to be careful how she responded to this information. "I see." Gemma sighed.

"Do you, Momma?" Suddenly, as though an emotional switch had been turned on, Anna jumped up from bed. "Momma, can you play Caro Nome for me?"

Gemma stared. How ironic the Victor Hugo tragedy made into Rigoletto by Giuseppe Verdi. A chill of horror came over Gemma as her daughter chose this aria to reflect her mood.

Gemma acquiesced to accompany Anna and found the score. Gemma played the introduction as Anna shut her eyes and sang "Caro nome." As she sang, her voice soared to its upper register and filled the room with sound.

Grandma Anna came in from the kitchen and listened to the passion of Anna's interpretation. She was mesmerized by the intensity of emotion pouring out of the glorious vocal instrument of her granddaughter. She swelled to crescendos and decrescendos, creating the entire spectrum of the color of her voice. When she finished, Gemma was moved, and she opened her arms to her daughter. They held each other.

"Giuseppe Verdi himself would have wept," Gemma whispered.

"Did my broken heart show, Momma?" Anna asked.

"What's going on?" Gemma asked.

"Al, the sweet name of the man I love, mom." Gemma put her arms around her daughter and held her.

Anna changed into sneakers, slacks and her sports jacket and went for a walk down the city streets. She noticed people brushing past each other, in a hurry. She melded in with the expression-less pedestrians. She recalled the time when she and Al went for a walk downtown and had to hurry their pace in order to keep up with the tempo of the crowd. She smiled as she remembered Al's quip, "so, how do you walk when you're going nowhere?" She remembered how he put his arm around her waist and they started to run. They had laughed so much.

After a couple of drinks with George and his fiancee, Al went home and put his arms around his mother.

"You saw her?" Biaggia Russo said.

"Yes, Momma," he said.

"It's over, isn't it?" she asked softly.

Al laughed sardonically as he walked to the kitchen window and looked out.

"Ah, figlio mio," she said "It's not over then." She sat down, feeling weak in the knees.

She couldn't fix it for her beloved son, not this time.

"Momma," he faced his mother, "some day she's gonna turn to me, and I'll be there for her. I'll wait for the rest of my life if I have to. You'll see."

Biaggia was stunned. He walked past her into his bedroom and shut the door. She followed him and hesitated when she heard his sobs coming in waves as he tried to muffle them in his pillow. She went back to her rocking chair by the living room window, took out her rosary beads and prayed.

Chapter Fifteen

1947 PREPARATION FOR LA SCALA

Gemma took time to be with her daughter as they went downtown to get their passports to Italy. Anna was going at the end of September. They would have two weeks of rehearsals and staging. Though she was excited to see her "Patria,"—fatherland-- she was apprehensive because she was going alone. Anna wished her mother would come with her, but much as Gemma wanted to, Maurizio didn't approve because it was time for his little bird to spread her wings and fly solo.

Santo and Kay were going a week before her performance. Santo also felt that Anna had to fend for herself. Maurizio asked management of the orchestra for time off for a week so as to be present for his daughter's La Scala debut. The orchestra members who were pretty much like a family rather than colleagues were very supportive of each other. They felt like a group of collective godfathers to Brescia's child, having been to their home over the years for many occasions.

Gemma enjoyed shopping for her daughter. They went to the best department stores, and Anna opted for severe simplicity out of sensitivity to the war-torn Italian people. She did not wish to flaunt her wealth, nor her station in life to any of the Italians. She needed them in her corner; she did not desire to create adversaries nor set herself apart.

Her cotton-white skin against a frame of jet black curly hair as well as her statuesque physical beauty did set her apart. No matter how she down played her appearance, she was always noticed even by people who did not know her identity. A month alone was going to be an adventure.

Before she left, she called Chet and asked him if she could use his studio to make a single recording of one aria. At this time, right before the baby Adam Sidney Simon was born, Chet had opened a recording studio in the city on 55th Street, and had expanded his income as proprietor and chief engineer of recordings. Anna called and made an appointment. She didn't want her mother to know that she was making a recording of 'Caro Nome"--dearest name--for Al, so she asked Aldo Di Tullio, her coach, if he could fit it into his schedule. The only time Aldo had was after 8:00 p.m., after all his students left. She confided in Aldo that she was making this recording for someone she loved. He asked her to come to his place and rehearse it that very night, because the following night, they'd record it. Chet had given them a two hour time frame from 8:30 until 10:30.

Carli asked her husband if she could come into the studio and have her mother-in-law watch Adam. She was dying to hear Anna sing. Chet asked her to clear it with Anna, since there seemed to be some intrigue over this single piece of music, and Carli guessed right away. Maybe they hadn't broken off, but she wouldn't ask. The Sicilian "omerta"-- silence--and respect for privacy prevailed. Also, Anna had too many commitments at this time, and intensive coaching and learning. Bad timing.

Anna rehearsed with Aldo, and he was enthralled at the depth of emotion in one so young. There was something deeper than a performance here.

Aldo was a very personable coach. He always inquired about his student's lives, expressing concern over their sense of well-being. Whoever worked with Aldo considered him a friend as well as a coach.

"Brava, Anna!" he said with a warm smile "who is he?"

"A jazz musician," she replied, and Aldo immediately thought, they're breaking up.

"Uh huh, how much time has Chet set aside for you?"

"Two hours. Can we do this in one take?" she asked.

"Not without vocalizing," she said, "I know."

The following day, Anna was busy with rehearsals of Rigoletto, and since she had one more performance before she left, she took as many rehearsals as they would give her. She enjoyed working, and since the La Scala engagement was now a reality, her colleagues as well as the assistant conductors looked up to her. She was a big name already.

She called Chet.

"Chet, this is a gift for Al. Would you give it to him after I leave?"

"Sure. Any message?"

"It's in the aria," she answered.

"What time you coming tonight?"

"8:30"

"He won't be here. I'll tell him I have another assistant requested by the artist--he won't get suspicious."

"Great, that'll work, I hope." Anna didn't want him to hear her record it, she wanted to surprise him, and subconsciously this was a farewell gift.

* * *

At 8:30 sharp, Aldo and Anna came into the sound studio, and after a couple of rapid scales to a high C, she then went beyond to the E above high C. Chet was beaming. The guys in the sound booth never heard sounds like that in this studio. They were mesmerized. It was beautiful, almost like hearing a bird so involved in his song he was totally unaware of the world. Anna was focused and intent; she was in the moment. Aldo watched her, and then she signaled Chet, with a slight nod, and Aldo began the introduction.

She sang with her eyes shut. The expression on her face was pure rapture. The recording staff had never listened to opera and were enthralled.

At the end of the recording session, they applauded. Chet was impressed. The men in the sound booth came out cheering. They were speechless. She was so young, so beautiful, and so professional.

At 9:15 when they finished, Chet wished her a bon voyage, "knock 'em dead, okay?" they embraced. "I'll give it my best." she replied, "hugs to Carli and Adamo, okay?" Chet nodded.

Aldo and Anna left.

"She's gorgeous!" the assistant sound man said, "I thought opera singers were fat ugly broads." He was surprised. "This one looks like a movie star Damn! Hey, Chet she going with anyone?" Chet laughed.

"She's an opera singer. You buy tickets to see her--you don't marry her, you don't even date her. It's a dead end street."

Anna went home and called Carli. They talked about every thing.

"When are you leaving?" Carli asked.

"Next week," Anna said. "I'd love to have lunch with you before I go. Is it possible?"

"Yes." Carli said, and they made a date for the following afternoon.

The next day, Al came early and asked how the session went the previous night and Chet was uncomfortable. Lying didn't come easy to him, and he gave short perfunctory answers. They worked well into the morning, tying up loose ends, setting up schedules for recording sessions of the local talent in the city, some of which was very good. They took a brief lunch break, and Al brought Chet an eggplant parmigiana sandwich. Chet laughed.

"I need a large napkin to eat this. Did your mom make the bread?"

"Yeah," Al said, "it looks like a mattress. You gotta get these thick slices or the bread falls apart. I made the eggplant. I used to make it for Anna. She loved my eggplant." Chet shook his head as Al kept adding more facts, trying always to mention her name.

They sat in the office and had the wonderful food. Al took out two cloth napkins and handed one to Chet. They talked, and, as always, Al asked about his godson, and they spent the next twenty minutes talking about the baby. Al started cleaning up, handed Chet a cold beer from the small cooler he had brought, and Chet guzzled it down.

"Man, that's great food," Chet said.

"What happened last night? Did she come here?"

"Why?" Chet asked.

"That weak story you trumped up was bullshit. Come on, man, don't tell me my favorite diva came here to record."

"She did. How d'ya know?"

"All I had to do was to ask your wife. She can't lie, either. Look, I'm hurt. Is it that Anna didn't want me to be here? Damn! What am I, a murderer that I gotta be discarded like that?" Chet got up. He handed him a small package of a recording. "She made this for you. She's leaving for Milan next week. I tell you man, we were all crying when she got through with this aria. One aria, man, that was it. You hadda see it. It was like she was in a trance. Awesome! She told me you'd understand it." Al's expression went from anger to surprise, then distinct pleasure as he realized that Anna had gone out of her way to do this. It was all he wanted.

"Sorry man, I didn't know." He looked at the single selection recording, and went into the sound studio to play it. He listened and sat still with his head in his hands until the very last note. Chet came into the sound room and rubbed Al's back. Al sat up and wiped his tear-stained face with the back of his hand.

"You okay, man?" Chet asked.

"Yeah! Now I am." Then he stood tall, straightened out his slumped shoulders, fixed a wide smile on his face, and said, "Okay, I'm ready to work. Let's go." He joined Chet in the studio. There were invoices to send out, and though there was a lot of paper work connected with a new business, Chet thought it best to keep his operating expenses low. Al had a piece of the business so that he'd be loyal to it.

The ladies met for lunch at the Astor Hotel in the city, then took a cab up to the studio. Anna was anxious to see Al before she left. Al didn't know about their luncheon date, since Carli was bound to her apartment in Riverdale taking care of the "big man," as Al called Adam.

Al thought that Anna didn't want to see him again. Until Chet had given him her recording, he'd thought he was history in her emotional book. Anna had called Al several times at his home in the Bronx, and each time, Mrs. Russo said that he was out of town. That, for her, could have meant down the corner to get a quart of milk. It was selective truth. Beniamino Russo didn't like his wife to lie.

"You interfere with destiny," he said, as his proclivity towards Anna being his son's wife fascinated him more and more. So she wouldn't be an ordinary wife. He'd cook and she'd work. What was wrong with that arrangement for a change? Simplistic, but beautiful. He, however never "sold his wife down the river" with his son by revealing to him that Anna had called a number of times leaving messages which Al never received.

In the Brescia household, pretty much the same "omerta" was adapted when Grandma Anna took the phone messages. Her answers were also selective truth.

"She's away." That could have meant down the block getting a quart of milk, or out of town for a performance.

"I have no idea where she is or whether I'll see her within the next few days." This intimated that she was out of town. This precluded Al's next question of "do you know when she'll be back?" to "will you give her a message?" The answer was, "I give her messages when I see her."

It was a losing situation on both sides of the fence. However, the force of destiny being stronger than people, Al and Anna decided that there was a conspiracy against them by their families. After they figured it out, circumventing them was the only way. In addition to families, there were insecurities in both Al and Anna. He felt that he wasn't in her class. She was certain that she didn't want a permanent alliance. Hence the yo-yo syndrome of their relationship. Too many factors were involved in the mix in order for it to resolve in a mutually emotional manner. The constant, however, was their love for each other. That grew with each obstacle, and the indelible emotional experience of her first love affair.

After lunch, Anna urged Carli to come with her to the studio so that she could see Al in person. She had to get back for a coaching lesson with Aldo at 4:00. There wasn't much time. Carli, of course, was happy to see that Anna was making some positive moves.

They took a cab and got off in front of the studio. They went up the stairs of the old building where there were lofts for rent, and Carli unlocked the door.. Chet and Al were in the office with a mountain of sealed envelopes in front of them. They had worked hard all afternoon and in the evening various jazz groups were expected to cut a solo number on a single record. At 78 r.p.m. usually it was all one could put on a recording.

They didn't even hear them come in, and Anna tiptoed behind Al and put her hands on his eyes to blindfold him. He stiffened up, and felt her cool hands and slender fingers, caress his face. He pulled her hands away from his face and kissed first one hand and then the other.

"Al, how did you know it was me?" she said

"You smell like the woman I love."

"Oh, God, Al." She bent over and kissed his ears, his cheeks, and his neck. He was moaning with the pain of wanting her.

He stood facing her, then covered her head with his hands and asked her to shut her eyes. She did as she was told.

"Remember me, Anna. You're going to Italy; you'll meet other people, other men, you'll connect with them. You're too beautiful to be ignored. You belong to the world, and as much as I want you to belong to me, it's not gonna happen in this lifetime. But all I ask is that you remember how much I love you. So help me God that will never be said in the past tense. I'll always love you."

"Oh Al," she cried and she clung to him tightly. They could even feel the rapid pulse beat of their hearts as they embraced. "You saved my life, my darling. How could I forget you? I don't want you out of my life. I'll write to you."

"Write me here, not my house. I'll never get it." He said huskily as his hands continued to caress her body.

"I know that, Al. I have to go. I have coaching in an hour. Did you understand my recording?" he smiled. "Loud and clear, Anna. Too bad you didn't sing in Sicilian." She giggled. "I would have, if I could have pronounced it." He could change her mood in a moment--with a word, a gesture, a facial expression. He stood there by the curb, frozen in time, with his right hand up like a statue's. She wanted to remember him exactly like that. He had, after all, touched her psyche, given her a stronger sense of self. She would never forget that.

The lovers had come to the inevitable crossroad of separation, yet Al felt a sense of peace and resignation, because she loved him, and because, il primo amore non si scorda mai (one never forgets the first love)

Chapter Sixteen

ANNA FOCUSES ON THE CAREER

Anna had a residue of sadness after she drove away in the cab from that forlorn figure of the man she loved. She had to refocus her energies on her music or she would not be able to function. She looked forward to Aldo Di Tullio's coaching lesson; he had scheduled it on a lighter day for him, as the last lesson in the day. This was always advantageous to Anna because Aldo would not watch the clock but allow time for her to question the dramatic impact of the role she was studying. Aldo discussed Gilda from Rigoletto as a real person. For him, the characters came alive, and for Anna, this was of tremendous value.

After the coaching lesson, they spoke of the Italian mentality. Aldo had worked at La Scala earlier as an assistant conductor and he was able to give Anna some pointers on the passion and severe criticism of the Italian audience. She was mesmerized with what he had to say. She never heard La Scala discussed at home.

Italians did not take their opera sitting down. They whistled if they didn't like someone. The whistle, in America, was a sound of approval at sports events, not in opera. In Italy it was a sound of disapproval. Another thing which Anna had no idea about was the young music students who usually sat at a performance with an open score to check out whether the singer was accurate or not. She was shocked. Her father had not told her that, but then his perspective was as a musician not a singer.

Aldo told Anna that she had to develop a thick skin to be in this business. Eileen asked Anna to stay for dinner so that Aldo could continue to brief her on the operatic scene in Italy. Anna's curiosity was piqued, and she called her parents and told them she was dining at Aldo's. As they dined, Aldo told her a bit about the history of premiers.

The criticism against composers whose works today were so brilliantly acclaimed and received sent them in a downward spiral at the time of their opera's world premiere. Though Bizet's Carmen today is one of the most popular of operas, initially most critics lambasted it brutally. After fifty performances, it disappeared into the annals of the silent world of ignored operas.

"So, what you're saying to me is that this is a business similar to the early Christian days, where the ancient Romans could decide the death of gladiators," Anna said as Aldo pointed out the dark side of this business.

"Anna, you must brace yourself for the criticism. Right now, I think you're in the best position. Your fame has preceded you to Italy, and from the newspaper articles being sent to your Poppa Santo, I suspect you won't have too much difficulty. Don't expect a smooth ride, is what I'm telling you. You're young, no family is with you and--"

"On purpose," Anna interrupted, "they all agree that this little bird should fly without them. If I fail, I'm alone; if I succeed, I'm alone. Scary, Aldo, scary." She poured herself a glass of wine and drank it in one continuous flow, and Eileen, Aldo's wife was shocked. Anna didn't drink.

Aldo then talked of the setbacks of Giuseppe Verdi, one of the greatest composers of opera Italy had ever produced. He told her of the public's reception to his opera Un Giorno Di Regno. They were rude and vociferous about their dislike of his work—and this after his wife and two children had died recently. He was ready to hang up his career, but a libretto was slipped into Verdi's pocket by Merelli who was his publisher's agent. The rest is history. "You know of course that Nabucco's chorus became the cry for freedom from the Austrian rule in Italy. It became the anthem of an oppressed people." Anna's eyes widened, and without thinking, she filled her glass with wine, but Aldo took it away knowing that she never indulged in alcoholic spirits. She thanked him and drank water instead.

"Aldo, you're trying to tell me something."

"Anna, I see how many people surround you with their love and their protection. You have no idea what the world is out there. You want this career, don't let anyone or anything stand in your way. They'll shoot you down, they'll mortify you, they'll upstage you, the critics will lambast you, and you either pack it in or keep your eye on the golden ring and go on."

Anna got the message. There was so much Aldo was trying to tell her. He didn't want to get personal about the family dynamic, and, besides, he was good friends with her father. She needed this talk. She needed to hear how the giants in the world of the arts had overcome huge obstacles to make it to the finish line. After dinner, she thanked the Di Tullios and went down to her apartment.

She had six more days before she left. She went to her wardrobe closet and pulled out her new clothes. There was one beautiful evening gown in lavender and dark purple hues, like paint one would mix in a palette. She tried it on and realized how very sensuous it was even though it covered up her torso and arms. It was high-necked, yet clung to her very curvaceous body, leaving very little to the imagination. Yes, she would take this along. Her grandparents Brescia had bought this one for her. She took off the gown and made a call to the studio.

Chet answered the phone and Anna asked if Al was around. Chet said he had gone home for the evening, but she could try him at home. He gave her the number, which she had thrown away after repeated attempts to try to speak to Al. Finally she dialed and got through. Mrs. Russo answered the phone.

"Allo!" she said, "who's this?"

"Signora Russo, sono io, Anna Brescia. May I speak with Al?" she asked.

"No, wrong number. That's okay, you check your number." And she hung up on Anna. Anna was mortified. Aldo was right. She had to focus on the career. She had wanted to see Al privately. She wanted to make love to him, but on second thought perhaps Mrs. Russo's "act" of the wrong number was an omen from God. Anna decided that moment to listen to her intuitive voice, and "hang it up," as Aldo would say.

She lay on her bed, and, with her score in front of her, went through the aria a capella. She had perfect pitch and didn't need accompaniment. The phone rang, she didn't pick it up, leaving it of course to Nonna Anna to take a message. Anna continued to go through the score and was totally involved in the tragedy of Rigoletto. She wept as she went through the story of infamy, seduction, treachery, and murder. It was heavy duty drama, and it touched her deeply.

"Hello?" Nonna Anna said as she answered the phone. "Who's this?"

"Hello, Signora, I'm a friend of Anna's. Is she at home?"

"Who are you please? I'm taking messages for her. I don't know when she's returning."

"Tell her it's the conductor Maestro Matarazzo," he said as he laughed into his hand.

Nonna Anna walked across the large living room and knocked on Anna's door.

"Anna, it's Maestro Matarazzo," Nonna Anna said.

Anna almost fell off the bed with laughter. It had to be Al. What a put-on, she thought. "Hello?" she said as she slid up to her higher register, "Al, don't talk, wait until she hangs up the telephone. It is you isn't it?" she whispered.

"Yeah, okay, let's do a little bull-throwing here. Hold on, so Signorina, your arpeggios should go as high as you wish, then you can slide down in a glissando and fall into the final cadence with a great thud. You have to know that as you do this you must enter into a crescendo so that the audience will not demand their money back. Endings have to be dramatic. You can even scream the finale at the top of your lungs until they throw tomatoes at you. My suggestion is that you vocalize every hour on the hour in order to achieve this effect."

Anna was laughing so hard, she fell off the bed. Finally they heard Nonna Anna hang up. She must have been listening.

"Baby, I'm gonna die," Al said, "I'm mortified that my mother spoke to you like that. I heard her, too. I knew that it was you. So I figured what the hell, let me try her house, and I get the same kind of bullshit, excuse the language. Does this remind you of Romeo and Juliet?"

"Al, it's what it is. I want you, Al. Tomorrow I have four hours in the afternoon. I want to be with you."

He almost choked. He couldn't believe that she would be so forward, that she would initiate an act of love. "I was afraid to ask."

"I'm not afraid to ask, Al. I want you, you want me. My career is taking off, but we don't have to stop loving each other."

"Amen, baby! Where do you want to go?" he asked.

"The Waldorf. I'll pay for it."

"No, it's my tab. What time?" he asked anxiously.

"Tomorrow at one, okay? Tell them you're my husband, they'll give you the room number. I'm registering under Russo, okay?"

"Sounds good, Baby I love you," he said.

Anna made reservations at the Waldorf, then felt satisfied with herself. There was no guilt. She knew she was going into a world of many obstacles, and unless she was in control of herself and what she wanted, those obstacles would have one of two effects: to destroy her or to strengthen her. She chose the latter.

That evening, when her parents came home, they asked her to join them in her small sitting room with the white wicker cushioned chairs. The room was filled with large plants and mirrors. It looked like a room in a Floridian home. Paintings of spring landscapes were on two walls. The three of them sat with a pitcher of water, fresh fruit and crackers, and snacked together.

Maurizio commented on what he perceived to be her sense of calm. He apologized and explained why she had to go through this alone. She assured them that she was alright with it. Gemma told her that a limousine would pick her up at 5:00 in the morning to take her to Idlewild airport in Long Island. Gemma asked, "are you afraid to fly?"

"Momma, if God wanted me to fly He would have given me wings. Yes I'm afraid to fly." Then Anna almost lost control as her father asked who Maestro Matarazzo was?

"Oh, Matarazzo?" she giggled then covered her mouth. "Sounds so funny, Daddy. He's a conductor from San Francisco. He called to wish me well."

"My mother told me that the musical talk from him sounded strange."

"Daddy, it was Al. We have to circumvent both our families in order to speak to each other. His mother hangs up on me, telling me I have the wrong number. Nonna tells him that she doesn't know if she'll ever see me to give me his message, and on and on it goes."

They listened as their rather self-assured daughter went into her soliloquy about their past, and her relationship with a man who had helped turn her life around, and they had no argument. She told them how she preferred honesty to subterfuge. They didn't deserve lies, and she hated telling them.

"Don't judge me. Your families didn't judge you. Momma, your parents were like gold to you, supportive and loving. They stuck by you in a difficult time. Daddy, when Momma and me came to you, your parents took us in with open arms. Nobody was giving anybody a guilt trip. Don't do it to me. You've been lucky. Please give me the same support."

Maurizio looked at his beautiful vibrant daughter, filled with confidence and resolve, and he put his arm around his wife and said, "Gemma, our little girl has grown up." He turned to his daughter "Anna, I do support you. You're right, but I don't approve, however, I respect your choices. We've tried our best." And soto voce, muttered "I hope that we've succeeded."

"Daddy. You have succeeded." Anna embraced her parents. "I love you both with all my heart, and if I could have had a choice in parents, I would always choose the two of you. You're very wise, you know, for pushing me out of the nest."

Anna went to bed ecstatic. Just thinking of the trumped up musical dialogue with innuendoes was enough to send her into gales of laughter again. Her parents heard her through the closed doors and across the corridor.

"Have you ever heard her as happy?" Gemma asked her husband.

"He's good for her right now. We'd better not interfere or the law of nature will take over and they'll marry. Once again, we must look the other way."

Maurizio put his arm around her.

"Wow! She exposed us. Our parents were spectacular, yours as well as mine. Without them in our corner, none of the early days after that reunion would have been as smooth. Gemma, I know what your mother was going through in those early years. She simply didn't want to be here."

"I know." Gemma said.

"Charlie was the matchmaker there, it's good to see your mother so happy."

Gemma snuggled closer to him.

"Another Sicilian," she muttered.

"So?" Maurizio asked.

"Rough around the edges. Not like your father, gentile, soft spoken. I suspect that Al's the same. However, Anna laughs with total abandon. She's seems happy with him."

He commented that they shouldn't worry about a future for the relationship. Because of the regional differences, Anna would never fulfill his requirements for a wife. The career, and her lack of domestication would terminate any alliance with a Sicilian man.

"Some day she'll meet the right person," he said.

"Don't bet on it, Darling. She's attracted to the wrong kind."

They talked a little longer, then fell asleep.

The next few days were a frenzy of activity for Anna. She had coaching in the morning with Aldo, then at noon went to the Waldorf Astoria and checked in for the day. She left a message at the desk to page Al at around 12:45 to 1:15 and tell him that his wife was waiting for him upstairs.

At 1:00 sharp, the desk called her and told her that her husband was on the way up. He knocked on the door, and Anna opened it. She was in a black negligee looking beautiful and mysterious. The shades were drawn, and she had a bottle of champagne on ice for them. He was taken aback by her beauty, and her ease with him. The shy conservative Anna was gone, and he noticed a change in her. Determined was the word that came to mind.

He kissed her lightly and she sat on the bed watching him. He opened the champagne and poured two glasses. She sipped hers once then put it down. Al drank a bit of his, and then got in bed with her. They held each other for a while and talked. She spoke about the rapid changes which were happening in her life, and he listened. Knowing that their paths had possibly crossed for the last time, the sense of the end of the road was so strong in Al. He remembered the previous year when this intense sadness about losing her overwhelmed him.

Anna talked about her fears of what she was going to face in Italy. The war-torn country, her fatherland, and her debut in a country of severe opera critics. She told Al what Aldo had told her, about Italians taking their opera seriously. He was surprised to hear the apprehension of this magnificent experience she was about to have. She was afraid, yet she had nothing to fear, for she had proven herself to the New York operatic scene with great success and grace. Then, almost as an afterthought, she said, "Al, what if I don't go and we get married?"

"You'd grow to hate me. No, Anna, I have to be your whole life, but it's not possible, not with the entity as your master. I want a traditional marriage: kids, a woman who can cook and darn my socks. You don't fit the bill."

"You have other plans, right?"

"I hope so. I'm 28 years old. I want kids myself. I want the normal cycle of life, Anna. That entity you call your career will always come first. I can't deal, I have to be on top," Anna grimaced, he added, "in everything, sweetheart, we've already drifted so far away from each other, and you know it."

Anna felt a thud in the pit of her stomach, she took her nightgown off with her back to him totally naked and slipped her dress on. She was mortified. She had to run out. The moment had passed. He slipped to her side of the bed and pulled her back on the bed. He cupped her sad face in his hands and kissed the tip of her nose.

"Baby, you're not going any where, this is the final performance, don't blow it."

"Sounds as though I've been faking it, Al," and he embraced her and his eyes glistened with unshed tears. "There's no faking this, when we make love, that's real," he enveloped her in his arms and this time they stopped speaking, and if Anna tried to say something, he'd cover her mouth with his..she understood, They had managed to shut the world out, to set aside the fears and find solace in each other in the final act. She wiped the tears of joy with the corner of the sheet and said, "I"ll always love you," and he responded, "I know that thought will keep me sane."

Chapter Seventeen
AL'S FAMILY PRESSURE

Al had achieved idealistic love with Anna Brescia. He couldn't put their affair away as easily as she did. She had a demanding career and all of her focus was on it.

Al called every day. She asked her grandmother to screen her calls because she knew that she could not split herself emotionally on the eve of her trip to Milano.

Al was depressed. He took to his bed and told Chet that he was sick. He sounded beaten, so Chet went to his home to visit him. Mrs. Russo was livid. She talked about the situation steadily with her son and told him that he had to fill that void with the courtship of her best friend's daughter. It made sense to Al, so he succumbed to the pressure of his mother's suggestion.

When Chet talked to Mrs. Russo, he couldn't understand this Sicilian compulsion to orchestrate their grown up children's lives. However, he listened and offered no reaction. Her argument was that if you are concentrating on one thing so intently, you cannot think of anything else. Actually she brought out the fact that Anna refused to take his calls. She too, could have called Al's house and gotten through, since he took to his bed the next day.

"What's she like?" Mrs. Russo asked Chet as she poured him a cup of American coffee.

"She's talented, beautiful and loves your son, but she isn't an average girl." Chet dipped the home made biscotto into his coffee and studied Mrs. Russo's facial expression. She gave him a side glance, raised her eyebrow in disbelief, and didn't respond to his answer. A Milanese, from a high-class family, centered on herself. What could her son expect but heartbreak from such a woman? How foolish Chet was, she thought.

"These are fabulous, Mrs. Russo," Chet said and she immediately packed a basket of cookies for him to take home. Mrs. Russo decided to "educate" Chet. She spoke of the disadvantage of romantic alliances, the unrealistic expectations of these arrangements. Sicilians mistrusted the romantic notion of love. In fact, she had learned of the circumstances of Chet and Carli's marriage and disapproved.

Her plan to fix up her son with her friend's daughter Concetta, 28 years old, was already in motion. A formal proposal was requested by the Russo's for Concetta's hand in marriage. The families were in accord and so the stage was set to "settle" Al's personal life.

Act One of the proposal was the official request of the Russo's. Act Two was the second visit with Al present.

The night of the meeting was planned at Concetta's house. It was proper protocol to have dinner with the "intended" family. The Russos brought two gallons of home-made wine, one red, one white. They also brought a huge basket of anisette biscotti.

Concetta was delighted. She wore a paisley print dress; her hair was pulled back in a bun, and she wore no makeup. This pleased the Russos.

Al looked at her and saw great possibilities of a more attractive young woman given the right hairdo and makeup. No, she was not homely, and she was very attentive to Al. It made him feel good. The unwritten contract of a union was discussed, and the courtship began. Al would take her out on a Saturday night and bring her home by eleven in the evening. This was enough time for a movie and a brief snack at a diner. He liked her, and realized that because of the way she looked up to him, that "like" would eventually develop into a solid love and mutual respect. It would be a marriage sanctioned by both families, and he would respect and honor this young lady.

When the Russos got home, Biaggia Russo sat with her son at the table. He looked more animated than in the past two days and her timing on this matter was perfect. He mentioned to his mother that Concetta was so painfully plain that she looked like a nun. His mother told him that once they were engaged, she could Americanize herself more, which she would do for him. At least she wouldn't dress and make up like a slut to attract other men. Her loyalty would be to him. She had never been with a man, which meant that she had the desirable trait of being a virgin, his mother argued. Al agreed, and now his focus would be on a rapid development of a relationship with this young lady who received the stamp of approval from the Russos.

The end of the week of mourning, Al was ready to leave when the phone rang. His heart almost stopped. It was Anna.

"Hi, darling," she said, and he was almost speechless. He was hurt.

"Are you okay?" she asked.

"When are you leaving?" His voice caught, and he sounded raspy.

"Tomorrow morning at 5:00 a.m. I've been so busy."

"Have you?" he asked sarcastically, "I called you, and you don't return my calls. Did you get the messages?"

"Yes, I did. But I had no time. Last minute details. I'll write you Al." Her words sounded so unfeeling, and she almost regretted calling him. He was not his usual exuberant self.

"Have a good trip," he said, and he had to hang up for he was choking back the tears of anguish, as he realized that the final chapter was at hand.

"Al?" She heard the phone click, and realized how callously she had treated him this past week. It was unavoidable. What was it he had said to her? "The entity owns you." Yes, it did. She sat down and wrote him a letter before she finished her packing, and would mail it herself not trusting her family to mail it.

"Dear Al: I am so sorry that we drifted so far apart this horrendously busy week. I heard it in your voice, and you were right. I should have called. Your mother would not give you any of my messages. It's not as though this is news to you, but I hoped you'd understand my motivation for not persisting.

The entity, as you said, owns me. I'll never marry, or if I do it has to be unconventional. Let's put it this way, he'll have to pour my juice in the morning. Besides the mundane little things in life, my work is highly demanding, and I think of nothing else. Why? because I don't live in the real world, I live on stage, and being there, I give so much of my art, of my self to what I do, that when I come off there's little else left of me.

Casting all the rhetoric aside, we love each other, but it's not enough, so our decision to walk out of each other's lives, was instantaneous. We came together from two different worlds, and we knew from the first that we could never make it into a permanent arrangement. Yet, I'm grateful that I had the privilege of knowing you and loving you. All I ask is that there is no rancor in this mutual decision. I know we'll cross paths again, and I hope that there will be no resentment. I shall always remember your profound statement that the only real thing between us is our love for each other, and that, you shall always have, Love Anna Brescia."

Two days after Anna left, her letter arrived. Al came home from the studio at midnight, and Biaggia got up from her bed and embraced her son. They sat and talked, and Al seemed more animated than usual. Biaggia panicked at first when she saw Anna's letter. She had mixed feelings about the letter arriving at the house in such an untimely fashion, for the propelling of Al's pending betrothal was in full gear. Though Biaggia was tempted to throw it away, the repercussions, if Al ever found out, would polarize them. Therefore, she placed it carefully on the kitchen china closet tucked under the other mail. Biaggia weighed all the circumstances. Anna had physically left Al. Biaggia wasn't worried.

Saturday night came, and Al had to call Concetta to tell her that she had two choices for their date. She could cancel the preplanned movie and snack date or come with him to the village for a gig. She opted for the gig after asking her parent's permission. Al talked to them and told them that they'd be home very, very late, like two in the morning. They refused him, so the first date was cancelled. Concetta cried when her parents didn't permit her to go with him to the village.

Already Al could see that contention was a part of his life. He did his gig and told Chet about the situation with his fiancee's family, and

Chet was shocked. Carli performed with them that night, and between shows, held Al's hand figuratively. Carli congratulated him on such a quick emotional recovery as he spoke about his verbal commitment to Concetta.

"How do you do that?" Carli asked, surprised at this old world setup.

"It worked for my family, my sister included. Look, Carli, I want a life of my own. I want kids. I'm so damned jealous of all my friends. They have wives, kids, and all that goes with it, a home. Stability."

"You and my friend are no longer an item, then."

"We never were, Carli. Make no mistake about it. If she ever gets married, it can't last, unless a man is willing to play second fiddle to her career." Carli was stunned at how quickly Al had shifted emotional gears.

After the last show, they packed it in, and went home sharing a cab. Al got home at 2:00 and Biaggia Russo got up from bed. She slept lightly until her son got home. She expressed deep concern over the broken date with Concetta and admonished him to get himself a substitute for the following week because her friend Gina, Concetta's mother, called her and complained over the lack of responsibility Al showed her daughter.

They talked about the engagement and how heartbroken Concetta was that Al missed their first date. Biaggia told her son that they plan a marriage right away or the Butti family was going to withdraw their daughter from the agreement.

"Ma, is this the way you guys do it in Sicily?" he asked angrily.

"Fighiu mio"--she said, "We need to focus on getting you settled. We are Sicilian. This is the way we do it."

"No wonder she's 28 years old and unmarried still. Damn it, I'm earning a living. Saturday nights is all he said I could date his daughter. They either work with me, or the deal is off."

Biaggia cried. Al hated to see his mother cry. She was his comfort, and seeing her so unhappy upset him.

"What do you want me to do, Momma?" he asked.

"Set a wedding date. You go there, and we'll come with you, and we'll make a formal declaration of a marriage offer. You have to do this." Biaggia blew her nose, and woke up her husband Beniamino.

He shuffled into the kitchen in his long johns, wondering why his wife was crying.

"Chi e?"--what is it?--he asked.

"Poppa, I'm sorry. Go to bed. Momma is just upset because the Butti's are threatening to terminate my courtship with Concetta."

"You blame them?" Beniamino said and he shuffled back to bed.

Al promised his mother he'd go there on Sunday morning after Mass and do a formal declaration, set the date, and start his life right. At 3:00, Al went to bed. He couldn't sleep. It was so weird this entire thing of getting settled as his mother said, that he wondered if this was the way Sicilian people started their married lives. No dating, no touching, no unscheduled time together. He realized that marrying a bona fide virgin like Concetta was a badge of honor for the Russo family. He tiptoed to the kitchen and made himself a cup of chamomile tea. This was the beverage that would calm him down after he returned home from his village gigs. He sipped the tea and found it to be awful tasting, so he went to the canister to get a teaspoon of sugar. He saw a letter with his name on it, tucked under the canister. He took the letter and read it as he sat down to sip his tea.

When he finished it, he put his head on the table and wept. By writing this letter, Anna had filled the gaping hole in his heart with her declaration of love towards him. It was a healing closure to their affair. He read the letter five more times, dwelling on "the only real thing about us is our love for each other". In reading this letter, he realized how very much he meant to her. At last he had a sense of peace with it. He realized that his mother had not given him the letter, that she had tucked it under the sugar canister.

On Sunday morning at ten, Al went to church with his mother and father. They reminded him to put in a call to the Butti's. He said he would, but first he wanted to talk to them at home after Mass. Biaggia got nervous. He probably found the letter. Sure enough she didn't see it and thought she had misplaced it. Throughout the Mass, she couldn't concentrate, anticipating her son's anger towards her. She would say she forgot it, and if she didn't want him to receive it, she could have simply thrown it away. She had been tempted to do so. She felt justified in doing so. Parents had the right to intercede when they saw that their offspring needed help.

After Mass, they came home, and Al sat his parents down at the table and talked to them. He assured them that his intentions towards Concetta were honorable, which meant marriage, and that after his talk with his parents, he'd call them and pay a visit to schedule a wedding date. Biaggia and Beniamino were relieved. Al then took Anna's letter out. Biaggia squirmed in her chair, and Beniamino didn't even know about the letter. He looked at his wife quizzically, and she took a deep breath as Al opened up the letter from Anna and read it to his parents.

After they heard the letter, Biaggia and Beniamino wept. They had no idea of the depth of emotions of their son's affair. It was so touching, so poignant and did not portray the "puttana" that the Russos had believed she was.

"Momma, Poppa, this is the woman I'll always love. I wanted you to know her, that's why I read her letter to you. Don't ever call her a slut to me again. If she ever calls or writes, you are to let me know. If you hide one more communication, you'll lose me."

Beniamino took his son's hand in his and felt deeply about his son's revelation.

"I won't," Biaggia said. "I was prejudiced against her. Show business personalities are not like us. Son, does this mean that Concetta is out of your consideration?"

"No, Momma, I'm calling and going there now. I think I'll invite myself for the Sunday pranzo there, so don't cook too much." Biaggia sighed deeply. Her son was doing the right thing.

Al called and went to the Butti's home which was on Digney Avenue near 233rd Street. They were pleased to see him, and Concetta's hair bun was gone, and her hair cascaded around her lovely face. She put a hint of blush on her cheeks, and she looked beautiful. She wore a sweater and a skirt and the sweater brought out her curves. As subtly as she could, she enticed Al to her.

The Butti family decided the wedding date, and, in two months, Al and Concetta would marry. Because of this, the flexibility of their future dates was opened up to Al's convenience. It would be a good marriage as his parents had predicted. Al's self-esteem grew as Concetta lived to please him. She poured his juice, and she poured his coffee, and served him indeed like a king. She was, after all a perfect Sicilian wife.

Chapter Eighteen
MILANO   1947

Daniele was walking across the piazza in front of La Scala and observing with pride how the Italians worked non stop to rebuild their fractured nation. The Marshall Plan was already in effect, and its aid from the United States was more than a band-aid. It was a lifeline.

He smiled to himself as he limped with his cane, thinking of the benevolence of the conquering nation always with its arms open to help those nations who had fought against them. This was forgiveness in the grandest style. In God we trust.

The operatic season was going full swing, and the populace in Milano was back doing their verbal posturing on all subjects, mostly the opera season and the new house. Bombs had almost leveled the magnificent opera house, and in one year it was rebuilt exactly the same way--with improvements.

He clutched the local newspaper under his arm and was perusing the story of the young, brilliant, soprano Anna Brescia. She cut quite a figure, and he couldn't understand why his lack of enthusiasm over her arrival. She was booked for concerts around Milano, and her Italian debut was imminent in Rigoletto. Talk about her brilliant debut as Queen of the Night in Mozart's "Magic Flute" was still resounding. A contingent of aficionados of opera wanted her to debut with this opera. However, it was not being done that season, and the offer was for a debut as Gilda in Verdi's "Rigoletto."

He saw his colleague walking quickly behind him, and he stopped as Franco Franceschi called out his name. Franco was a bubbling personality, totally involved in his voice. He was a brilliant lyric tenor and his right hand was always on his throat as he cleared it. The man was talented but nervous about that talent. He was not anxious to be working with Anna Brescia. Too beautiful, too much great publicity and he felt intimidated as well as replaced by her since he was a leading tenor. He'd be playing the Duke to her Gilda.

"So, Maestro," Franco said as he slowed down his pace and put his arm through Daniele's arm. "What do you think of the American diva sweeping into the operatic scene in Milano?" Franco was hoping for some criticism or reservations. It would affirm his own feelings of antagonism.

"Franco, I reserve judgment; she's one of ours," Daniele said.

Franco told Daniele that he was aware of the history of the family from Milano and their emigration. Since he had no real bone to pick just yet, he mentioned the fact that they abandoned the patria to embrace another nation. He questioned their patriotic position.

"Franco, I can't get into it. But I'm kind of apprehensive about working with someone with an American mentality. All her photos show her to be proud and arrogant." He stumbled on a cobblestone and Franco steadied him. Daniele had a piece of his leg and bone shattered in the war, and was lucky to have a shriveled leg to walk on. It was weak, but with the use of a cane, he was able to walk.

"Then you do have judgment," Franco said with relief. "I wonder how she'll take your stage directions. What if she has this attitude that she knows best? Remember Sol Hurok, the biggest agent in America, works for her. She doesn't come from peasant stock. Her parents are classical musicians, both educated in our conservatory. I wish you luck."

Daniele quickly answered, "I wish you luck. You're the one who's going to make love to her on stage. Should be very interesting." He chuckled, and then the talk drifted to the rehearsal schedule and working around other directors. Daniele was a serious young man, having been schooled directly in the operatic theater. He had been sent to Covent Garden in London to apprentice his craft, an age-old discipline, so that he would be capable of working in Milan's critical climate. His father had held the position of impressario for many years before the war, and Daniele had listened to no other music other than the operatic and vocal repertoire. They had so much in common besides being native born Milanese. Early in their lives, their music education had been focused totally on opera, excluding other music.

Suffice to say the affable climate Anna Brescia expected at La Scala would not be in accord with the printed accolades about her talent. Italians, being a population of strong individualists, differed with each other about everything including their taste in divas.

Daniele and Franco got to the opera house and checked in for room schedules, appointments and rehearsal information pertinent to their respective fields.

Daniele went into his office and shut the door. He wasn't expecting anyone for a while. He pulled the bottom drawer open and took out a file. He laid it on his cluttered desk and opened it. It was a collection of newspaper articles from the inception of the publicity barrage of the Hurok office.

Daniele's horn-rimmed glasses slipped down his slender straight nose, and he muttered as he re-read the story of this incoming "diva" from America. His comments were barely audible, but at one point, as the office door opened, Franco peeked in, ready to knock, when he saw Daniele D'Andrea deep in thought. He heard him say, "arrogant" "Typical American" "I don't believe it." Franco laughed, and Daniele sat up.

"May I come in, Maestro?" Franco said, very much amused. "I see you have the diva's publicity machine in front of you. You don't believe it either, do you?"

Daniele stood up and offered Franco a chair.

"It's like the propaganda machine we were subjected to in the war. It's all phony. She's a phony. Ah, what's the use? I'm working myself up into a froth and she hasn't even arrived yet. Here I am almost 32 years old, having survived the hell of a world war, and I get myself all worked up over a snippet of a young girl with an air of a queen, a lineage of her own making. No, I'm not looking forward to it. So Franco, what brings you here?"

Franco told Daniele that he wanted him to come over on Sunday for a pasta dinner which his Neopolitan wife Francesca was making.

They had finally gotten some exquisite cuts of meat and were anxious to share a Southern Italian cuisine with their Northern brothers from Milan. Daniele laughed and said yes. He had never wanted to socialize with the "plebes," so to speak, since he was in the upper echelons of the operatic pyramid. But when Francesca and Franco's son had been born last year, they asked Daniele D'Andrea to be the godfather. He'd said yes, enthusiastically. It had been such a refreshing time right after the war to engage in such social and religious rituals.

"I have to check with my parents," Daniele said, "and then I'll let you know. How is my young godson MichelAngelo?" Of course Franco took out the photographs of the child eating, sleeping, bathing and throwing up which they enjoyed showing to all.

Franco was a nervous but cheerful person. He adored his wife Francesca, who had been in the chorus of La Scala, never quite having made it to the solo category of singers. She couldn't care, for her sole ambition was to capture a tenor and marry him. She had. She also had lived "happily ever after." They were made for each other, mad for each other, and created an aura of joy whenever they were together. People never turned down invitations from the Franceschi's.

There was an air of excitement in the company as the time for the young American diva was coming closer. The publicity machinery preceded her with invitations to all those who were going to work with her to meet at a private party. There was a possibility of Anna doing a post opera concert at Ferrara, or La Piccola Scala, according to Hurok's office.

As smooth as it could possibly be for her, Santo Averso had managed to work hard to achieve comfort as well as welcome from the critical Milanese people, especially those directly involved in any of her concert or operatic performances.

Daniele D'Andrea was all set to dislike her. He had fortified himself with every rationale to do so. None of it was logical nor made sense on the surface, but beneath it all, he was intimidated by a star from America. It all was wrapped up in the loss of the war for the Italians, the devastation and toll on human lives, and the mortification of Mussolini's death. It was a matter of national shame for him. Daniele had believed in the Fascist movement and, as though a parent had disillusioned him, he felt that he, too, had been betrayed. None of this was Anna's fault, but she represented America, the victors, and she represented youth, wealth, and success. Daniele was envious on every level of her achievements. This built in mindset worked against his participating in the most sought after experience of being part of an international name. Just the sight of her picture in the newspaper caused disdain in him, and he was quite generous in his expletives against her, particularly when he had the luxury of doing this by himself, with no witnesses. He indulged himself in self-pity as well as hatred for the daughter of the victorious America. Even though Anna Brescia was born in Milano, he discounted that fact and never considered her as being Italian-born.

Anna had these strikes against her even before she landed on Italian soil. She, too, had a mixed bag of emotions and mindset. Her coach, Aldo Di Tullio, had told her of the severity of the Italian critics, in essence the general populace. He had worked at La Scala as a visiting assistant conductor years earlier and was aware of the differences in mentality, even though he was Italian-American. Aldo could only equate that attitude as arrogance in knowing your company is the best in the world.

She wasn't sure if she was fish or fowl as a representative of a country. In America, she was the young immigrant from Milano. In Italy, she was l'Americana from New York. These categories created confusion in her own mind. Alone, without family, without a familiar face, Anna was extremely apprehensive. Yet, as Aldo said, she could show neither fear, nor insecurity to the Italian populace. She was, after all, prepared for what was happening, and that was to have the lowest possible expectations from the experience. She was prepared for any obstacle or barrage of negative attitudes which would come her way.

Her Poppa Santo told her to win everyone over. He told her to do it over food to which Italians responded to. He gave her a huge amount of money to wine and dine her co-workers as well as her superiors in the opera company. He also admonished her not to flaunt her wealth, but to go slowly in wooing them to accept her. With a laundry list of admonishments from Poppa Santo, Aldo Di Tullio and her own parents, Anna had only one desire. She only wished she could have stayed at home, married her beloved Al, and lived happily ever after just like Cinderella. But that wasn't her world, and she knew that, with a gift as large as she had been given, her responsibility was to pursue it, and nurture it so that she could share it with the world. Humility towards her gift began to grow in her, and Anna truly remembered the words of her beloved Al: that she had to march to the tune of the entity which owned her. However, with one difference than Al's take on it, it wasn't the entity that owned her, but she who owned the entity and had to honor its hold on her as a gift to the God who had given it to her. This she could live with; this she had to live with. She also faced the fact that her real life would never be her own. She might never have a life like Carli, a baby like Adam, or a husband like Chet. She was ready to face that. Emotions had to be put in places in her psyche, which would serve her rather than dictate to her. She was, after all, according to her father's last words, "growing up." She was becoming a woman.

Anna Brescia arrived on the last weekend of September. Her emotions were put on hold as she landed in the noisy vibration filled flight she got off from. She was met by an envoy from the Sol Hurok office, a Grace Giordano fellow Italian American who took care of her arrival and customs. The limousine was waiting auspiciously right outside the terminal, and as they got in, the photographers snapped her arrival and stopped her for a short interview.

"Are you happy to be in your homeland Signorina Brescia?" one gentleman asked.

"Yes, very. I'm deeply touched to walk the Italian soil after all this time." Her answers were to the point, and she made a good impression. Grace Giordano told her to take on several more questions, then she would whisk her away. Anna was to act from this moment on like the epitome of graciousness no matter what she was feeling.

At the hotel near the opera house, she was met in the lobby with more reporters, more questions and lots of picture-snapping. She smiled graciously and found them to be very aggressive and unrelenting. Grace finally took her upstairs, knowing that Anna had not slept at all on the long flight, and was exhausted.

By this time, after months and almost a year of feature stories, and anticipation of the Milanese soprano, Anna was familiar to the Italian populace. Anna changed into casual attire hoping not to attract attention to herself. However, she was surprised, when photographers recognized her. Italy was tired of war, and Anna became the respite of good news in a cauldron of war stories and devastation.

"Are you excited?" Grace asked her.

"Oh, yes. I'm looking forward to it. Grace, can we go to Mugenta?"

"That little town? Why?"

"I was born in a villa there. I want to see my first home."

"Oh? Is that where your Milanese father Brescia lived? I thought he lived in Milano."

Anna realized that the dirty laundry of her illegitimate beginnings must remain a secret.

"He did, but for a while we lived in Mugenta." Anna realized that this quest to seek Santo Averso's home was ill-conceived. This surely would expose that part of her life which would be a huge scandal. She would be the bastard diva in the eyes of the Italian public, not a palatable position for her family or her. No one would even remember how well she sang or acted. The only thing they'd remember would be negative press.

"If you wish, I can arrange this trip for you tomorrow," Grace suggested.

"On second thought, I'll pass. If it's bombed, I don't want to see it. No one is there anymore. It would be an exercise in futility. But thank you, Grace; you are very kind. I think I can get around by myself. I appreciate you meeting me and bringing me to my hotel. Suppose you let me know how to reach you and what my itinerary is. God knows you have so much to do."

"Yes, thank you Anna. You're sure you're alright? I can get you an escort to take you around." Anna assured her that she would just go in the environs of the opera house and the shops around the piazza. Grace warned her not to carry a lot of money, to keep her bag hidden on her body, and to try to be unobtrusive. Anna put a kerchief on her head, as though she were a peasant, put on a dark navy pea jacket from a neighbor's naval days in the war. With dark glasses, and a man's clothes, she looked like a man, hoping no one would know who she was.

Franco Franceschi found Daniele D'Andrea in the coffee shop to the right of the opera house. He was sipping a cappucino and reading the Italian newspaper with accounts of the arrival of la diva Americana, Anna Brescia.

"So, what do you think?" Franco asked as he pulled up a seat next to D'Andrea after getting himself an espresso with sambucca.

"I don't think," Daniele responded. "I don't even want to meet her."

"I've had her moves followed by my cousin Domenico. He told me that she was somewhere in the piazza because they saw her walking out of the hotel. But I haven't been able to find her. Keep your eyes peeled." Daniele told him to change the subject or he'd walk out. Franco couldn't. He was stunned to see Daniele finish his cappucino, get up, and walk out. He started walking towards the left side of the piazza under the buildings, and he bumped into a person whose gender was not obvious due to dark glasses, a masculine jacket, and pants.

"Pardon!" he said as he almost knocked the person off his balance. why it was a woman, he thought to himself.

"Why don't you dress like a lady?" he snapped. "Would that have made you act like a gentleman?" she snarled. He was mesmerized by her magnificent white skin, and full sensuous red lips. He caught his breath as a chill came over him. She turned on her heel, grunted disdainfully and walked to the coffee shop.

He watched her walk away. Who would wear such clothes? She smelled expensive and looked like a foreigner. Daniele laughed aloud.

"That," he said audibly, "was the American diva. Dear God, what nerve. This should be very interesting. We'll see, my caro Daniele." He walked on, pleased that he was in a position to be able to teach her a thing or two.

Chapter Nineteen

LETTER TO CARLI

Carli! I miss you so much. So many things going on inside as well as around me. I hardly know where to begin. Let me preface this by saying that I'm glad I came. I see my homeland shaking off the rubble of war, running towards a new chapter in their history, and making it. Oh, God, are they making it. There is great love for the Americans in most quarters. I don't think the Axis were ever joined at the hip. Too much antagonism between the Germans and the Italians existed even before their war machine began to disintegrate.

I've met the cast of Rigoletto. Nice, but reserved. However, I'm still Signorina Brescia to them (l' Americana)…would you believe? Just as I feel that we're getting close, I almost expect them to use my first name, but you know? They don't. There's such a caste system: formality and protocol. Dining is formal. No buffet dining. Every meal, even a cup of espresso is a ritual of serving the consumer. It's queenly, Carli. Grandma Anna waited on me as though I were a queen, so I'm used to it. She'd always pour my juice, tuck my napkin under my chin and la de da it was nice. Gotta make sure I wash my hands frequently. Men meet you and then kiss your hand. ALL OF THEM. Wonder how you'd react to that?

However, not all is perfect. The stage director growls when he sees me. I don't hear it, I FEEL it. He's got a major problem with me. I understand that he learned his craft at Covent Gardens as a young man.

He looks at me as though he's concocting some evil deed. It makes my skin crawl. Of course he's on my shit list. So far, he's the only one on it.

I miss you-know-who. How is he? I haven't written. He wouldn't play second fiddle to my "entity," as he called my career. I know you were surprised that we didn't make it. I could never fill his domestic needs as a wife. You know what, Carli? He never did ask me to marry him, oh I think he mentioned it once or twice, but he knew that it wouldn't work out. I think it would have been demeaning to him as a Sicilian husband to have to make the eggplant parmigiano because I couldn't even boil water. I'm telling you this because the whole thing was an enigma to you, though I don't know why except that you have an unusual grandfather who takes over the kitchen on Saturdays. Sooooooooooooooooooo..

I have to go. Rehearsal with the director on my S. list. Oh! I like the way he thinks artistically. He's good, Carli, but I'll be damned if I'd ever admit it. Ciao for now. Luv ya, and …damn! I forgot what I was saying. Oh, yes, I remember now. I'm shopping for my godson every chance I get. Shops are coming back, and baby things all hand-made here are so beautiful, but I'm buying big sizes, because I know my beautiful godson must be on pasta now…talk to you later, love ya.

Hi, it's me. Just came back. The bastard set me up for mortification in front of the cast. I almost cried, but I wouldn't give him the satisfaction. I did Caro Nome, and he sneered and said, "you're playing the virginal Gilda like Salome and the seven veils, you must float on stage, not slink, okay?" I hate him and I always shall. soooooooooooooo…

Tuesday: Hi Carli, I'm doing better. We're getting close to performance time. My parents are coming in a few days. Poppa Santo and Kay are also coming, but they're staying with the D'Andrea family (the hateful stage director's parents.) I've written Daddy to try to be civil to Poppa Santo. He said he'd be good (whatever that means). What are you doing? I know you're busy with diapers, baby food, pastina. Sometimes I wish it were me. I think. Sometimes I want to settle down, and other times I don't. I'll let you know. My famous phrase--do you remember when we first met at Sacred Heart school, and I said I'd let you know if you could be my best friend or not? What arrogance! Why didn't you sock me? But that wasn't you. I think of what daddy's thought will be when he comes to La Scala to hear me sing. I just can't think about him, because I'll cry. This is where he wanted to be. This triumph should have been his, and you know what Carli? I swear to you, my triumph is for my father, and so it means more to me than just a debut at La Scala, it means years ago, someone in this opera house blocked him, and he had a nervous collapse, so he left Italy for America a desperate man.

Wednesday: Hi, it's me again. Well, one American arrival was emotional. Poppa Santo couldn't stop weeping. Kay tells me that he does that a lot. Just cries all the time. I hope he doesn't crack up or lock horns with Daddy. That is a scary thing. But, I hope, for the best.

You're never going to guess who we went out to dinner with. Yep, the psychotic stage director, his father, Santo and Kay, and me. Poor "Psycho" had to sit opposite me. I hope he choked with aggravation. He talked about the opera, of the past. Psycho kept glaring at me, and I was good, Carli. I pretended he was invisible, and he pretended not to be looking at me, but I saw his side glances darting at me like so many spears…I hope he was angry. The old impresario was frail, and he kept saying "Brescia," and nodding his head. He just met me, yet he calls my name, strange man, that's where psycho gets his genes from…his mom's nice, I mean really nice.

Observation: if I'm considered an "Americana," they like America. If I'm considered Milanese, they hate America and feel that only Milano could have produced such talent. I wish I had Al here; we'd have a field day peeling off the skins of the operatic ruling class. Can you just hear the Bronx cheer? I miss him. Well, gotta go. I have an appointment today with a woman who does custom-made sweaters. I'm ordering a size for a two year old boy. Two more entries, I promise you and then I'm mailing this…

Thursday: Carli, you won't believe this. Only for your eyes. Promise? Okay, we had the dress rehearsal the other night on stage, it was magnificent. I couldn't get over the sound of all of us with the orchestra. Psycho man made sure that I got a last minute lecture from him about floating and little does he know how I pull the sheet off the bed, drape it around me so that I can practice how to float in front of the mirror..I'm looking so queenly, I don't know about virginal, but then

153

that's his problem, the son of a bitch.. After rehearsal, I invited the cast to Poppa Santo's former restaurant. They accepted.

The only one who turned down the invitation was the stage director. I begged Franco to get him there no matter what. I had to "get back" at the dissonant director. Franco did. Daniele was told to sit on the makeshift stage because I had a performance to do for him. Well, I changed into see-through veils and did the dance of the seven veils. It is a sensuous and horrific dance, for Salome asks Herod to behead John the Baptist and to put his head on a silver platter. The cast was mesmerized, and Daniele was horrified.

At first the cast snickered, then fell silent. It was frightening. It was exactly as I intended it to be: ugly, Carli. It was the weirdest thing. Here I was creating this to get even with a man who's aroused such anger in me that I literally lost my head. Never mind John the Baptist. It was I who lost my head. When I finished the dance, I was gasping for breath, and my half-naked form was limp on the floor. The cast stood up and, one by one, applauded and said "Brava". It was my way of giving him a moral slap in the face, but it backfired. I felt dirty, real dirty. I learned something. I got myself up on all fours like a dog, stood up with my head bowed low, and guess what he did? He took his jacket off and covered my nakedness, and I wanted to die. Everyone was quiet. Daniele motioned to Franco's wife to get me dressed. He left in his shirtsleeves, never said a word, and left the restaurant. The cast was wonderful. I came back, sat down, and no one said a word about my Salome'. Carli, I'll never do that again. I lost my dignity in front of him; the whole stupid thing backfired. I don't know how I'm going to face him again. After the performance, I'm leaving Milano and spending a week in Florence with Kay and Poppa Santo, and just connect with the muse of art. Ciao for now.

Friday: Hi, it's me. Well, my parents came in (another trauma), and they were civil to each other. I mean, Mom has no quarrel with Kay. She likes her, she has forgiven Poppa, but she is uptight because of my father. He won't even look at Poppa Santo.

Now for the performance. Remember I told you about D's directing?

By the way, I won't refer to him as psycho man any more. It's not fair now, not when he tried to protect my dignity with his jacket. I am so ashamed. I can hardly look at him again. Soon I won't have to.The Italian audience is passionate! I'm glad they liked me, otherwise they probably would have littered the stage with tomatoes. Yes, Carli, this is how very outrageous some of the behavior is towards opera singers..standing room only carry their scores and keep them open to see if the singer goofs or not..interesting? Aldo was right this is an intimidating audience to work for..I'm expounding so much energy these days…however, the performance was brilliant. D. had a special pale blue gown made for me by one of the best designers of costumes. I looked as though I had just stepped off a cloud from heaven. Guess what? I floated, I didn't slink and, I knew that it was brilliant, cast were wonderful. One of them whispered, "Brava Brescia," I wanted to weep. Before the performance, my parents were with me backstage. My father, oh, God, how he touched my heart. He was shaking. I had no idea how deeply being here would affect him. Momma looked like an angel and turned more than one eye backstage. Then the sound of the stage manager's voice came on, and it was time to begin the performance. Brilliant! The orchestra was formidable, like holy communion, they connected with their musical god:.Toscanini. No other conductor can evoke such musicianship, precision and integrity as he can from an orchestra. Suddenly I thought of Al. I remembered he called this my entity. It was, oh, Carli it was. The entity connected the cast with a golden thread of excellence with this performance. I have never heard anything like it. Awesome, we put our best foot forward, and made it. We adore Toscanini, he's intimidating, but he's got integrity, always keeping in mind what the composer wanted..singers are not allowed to hold a note forever, because the singer is the instrument through which the genius of the composer is expressed. We adore him, and we're scared to death of him….in rehearsals he curses, and yells, and I even heard him say, "bestia cane"..which is beastial dog..wow..that's enough to give anyone the shakes..If he gets angry to the point of losing it, he walks away, and has been known to do that…let me tell you, you really feel the difference working under this maestro..the result is celestial.. We all behave, yes even D. The performance resulted in a thunderous ovation. Every singer on that stage behaved like a god. I took my solo bow, they screamed "Brava, l'Americana!" Then from the other side came the opposing group of shouts: "Brava la Milanese." So I guess I've arrived. Daddy was so proud of me, and I told him, "Daddy this was for you," and he broke down and cried in my arms....how can I sleep after that? It's 3:00 in the morning. Momma and Daddy are in my room sleeping with their arms around each other. They wanted to be with me tonight.. They are so in love, I'll never know love like that..I have this strong feeling in my gut, that for me it's not going to happen.. so..I'm resigned..

I just had to finish this letter. Momma and Daddy are coming home in two days. Daddy wants to tour the familiar places they knew together. After they leave, I'm going with Kay and Poppa to Florence. I'm buying you an original painting of the Ponte Vecchio in Florence for your home. It was the only edifice which wasn't bombed in the war. Interesting? I have a few more concerts of art songs, from the Italian Anthology, and then I'll be home.

I can't wait to see you, but what are we going to talk about when I've told you everything? Anyway, I know. It'll be your time to give me your reaction. Can we spend a day together? Please. I NEED to see you. Ciao for now. See you soon. I won't be writing any more. Just too friggin exhausted. Love to my bambino "Adamo"-- (as your Grandpa Charlie calls him) and love to Chet, and you-know-who if possible. by the way, nothing could have taken me to such heights in the real world, this was a spiritual experience, we were woven together by a magic thread of the muse of music, I'm sure that St. Cecelia, the patron saint of music, was glowing as she watched this performance from her throne, and so was Giuseppe Verdi..Indimenticabile, (unforgettable)...Love always, Anna or Brescia as other singers call me around here, especially the men..I think it has to do with a sign of respect for me, yes, I think so...ciao. A.B.

Chapter Twenty
RECONNECTING TO THE PAST

Maurizio and Gemma were ecstatic at the reviews and excitement over Anna's La Scala debut. It couldn't have been better than it was. Interesting to Maurizio was the diversity of the outbursts of "Brava la Milanese" as opposed to "Brava l'Americana." He chuckled when he heard his daughter's interpretation of it, because it made sense.

Maurizio and Gemma waited until noon to see their daughter. After a performance, it was difficult to wind down the body to go to sleep at a normal hour, so they slipped out, had a continental breakfast of coffee and a briosche--sweet pastry--and took a walk around the piazza. Gemma talked sadly of the time she was walking across that very piazza knowing that she was pregnant and waiting for Maurizio to come back from Switzerland. She relayed the "chance meeting" with Santo and what transpired between them. Maurizio listened to her narrative with renewed anger against Santo. They even went to the same coffee shoppe where she had run for shelter in the middle of the storm.

Yet, after visiting the grave of the ending of innocence, and the world of intrigue, they put it aside. Too many wonderful gifts had developed over the past fifteen years, enough to give them faith in God and in each other. Anna had changed. She seemed so self-assured, and had come a very long way in such a short time since her debut at the Metropolitan Opera house. Their young daughter was now capable in their estimation, of dealing with the stress and the curves of this very demanding career. La Scala was the testing ground, and she had passed.

Maurizio read the program very diligently at coffee, because the excitment of his daughter's debut, he had not read the other names on the program. Brescia and Toscanini were the only names that he focused on.

Gemma had her own copy, and she took it out as they sat opposite each other at the small table in the coffee shop.

"Gemma, look at the name of the director," he said. Does that ring a bell?" He looked at his wife and she grimaced as she saw it.

"What are you thinking, my darling?" she asked.

"Only that his last name is spelled exactly as Donato D'Andrea's. Gemma, they're related. They have to be." Anna had not told her parents of the dinner Santo and Kay had taken her to when she did indeed meet the old man. She didn't want to aggravate her parents with how she spent her time with Santo, unless there was pertinent information they should know. The mystery remained just that, a mystery. They walked around a little more and decided not to dig up too many bones from past painful memories, for, inadvertently, hadn't they been the victors in that intrigue?

Gemma looked in the jewelry shop for a piece of gold she could bring her mother and mother-in-law. The stores were closed for it was Sunday, but at least they could look in the windows to see if anything interested them.

He promised his wife that they would return again when the time constraints were not as limiting. They had to see Italy again as it grew back into all of its glory and splendor. Gemma had never been to many of the cities in Italy; nor had Maurizio. Years earlier, they were deeply involved in their careers, and travel for pleasure was not an option.

At noon, they returned to the hotel on the other side of the Piazza della Scala, and woke Anna up with a phone call. She had showered and was ready to come down. When she did, the people in the lobby recognized the young diva, and smiled at l'Americana, for she looked casually dressed in slacks, her father's shirt and a jacket, wearing a trace of lipstick and bouncing into her parent's arms. They took her for a coffee, then, arm-in- arm went around the environs of La Scala.

They took a bus to the old neighborhood where Gemma lived with her parents. Much as Anna wanted to go to Mugenta, Gemma didn't even mention it. It would be a blatant act of insensitivity towards Maurizio. So they didn't, though Gemma was very curious as to whether the bombs had leveled the sumptuous villa she had once lived in as Santo's wife.

Anna had received a number of invitations from the cast to dine with them on Sunday, but she declined and chose instead to spend this precious time with her parents. They asked her what her itinerary was for the month, and she wrote it down and gave it to them. She also felt that she should tell them of her visit to Florence, to visit the Uffizzi palace and shop for herself as well as Carli. Gemma asked her to bring home a painting for her, too. The mecca of the world of art was in Florence, and the city looked like a virtual museum with statues all around. Gemma did not want to leave, but Maurizio had to get back to his work in the orchestra. He did not want to jeopardize his position.

They got off at the old stop near Gemma's house. Much of it had been bombed, and reconstruction was going on, as in most of Milano. It was a Sunday, and at 1:00 p.m. most of the late Masses had ended. Gemma stood in front of her old building and remained silent, as one would in front of a holy relic. Maurizio had his arm around his daughter's shoulders, and they were staring at the building, not recognizing it as it got its magnificent new façade replaced. There was a sense of keeping the architecture of the past in the reconstruction, particularly if most of the building was salvageable.

As they stood in front of the building, a woman walked out, practically bumping into Gemma. She said excuse me, and then stood there with her mouth open in shock.

"Gemma?" she said incredulously.

"Carla?" Gemma screamed, and the two former neighbors hugged each other.

Carla and Maurizio embraced too, and then she saw Anna, and wept, "oh my God, here she is the fruit of your love. She's all her father, Gemma," and Gemma said, "even her talent is his," and he said, "you had the biggest part in this child, my love, she has your heart, your courage, not mine, and your stamina." After that discussion Gemma asked about Carla's twin boys, Pippo and Pietro. Carla invited them upstairs. She shared a huge apartment with Pippo who was married and working as a polizia per il stato, a state policeman.

The apartments had been worked on to recreate the fidelity of their original classic design. These, however, were greatly improved. The six-room apartment was spacious, and had long windows, and 20-foot ceilings. When Pippo saw Gemma, he confessed that both he and his brother had been in love with her when they were twelve years old. They laughed as she reminded him that his mother had to cut a lock of his hair in the front so that Gemma could tell which twin she was giving a piano lesson to. Coffee was made and served as one, by one, the missing gaps of information in each other's lives were filled. They also did age inventory, and Carla was 53 years old, five years older than Gemma. She was older-looking than her years due to a matronly figure which in the old days was corpulent. Anna loved being the bystander in all of this, for she heard a part of her mother's life narrated right before her, and it was so nice, for a change, not to be center stage. Maurizio was enthralled with this reunion, and he urged Gemma to invite Carla to America. Carla said she would come.

"You smell wonderful, Carla," Gemma said as she embraced her again.

"Sure, I don't smell of garlic anymore. I quit cooking when my husband died during the war. He worked at the cemetery and the bombs fell on people who already were dead, so he died for nothing. You couldn't even say he was defending anybody." As she giggled at her observation everyone laughed.

"I saw this beautiful child of yours in the newspaper, and I knew that she had to be yours. I wanted to go to the opera house to find out, and somehow I didn't have the nerve. Pippo was going to go. We weren't sure how you and Maurizio got together, when the last time I saw you, you were married to the Count. It was confusing, and I didn't want anyone to know your story for fear that it might hurt your daughter, so we tried to be discreet. You have no idea how happy I am to see you." She was holding Gemma's hand and kissing it.

Maurizio then stood up, and told Pippo's wife to put the food away, for they were all going to a good restaurant down the road and he was treating. It was wonderful. Pippo sat next to young Anna, flanked by his wife Nini. He talked to Anna about the old days when her grandmother Jenny and her grandfather Luigi were their adopted family. He told Anna how Luigi had taught him and his brother how to cheat at cards. Anna absorbed every word with great interest. Life had become so busy for each of them in America that the past was all but forgotten. This was the missing link that Anna was thrilled at finding.

She continued to wonder about Santo and how he managed to fit in to her family's history. There had to be intrigue and betrayal on some level, because her very peaceful father never got himself into a rage except when it came to any mention of Santo Averso. Much of the mystery was being revealed to her as she heard the stories in snippets of the past. It was beautiful to see her parents still holding hands, her father still pouring his wife's wine, and when he wasn't dealing with food, his hand would rest on her shoulder, or caress her arm. It was truly the deepest love between them, and no matter how much they had gone through, the finding of each other was a dream of idealistic love fulfilled. This is what Anna wanted. A lifelong devotion, something which she felt unattainable because of who she was. She felt that who, in his right mind, would want her as a wife? He'd never be first in her life. Men didn't like second place... As she watched, listened, and studied the interaction of this wonderful reunion, clarification of her own personal goals were coming into solid focus for her.

"So Anna," Pippo said, bringing her back from her reverie, "when did you know you could sing?"

"I think at the same time that I learned how to talk. Opera recordings were played and sung by my step-father Santo. I was also given a voice as a gift and I could think of nothing else but to use it. Pippo, tell me about your piano lessons." She sat back as they finished the minestra, and waited for the "primo piatto"--first course--of pasta.

"My brother and I were very mischievous. We came home from school with our grempiulini dirty or torn. Your grandmother repaired them and then made another set so that we would never be without them."

"Grempiulini?" Anna asked, not knowing what they were.

"Dresses," Pippo answered. "All boys in Italy wear them, it's a compulsory uniform, but they were a hindrance to our boyhood--that's why they got torn."

"Ah," she was getting a picture of life in Milano in the 1920's, "and when did you take your piano lesson?"

"Once a week on Mondays. Momma would pick us up, hurrying us because we had to wash before we sat at your mother's grand piano, and our snack had to be delayed if we didn't get home on time. We were always hungry, so we ran home and left Momma behind. We laughed our heads off hearing her curse us as she tried to catch up with us."

"And the snippet of short hair? Were you really identical?"

"Not to my parents, but to Gemma, yes, except when we sat at the piano. Your mother used to give us different piano method books to work on, so she could tell who was who by the music book. The hair was a back-up identification for her to tell us apart. You see, when she wasn't home, we ran in and practiced on her piano. Ours was so badly broken that one out of 3 keys wasn't playing. We played well, she said. But your mother said that to all kids. Encouraging us all. We loved her, therefore we practiced. When she left, we never touched the piano again." Anna moaned regretfully. "Oh, why not?" she asked sadly.

"Because we studied and played to please her. Hey we were kids, and we'd rather play cards and learn how to cheat, or run in the street and scare a cat. Besides, the only talent we had was to confuse your mother. She went nuts one afternoon as both my brother and I came in with the same short hair in the front. He was amused by driving her crazy. As a matter of fact, I was, too. We played tricks on her constantly."

Carla wanted to know about Jenny, Gemma's mother, and that story was told to her as everyone listened with great interest. How her grandfather died had never been told to Anna, and she was horrified at the stories of the fascist regime. She knew though that Poppa Santo's emigration from Italy was because he was with the Democratic Socialist Party and was afraid for his family to remain in Italy seeing how the Fascists wiped out all their opponents.

After the fourth course of food, everybody was ready to collapse. Pippo tapped his wine glass with his fork, suggested that everybody go to sleep for the afternoon siesta. Maurizio and Gemma immediately agreed. The wine had gotten to them. They emerged after a two-hour nap, and at 7:30, refreshed from their "pisolino"—nap--they went back out to a trattoria for a pizza and beer. The pizza in Milan was not like

Naples, but then nothing in Italy was quite like Neopolitan cooking. Every city and province had its own cuisine and dialect. A country of varied city-states in the middle ages, each city and province continued to maintain their own characteristics. Food in Northern Italy was more delicate in taste, with a base of rice instead of pasta and in the southern part of Italy, pasta was the mainstay, as well as richer and redder sauces.

For Anna, sharing in her mother's reunion with Carla and her family was indeed a wonderful adventure into the past. Gemma, according to Carla, had not changed. Her body was tall and still slender, her beautiful blonde hair now had many wisps of white going through it. Maurizio tall, and still athletic at 52, still cut a fine figure for a middle-aged man, with everything being intact.

At ten in the evening, they all broke up and said goodbye. Gemma and Maurizio had some serious shopping to do on Monday before they left on Tuesday. They only had one day left in which to buy gifts for both sets of parents. They had to get Vittorio a piece of gold, too, so their decision was to buy gold chains with a religious medal or crucifix.

On Monday, Maurizio asked Anna if she would accompany them on their shopping trip, and since he had mentioned it to Pippo who had suggested they go to his personal friend the jeweler on a side street near their house, they agreed. Italians bargained for everything. It was an art, and Pippo was large, imposing, and strong-willed. Maurizio appreciated his taking a day off to do this for them. Of course, Carla came along, wishing to take advantage of seeing Gemma and her family again. Once more, they trekked together, this time to the stores. They hit every jewelry store for comparison shopping, and did end up buying the four pieces of jewelry at Pippo's friend's store. Next door to it was the tailor shop that used to belong to Anna's grandfather Luigi Liguori. Anna took a photograph of her mother in front of Luigi's old store. Gemma even saw the spot where her father had been beaten and eventually buried alive in the woodsy grave outside of town. Maurizio held his wife's arm as she stared at the spot where her father had been beaten. They stood in a circle, heads bowed and prayed on that spot. Anna was deeply shaken by the tragic memory.

On Monday night, Pippo insisted they come to his house for dinner. He was cooking. Gemma asked if she could participate, and if they would just put aside the formality of Italian dining and adapt some American customs. She introduced them to the buffet. They went along with it, as all the courses were put on one table with serving spoons and large dishes on to spoon the food.

During dinner, Maurizio invited Pippo, Nini and Carla to come to New York for a visit. They were thrilled at the invitation, and agreed to come. It was a mutually satisfying reunion, one which touched each member so deeply, especially Anna.

The next day, Pippo rented a limo with a chauffeur, and accompanied the Brescias to the airport. Pippo, Nini, Carla and Anna went along. It was the most stimulating and exciting personal time for all of them. Pippo told Anna, that his home was her home, that if she wanted to leave the hotel for the rest of the time, she had a room in their house. Anna thanked him but stated that she needed to be near the theater .

The Brescias were filled with emotion as they said goodbye to their former Italian neighbors, who had been a major part of their lives. They boarded the plane.

As they settled themselves in their seats, a window seat near the wing of the plane, Maurizio reflected: "We have not lifted a finger, yet, every moment of our return to Milano was special, particularly the irony of God's intervention."

Gemma knew where this was leading to. There had been some reference made to the D'Andrea name, and Maurizio concluded that the director must be the son of the infamous D'Andrea. A few days ago, it wasn't important enough to dwell on.

"What are you saying, my love?" Gemma asked.

Maurizio mulled over events, "if Daniele is his son, it's ironic that he was assigned to direct our daughter, wouldn't you say?"

Gemma sat back, and as the stewardess interrupted them to give emergency procedures before the flight, they paid attention.

Gemma was in awe of her daughter. Anna had sacrificed giving up a man she loved for the sake of her career. Maurizio was having other thoughts. All he could think about was the director's possible connection to the infamous impresario who had single handedly destroyed his career in Italy. Long after Gemma came to live with him, she finally confided Santo's infamous bribe to the impresario to block him from being hired by La Scala. Maurizio never got over it, it enraged him when he thought of it.

As the flight took off, and ascended to it's flight level Gemma held her husband's hand, and said, "Remember tesoro, we have had many blessings, each other, and our daughter who is more than any two musicians could ever hope for."

He sighed deeply, and her words were just the balm he needed to hear, he brought her hand to his mouth and kissed it, Gemma relaxed, she snuggled up to him and shut her eyes. They turned their thoughts to coming home with a euphoria of spirit, their daughter's triumphant debut at La Scala.

Chapter Twenty-One
DANIELE'S ANGUISH

Anna Brescia was through with her performance at La Scala. Since it was a singular performance, Hurok decided she should be booked for other singing engagements to perpetuate her versatility as a singer. The choice was art songs, which originally were scheduled for La Piccola Scala, the smaller theater of the opera house, or another communal opera house in Ferrara. It was sold as a benefit concert for the propagation of rebuilding art and artifacts. Anna believed in the arts. They were her whole life. A benefit concert in which a minimal fee, due to Sol Hurok's clever negotiations, was paid Anna, and Ferrara seemed like their best bet. Ferrara was not Milano, but the populace was extremely critical, perhaps more so than in Milano. There was a free week before the concert. Anna wasn't sure if she should take a brief holiday and art shopping spree in Florence with Santo and Kay, but she cleared it with Grace Giordano her representative from Hurok's office.

Grace told her to go, enjoy, and not stay away for more than five days. The accompanist Giuseppe Di Palermo, had to have a few run-throughs, and though it was a concert without costumes or staging, some staging was needed. They asked Daniele, who immediately gave his consent, waiving his fee.

Daniele D'Andrea had been shaken by Anna's display of defiance and anger when she set him up to observe the ugliest version of Salome that she could concoct, leaving her colleagues breathless and stunned.

Daniele hid well his real feelings about Anna. So well, in fact, that he hid them from himself too.

He was in great conflict. He needed to be alone. He took a cab to the outskirts of Milano. He walked on a dirt road and thought about all the scenes of the past month and a half with a woman he had set out to hate and destroy. Why? He had to answer that for himself. He never wanted to hurt this spirited, talented young beauty. It infuriated him, that she was not intimidated by him. She never cowered to his aggressive behavior. In fact, she had retaliated in unusual and creative ways. The piece de resistance was the dance of the seven veils from Salome, which she had managed to captivate everyone with. Her makeup was dark and ugly. By portraying a figure possessed by evil, she gave the role another dimension. He, as a director, was mesmerized by the intensity of her dance. Even her partial nudity was not sensuous. It was grotesque; so much so, that he felt compelled to cover her body with his jacket. He realized that it was meant to get back at him, and it sickened him to see how deeply she had been affected by his sarcasm forcing her to expose the dark side of her nature. He ran out of the restaurant right after that performance, wanting to scream from the bottom of his soul. Furious with himself, because he had reduced her to such a drastic retaliation.

Now she was gone. She was in Milano, but not even Grace Giordano knew where she had gone. There was a search by some members of the company to find her in the environs of La Scala piazza, but to no avail. He had to find her. He couldn't let this girl go home knowing that Daniele D'Andrea was a sadistic madman. Much had to be clarified. It meant so much to him now.

He took a cab back to her hotel at the piazza La Scala and checked to see if she had returned. He had left several messages, to which she hadn't responded. He grew frightened at the thought that she might be ill or dead; he asked the hotel management to open her suite of rooms. They searched everywhere, including the closet. He was desperate to find her. What would he say if he did? He knew that he had to set the record straight, and then perhaps he could approach her on a personal level, on a normal level rather than with the intense mind games they had played on each other.

He walked into the hotel bar and found a telephone, then ordered an espresso with lemon and two sugars, sipped them, and attempted once more to call the hotel room. It rang five times. Usually he made it ring for twelve times, counting each ring methodically.

"Hello?" she answered. His heart almost stopped.

"Anna?" he said breathlessly, not knowing if indeed he would ever hear that voice again.

"Daniele, are you in the hotel?" she asked as though she had just spoken to him yesterday. She suddenly realized that they were on a first-name basis.

"Downstairs. I've been frantic. I thought something happened to you." He was relieved to hear her voice. With a war zone mentality, one never knew if someone would ever see a person again.

"No, I've been busy. You must be calling about your jacket, shall I bring it down to you?"

"No! that is, uh, do you mind if I come up for it?" he asked. "Not at all." He knocked on the door and she let him in. He opened his arms and asked if he could hold her for just a moment. She hesitated, wondering what could possibly have precipitated such tenderness. He backed off, realizing that she was apprehensive.

"I was frightened. Thank God you're alright." Once more he extended his hands to touch her, then pulled away quickly.

"Why Daniele, you're concerned. You're not playing games are you?" she stepped closer to him. "Come, you can embrace me." He put his arms around her, and she could feel his erratic breathing, as though he had been running. She offered him a glass of mineral water and asked him to sit down at the glass table. He told her that the office for concert management had asked him to stage the concert she was doing, and she felt there was no need. After all, they were only art songs. He told her he didn't have to do anything to improve her acting, for she was a consummate actress. She was astonished at this declaration. Had it all been an act? Certainly it seemed as though a mask had been lifted. What volcano slept under that ice cold façade? How lucky the woman who could uncover it, she thought.

Gone were the sarcasm and the antagonism. She laughed.

"Daniele, can you stand it? We're actually being civil to one another?" She sat opposite him at the table, and poured herself a glass of mineral water, sipping it and peering over the rim of the glass at his blue/gray eyes. He agreed and let her know that frankly he was relieved. He discussed the change of heart he had towards her after building a case against her even before she set foot in Milano. She listened with interest and realized that this man was shedding every layer of posturing, subterfuge, and intrigue. His candor about his own part in the whirlpool of antagonism which had dominated their encounters was refreshing. She asked if all of it was because he had genuine antagonism against her as an American, or was it something else?

He said something which stunned her, and revealed more than he wanted her to know at this juncture.

"When I saw your picture in our newspaper, I felt a stirring within me. I fought what I was feeling. It would not do. You were unattainable, and my pride would not take rejection."

"What rejection, Daniele? I'd reject you as a stage director?" What in heaven's name was he saying, she thought to herself, rejection?

"I'm not ready to say more, Anna, but I have a file about you. Photographs, stories, anecdotes, and publicity articles. I have approximately twenty articles." She was astounded. She asked if she could see them, and he said he'd give them to her if she wanted them.

His eyes were softer. Gone was the glaring look, and the invisible fence he hid behind. He sipped his water, then stood. They joined hands, and Anna said, "Truce?"

He stared intently into her eyes, "Truce!" She walked him to the door, and before he left he asked her what her plans were for that week, and she told him she was leaving that evening with Santo and Kay to go to Florence. He asked her to call him when she got back. She said she would.

He was ready to walk out, and she walked behind him. He turned to look at her once more and put his hands on her shoulders then gently pulled her towards him, and he kissed her mouth longingly. She was surprised, but then she put her arms around him and kissed him back.

"Anna," he said huskily, "I don't want you to go." His face was flushed, and suddenly he left. She shut the door behind her and was still for a moment. Dear God, she thought; he cares for me. I can easily love this man, she thought. They had wasted all that time, and now there were only two weeks left, and she would be gone.

The thought saddened her, and, as she finished her packing, the phone rang, and it was Poppa Santo and Kay calling from downstairs. She told them she'd be down in a few minutes. They were early, but then she knew how anxious Poppa was to be with her.

Daniele went home. He spoke to his parents, had a bowl of soup his mother had prepared for him, then went to his office and started working on sketches of his staging of the next opera, "Traviata," by Verdi. He worked diligently through the early evening hours, and all the while he could not get her out of his mind. He didn't know how he could possibly bridge the emotional gap between them and accelerate his intentions. He wanted her as his wife.

Daniele put his head on his folded arms and was aware of rapid changes in him. Doors he would never open willingly, feeling such depth of emotion again, disturbed his emotional equilibrium. Yet, he felt ecstatic, like a fourteen-year-old boy discovering women.

After working for three hours, he emerged from his studio and sought out his ailing mother. She was in bed by 9:00 every night, exhausted from even the most simple chores.

"Momma," Daniele said as he kissed her, he held her hand and sat at the edge of her bed. She was propped up on several pillows with a magazine on her lap.

"Figlio mio." She caressed his face. "You seem so preoccupied. What's happened to you?" She smiled because she sensed and saw changes in Daniele's usual serious façade.

"Momma, I never thought after Margerita got killed that I would ever love again. I've been successful at keeping everyone out, and now? She's managed to come into my mind, and I'm anxious, yet nervous." She cocked her head and smiled, and kissed her son's slender hand. He was so animated, and flushed, and she could sense that he was about to share a great discovery with her. Himself. He had been frozen inside like an iceberg, and nothing could thaw him out. Women were flights of fancy, but his limit with any woman was twice, and he never chose anyone in the world of opera. Therefore, Daniele D'Andrea, handsome, and brilliant had become an enigma for the women who pined for anything with him, even one night of love.

"My son, life belongs to the living. You have buried yourself with your wife. Do I dare ask God to help you love again? Who is she?" He smiled. "Momma, you met her. Anna Brescia the American diva."

"Oh, my God, I don't believe it." She nodded her head back and forth. "She never even looked at you. You're joking." She studied her son's face. He then told her of how methodically he set out to hurt her even before she arrived. Elena D'Andrea was puzzled at her son's declaration, and by his confession. "Why in God's name did you try to hurt her?" she asked. "I was furious with her. She had touched my heart in a newspaper picture. I hadn't even met her, and I screamed: God No!" Elena was stunned. He had fallen in love with her from the first sighting of her picture? Incredible!

"You see, I had managed to live in a tall tower of my own making, where no one could touch me. I had my work. I had everything I wanted, then I saw her. We bumped into each other and she glared at me, and my safe tower collapsed before my eyes. I didn't want this to happen, but it did."

Elena had ambivalent feelings. Yes, she wanted him to feel again, but love was ecstasy and pain, the ying and the yang.

"An ocean between you, and she an opera singer? How cold your bed will be as she travels all over the world. Think carefully, my son." Daniele spoke softly, "Momma, I set out to destroy her. She wasn't afraid of me. She staged a brilliant retaliation and I? I fell madly in love with her spirit, beauty, and creativity."

He let go of his mother's hand, and it pained him to see how distressed she was over his choice. Truly it was an impossible choice, for all the reasons he had originally against her were valid reasons. However, she'd be here for a short time, and then she'd be gone. He wanted her.

"Then pursue her while she's still in Italy. It's crazy. Does your father know about this?"

"No, I never discuss things with my father. You know that."

"Insanity! But, do it. She has two weeks? Make them count. Do it strategically, as you did in war."

Daniele told her that Anna was leaving for Florence with the Averso's.

"What are you doing this week, son?" she asked.

"Planning the next opera."

"Why aren't you in Florence with her?"

"I didn't want to impose myself on their time together."

"You don't have the luxury of ceremony, there is no time, my son. You were a colonel, and you engaged in many battles, why are you afraid of this one?"

"I'm scared of rejection. I don't deserve her. I treated her like dirt. How do I make myself a good person again, and pursue her?"

"Son, you are a stage director. Go to the Teatro della Pergola in Florence, meet with the staff there. You're from La Scala; they'll welcome you with open arms. You then have an excuse that your work took you there. Ask about their staging for Traviata. There! You have your strategy. Why do you have to be so honest in matters of love?"

"Momma, you're an angel." Daniele kissed her, then thanked her.

The next morning, Daniele went to Florence to find Anna Brescia. Certainly, with the Count being so wealthy, they'd probably stay at an exclusive hotel. It would be easy to find them. The plan was perfect. First he would find her, then he'd ask her to come to the Teatro della Pergola with him, then they could be four instead of three. Perfect plan. Daniele planned his strategy accordingly.

He slept peacefully for a change. The agitation and sadness were gone. He pulled his pillow to him, and hugged it, hoping that soon it would be replaced by Anna Brescia.

Chapter Twenty-Two

DANIELE PURSUES ANNA

Daniele woke up the next morning, called a private chauffeur to drive him to Florence, thanked his mother for her support, and left to pursue his dream. He felt a renewed vigor he had not felt since before the war. Fired with resolve, he hurried to meet his destiny. Time was against him, and his awareness of insurmountable obstacles in the conquest of the diva did not dampen his impossible mission. The modern highway system begun by Mussolini circumvented the mountainous route by a series of tunnels cut through the mountains. What used to take six hours now took two. Roccio drove Daniele to the Grand Hotel and found that the Aversos were registered there. Daniele dismissed Roccio, and told him that he'd probably return to Milan in four or five days. Daniele asked the hotel clerk if the Aversos and Signorina Brescia had left their room. The young man smiled and said "I don't think so, or there would be activity in this lobby, sir." Upon inquiring for clarification as to "activity in the lobby," the hotel employee stated that with the arrival of the American diva, opera buffs gathered in the lobby to get a glimpse of her. Daniele smiled. Of course, they wanted to see her. She had everything: looks, and a smashing revue with photographs of her, her parents, her entourage of Hurok people. Anna was front page news.

He asked for her room number and called her as soon as he got to his room. The phone rang and finally she picked up. "Poppa, you've got to give me time to bathe, are you ready to go out?" she said without asking who it was.

"It's Daniele, Anna, I didn't mean to interrupt your bath." Dear God, she thought, is there a problem? "D'Andrea? Where are you?" she asked.

"Downstairs, I too have business in Florence."

"You do?" she was surprised.

"May I see you now?" he sounded urgent.

"My bath is running, I'll meet you in an hour."

Why was he here? Perhaps he was considering a directing engagement at the charming Teatro Della Pergola which she had only heard of. Maybe a performance in Florence? She'd love that. Salome? Anna burst out laughing, that would be total irony.

She took her not so leisurely bath. Now her interest was piqued. She dressed in a dress instead of slacks because Poppa Santo requested that she not dress "American" while she was with him.

She wore a navy dress with a navy jacket, and a long polka dot scarf around her neck. Simple pearl earrings, and sparkling pearl ring as well as gold bracelets, trying not to look flashy. She wore short heels for walking and she looked stunning. Her jet black curly hair as it was didn't require much attention except to be brushed. It was wet still, and curled even more than usual. It cascaded around her fine featured cherubic face like an exquisite frame.

She tapped on Santo's door and saw that he was rushing to get ready for the shopping spree of his life. Kay was so happy, as was Anna, and it was for them a special time, one in which every moment would be remembered by each of them, for it would be the last carefree and joyful time for them, as a trio.

He embraced her then fussed with pushing a few curls away from her forehead, as Kay watched with a smile.

"You're still his baby, you know, Anna," Kay said.

"And he'll always be my Poppa." He asked her to turn around to see that her seams were straight, and as she obliged, he grunted with approval.

Santo took his portfolio, in which he had all his money, and they walked out for the "ascensore"—elevator--which was like a cage. The view going down was unobstructed by elevator walls. It was unique to Europe, and Anna loved all of it.

She put her arm around Poppa and told him that Daniele D'Andrea was in the same hotel. Poppa was livid. He turned to his wife and said, "Kay, I told you, didn't I? He's out to get her, I won't tolerate it." Anna was thrown by Santo's insinuations.

"Poppa, we don't even like each other, he's not here because of me, he came for business with the Teatro della Pergola." Santo tried to rush out, but Anna went to the desk and asked for Daniele's room. She started to dial, but he was already behind her and she felt sensed his presence. "I couldn't wait to see you," he said softly.

She didn't know how to react to this change in him. Poppa Santo pulied Anna away from Daniele. "Let's go." Santo said gruffly, and he turned to Daniele D'Andrea and snarled, "It's our time together, I want you to keep out of my way and do your work on your time, not mine."

Anna wondered about his sudden interest in her, and she suspected that because of her success, he might want to hook on to her, for his own purposes. Well, why not? Everyone did it. Aldo had warned her as well as Santo. This was part of the mantra of success, the hangers on. But on the other hand, she enjoyed the attention no matter what the purpose of it was. He interested? No, she thought, impossible. They left, and Anna knew felt that he was watching them.

Meanwhile, Daniele walked to Ponte Vecchio which had successive jewelry shops next to each other. He walked in to one and immediately the saleswoman asked if she could help him with something. "A ring," he said, "an engagement ring," and the saleswoman smiled, "auguri signore," (good luck sir,)and showed him the inventory they had in that category. The woman was very glib in small talk, and suddenly Daniele said aloud to himself, "but what am I doing? Have I gone mad?" He turned around and left. The saleswoman was surprised and then she shrugged her shoulders and said to her boss, "you know, he probably hasn't even proposed yet, but he'll be back as soon as she says yes." Her boss said, "he'll be back." Daniele walked to church, and knelt at a pew in the front. The candles flickered in the darkened church and he thought about the rehearsals, and his cruel verbal attacks denigrating her. How could she react to him? He hated what he had created. She was twenty years old, innocent, not mauled by life's trials or war as he had been.

The only encouragement were his mother's observations when they had gone out to pranzo. There was such a strong disdain between them, that Elena D'Andrea stated that it was a cover up for what they were really feeling for each other. Daniele, hung on to that thought, but perhaps his mother had stretched her appraisal to include Anna, and now he wasn't sure. She was perplexed by his sudden attentions. She had kept him waiting for an hour, when he had called. Reality check, he said to himself, she has no interest in me, perhaps I have been too harsh with her, and she's still feeling badly.

This was war, his own war against his own isolationist mentality. Why was he afraid to feel again? Why did he think that there were guarantees doled out to people who fell in love, that they, indeed would live happily ever after? If anything, the dark side of love brought confict, turmoil, power plays, pain and reduced his sense of self. On the other hand, love was the antidote to death. How ironic, the resurrection would not have been possible without the crucifixsion, perhaps the message from God about life and love was hidden too in that one act of extreme love from Him..had we learned, anything, he pondered, probably not, but there was hope as he tried to fathom the meaning of the greatest miracle ever. On the other side of Love was the fact that you knew that you were alive. Everything functioned better, regardless of the down side of love. His decision would be whether to engage in this epiphany which he was experiencing or deny it. The moment of truth was upon him, and he chose his own war, "conquer thyself," he thought to himself, as the cliché, "Physician heal thyself" crossed his mind. Could he pull this off? He had to. It might mean rejection, ridicule, outrage, but if he turned away from feeling again, he might be doomed to live a life in limbo. "I'm ready to bleed for this," he prayed, whether he made it or not. As he made the decision, a blanket of peace overcame him, a soft billowing feeling and he knew that God's spirit had indeed awakened his, simply because he had asked. Filled with resolve, he left the church more lighthearted than when he had entered it.

At 3:00 in the afternoon, Daniele went back to the hotel and called the Brescia room and the Averso room in that order. They were not back from their outing.

He called his mother, and described the catharsis he had just experienced…"And?" she asked, "I'm ready to take on my adversary, me—then the Count, but how?" Elena never planned to tell her son the dark secrets surrounding Anna Brescia, but now she had to.

"The Count married Anna's pregnant mother and gave Anna legitimacy as well as his name. Your father knew, it was an incredible intrigue, my son, one which I cannot divulge. Suffice it to say, that Anna and the Count are very close. She has managed to balance her love for both her fathers, and I admire that. Don't come between them, you'll lose."

"My God, I suspected something, How did it happen?" Elena said, "I can't, don't ask me to, okay?" There was a long silence from Daniele, and he frowned wondering, "and so, the intrigue is a secret, will this be another obstacle?" she answered, "no, try, if nothing happens, what's important is that you will have tried, your first hurdle, and then your real freedom will come…God be with you, son." Daniele whispered, "Grazie, momma, t'amo."

* * *

At 6:30, Santo, Kay and Anna walked in carrying packages. The count seemed to be dragging his feet. It wasn't a good time to approach them. They took the ascensore and waited until they got to their respective rooms. After waiting in the lobby for two hours, the right moment to intercept had come and gone. Disappointed and anxious, Daniele took a walk to contemplate his next move.

Anna called his room as soon as she got in. Daniele wasn't in his room. Kay called and told her that Santo was taking a much needed nap. The rest of the late afternoon was hers. Anna showered and changed into her "American" clothes, casual slacks, sneakers and a blue sweater tied around her shoulders, and went shopping. Anna tried to contact Daniele, he wasn't in. She went shopping and saw the delicate embroidered garments in the window. Hand made lace on the tablecloths were displayed. She walked in to buy one for her mother's dining room table. It was lacy and scalloped, and the cloth was pure linen. She looked at the stitching, and the saleswoman stared at her as though she knew her. Anna was getting used to this in Italy. Everyone was involved with the opera, even the poorest of people, so being a

179

celebrity was common here. Even her casual clothes gave her away. Italian women simply didn't wear pants, not in post-war Italy. She purchased the tablecloth for her mother, all of five dollars, and held it under her arm as she walked out proudly with her purchase.

She continued to go down the small narrow streets, where no car could fit, then found an art gallery. Anna looked at the entire art collection. She asked the proprietor if she could purchase without a frame so that she could take it home. The proprietor, of course, said yes. He stared at Anna.

She asked him if he recognized her and he said, "Should I?" He was embarrassed. Anna was pleased. At least he'd pay attention to what she wanted rather than who she was. In an hour she chose ten paintings, and the man added the cost, which was close to 300 dollars, several of the paintings, originals. These same paintings in twenty years would be worth over a hundred thousand dollars. Anna gave him a cash deposit for her selections. He wrote her a receipt and she left, fully delighted with her latest art acquisition.

It was late. She supposed she wouldn't see Daniele again, so she walked back to the hotel, called Kay and told her that she was turning in for the night.

Daniele got back at 7:30, just as Anna was coming out of the art gallery, and he called the Count's room. He asked Kay, since Santo was not taking any phone calls if the Count would call him back at his convenience. Kay related the message and he snarled, "at my convenience."

Daniele's attempts to communicate with Santo and Anna were at an impasse, so he decided to turn in for the night. It was 9:30 when a phone call woke him up.

"Signor D'Andrea?" a female voice asked.

"Si?" he responded sleepily.

"It's me," she whispered. Were you sleeping? How about meeting me at the bar for a cappucino?" she asked

"Not in your room?" he asked, waking up quickly at the sound of her voice, feeling the surge of anticipation.

"I don't think so, Daniele. You know what?" She was tired and it was an ill-thought out phone call. "I'm going to pass. It's too late, it's been a long day. Sorry I disturbed you." She hung up. Then she said aloud to herself, "Damn!"

Daniele flew out of bed, dressed in a casual pair of beige pants and a black knit shirt, walked up the stairs the two flights, and knocked on her door rapidly.

"Open this door, Anna. Please, it's important." He sounded urgent. She was already out of slacks and into a long lavender nightgown with a matching lacy robe. He knocked softly and she let him in. He walked in and took charge, catching Anna off guard.

"Bella, come here quickly. Sit down, I have to speak to you." Anna could not imagine why this urgency and she was puzzled. He paced on the other side of the table as he spoke about his life. He had been married before, and his young wife seven months pregnant, had said goodbye to him as he joined his battalion. They had spent the night together, and he had made plans for that evening for a peasant to take her to Lake Como so that she could be safe. All arrangements had been made. The last mental picture he had of his wife was when she stood in the cobblestone street, holding her arm up in a wave, and with the other hand poised on her pregnant stomach. Within moments, the caravan sped down the road, and suddenly they heard an explosion. They turned around, and the entire block had been leveled by a bomb. His wife and their unborn baby were instantly killed. Part of him died during that air raid. He continued to fight for the losing battle of Italy's survival, and Daniele had grown disillusioned over the Fascist movement.

* * *

"I stopped feeling, on purpose. I made myself a promise that no one would touch my heart again until I saw your photo in a newspaper story, and I felt something, fought it like hell, folded the newspaper and put it away. What in God's name was I thinking? My mind was filled with you, day and night, and when I saw you I was furious at you. How dare you invade what had been well hidden?" Anna was frozen to the seat, and was shocked by his manner, a frenzy of purging which was on the verge of hysteria. Yet, his declaration wasn't a complete surprise, in view of that spontaneous eruption when he came to get his jacket. However, as sweet as it was, it was only for a moment, and it seemed to mean nothing to him for he had quickly walked out. Daniele continued to pace after a long pause of dialogue, then he opened his soul even further to lay out what he thought of himself and of her. "I'm crippled. My body and spirit, wounded. You? young, talented and beautiful, and I have no right—except for one right, I love you, would you consider marriage?" Anna stood up slowly, walked to the window, and looked out at the piazza with her back to him. She was speechless.

She heard him leave, and slowly the impact of what had just happened, began to penetrate. Her thoughts drifted back to every encounter she had had with him. Now she understood why he was antagonistic from the very first. She smiled, my God, he liked me, who would have thought? Many things fell into a semblance of order, and she too wondered why he liked her. She had retaliated with a vengeance she didn't even know she had with the Salome impromptu performance, and now this?

Anna did have to think about it, and she did for the rest of the evening and into the night. She couldn't sleep with the range of emotions going on in her. Perhaps her grandmother Anna's words were true, though at the time Anna didn't understand the oxymoron, "on the other side of hate, is love." With this thought, she finally fell asleep with very mixed feelings. In the morning her confusion would be gone, and she would understand that strange proposal of marriage which had been so unusually executed.

Chapter Twenty-Three

HESITANT BEGINNINGS

The next morning, Santo had plans to take a guided tour of Florence. He called Anna at 9:00, the middle of the night for her, but she forced herself out of bed, showered, and half groggy met with him and Kay.

"Poppa, I want to talk to you about Daniele."   He ignored her and took her arm and Kay's and walked them out of the hotel lobby as quickly as he could, afraid that Daniele would interfere with his outing. Anna wanted to leave a message, but Poppa Santo told her that today was probably going to be busy for him at the teatro. Perhaps he had told Poppa Santo that he was going to be occupied, so she didn't bother to leave a message for Daniele.

Out they went with their private car and guide, and Santo asked him to take them to a good restaurant for a breakfast. This was not easy to find. Italians didn't have big breakfasts, but Santo knew that he just wanted to get away. The guide explained that most Italians go to a bar for a cappuccino, brioche and a light breakfast. Santo feigned forgetfulness, but he did what he set out to do, which was to get Anna out of the area as quickly as possible to avoid Daniele's intrusion again. Santo succeeded. He was proud of himself and Kay whispered to him that he was acting like a young spiteful little boy. He bellowed, "AND I'm proud of it."

They spent half a day touring, eating, interrupting their tour to shop, and anything at all they wanted to do.

Anna asked Kay to go to the ladies room with her, and they had to have their own tissues because most Italian restaurants in post war Italy didn't have toilet paper, but coarse paper hanging on a hook. Some used newspapers.

"Can't you choose a better place for this tete a tete, Anna?" Kay admonished.

"Daniele actually wants to marry me," Anna said excitedly.

"Dear God! Why are you surprised?" Kay stared in disbelief. "But my entity owns me. Al told me that," she said sadly.

"But Daniele is in the same field," Kay said, "Al wasn't."

A beautiful young woman who was sought after, was insecure? How unusual, Kay thought.

"Daniele is afraid that Poppa Santo will block us. Will he, Kay?"

"Anna, he's ecstatic because he's got you all to himself this week. At home, you have your parents, and seeing you is limited; being with you now that you have your busy career is close to impossible. Daniele is a thorn in his side only because he wanted you totally to himself. Can't you see that?"

Anna wanted to know how he really felt about Daniele, and Kay explained that he liked D'Andrea's son, but not this week. His timing was way out of whack, and Santo was incensed over the director's intrusiveness. However, in their private moments, Kay said, he approved and liked the young man for his talent, and his elegance.

"Good!" Anna saw Santo looking for them, and she grabbed Kay's arm and said, "look, he's going to start shouting for us. Let's go before the "caribinieri" come and arrest all of us." Kay laughed and they ran towards him.

Daniele woke up at 10:00 a.m., for most of the cast and artistic staff worked late, and mornings began at noon. Daniele washed up, then called Anna, half-expecting her to be waking up. Instead, she was gone. He jumped up and limped into the bathroom for his shower. He could sense the hand of Santo in this. He got dressed in casual sports clothes, and went to the lobby. Upon inquiring about the count and the diva, the clerk told them that they'd be gone for the day since a private car and chauffeur picked them up at 9:00 a.m.

Daniele called a cab and went to the Teatro della Pergola. It was a cream puff of a small theater. Perfect stage and enough seats for people to enjoy an intimate performance. He introduced himself. Quickly the red carpet treatment was afforded him because he was connected with the apex of opera houses, La Scala.

He met the impresario Signor Orlando Di Giacomo. They showed him the magnificent acoustical sound by asking a young lyric soprano to sing a couple of arpeggios, and he was enthralled. He was shown backstage, rehearsal rooms, costume department, and anything he wanted to see. He spent the morning there, and decided that he'd like to work at this exquisite little theater. For a mad moment, he pictured doing Salome there. He shrugged the idea off, but it persisted in his mind, and then he snickered. Imagine approaching Anna with this idea, she'd either laugh, or get angry.

At the end of the tour, they asked him if he would consider directing an opera at their theater, prefacing that his fee would be met no matter what it took. Daniele was flattered and said that his fee was not written in stone, and that it could be discussed for the right opera.

Orlando Di Giacomo asked him what he thought would be the right opera?

"Salome," Daniele answered, tongue in cheek. Di Giacomo was shocked. Such a severe and horrible subject. In this small theater? Yet, he didn't wish to say no to this great talent and said that perhaps they would discuss this further, since his opinion was that the teatro was simply too small to stage this opera.

"Lights and a scrim could be used to give the special effect in the dance of the seven veils. I visualize it, and have worked out sketches on staging." Di Giacomo was shocked again. This man was on holiday, yet came in to see if they would give him the opportunity to do Salome. He was puzzled, for none of it made any sense. However, they exchanged greetings, cards, and phone numbers, and Daniele left to go back to the hotel.

When he walked in his room, he called his mother. He told her how Anna seemed indifferent to his proposal after he spoke about the loss of his wife and unborn child in a bombing. "Of course, Daniele. She sings tragic operas, but she hasn't lived them. You have. Did you expect her to rejoice after your narrative? Some things are better left unsaid. You have lost touch. What is your plan of action? Are you giving up?"

"I don't know. I think the next move is hers. I'm packing it in and leaving; however, I did visit the Teatro della Pergola, and they're interested in me. I blundered badly. Any messages for me?"

"The opera house wants you to call them."

"I'll call right now. Ciao, amore."

"You sound as though you've given up. Have you?"

"I don't know, I'll see you tomorrow." He ended the conversation, packed and asked the concierge if he would get him a private car and driver, and the answer was yes, within the hour. Daniele cancelled the scheduled pick-up from Roccio and penned a note to Anna.

Santo, Kay and Anna returned to the hotel at 2:00. Anna went to the desk to call Daniele, and was told that he had checked out and left. She was disappointed. However, the desk captain gave her the written message in her box.

Anna walked to the far end of the lobby to read it.

"Anna, I had to leave. I've been intrusive in your holiday. I am no longer familiar with the dance of intimacy between a man and a woman. What should have been a delicate moment, ended up by you walking away from me. I sounded like a military man giving orders. I'm sorry, forgive the bungling behavior, and if I don't see you again before you leave, I must say that you are a consummate artist for one so young, and it has been a privilege to work with you. My hope is that our paths shall cross again, Warmest wishes, Daniele."

Anna folded the note, and put it in her bra, mulling over the lack of confidence despite his almost arrogant façade.

Kay and Anna met, and talked about Daniele's incredible proposal. "Anna, Signora D'Andrea confided in us that he's detached from his emotions, would you marry him?""Yes!" Kay smiled, "Santo knew it even before you did. Before we left home he mentioned that D'Andrea's son would be stage director and he said, when he meets Anna, he's going to fall in love with her."

They joined Santo, who was filled in with the latest situation, and he relaxed. Anna asked him if she could visit the Teatro della Pergola, and Santo said he would arrange it.

After the midday pranzo, they went to the teatro after making an appointment, and Di Giacomo was thrilled to meet Anna Brescia. She was even more beautiful than he had imagined. Santo told him that she had worked at La Scala with D'Andrea. Di Giacomo was impressed, "he's the best stage director, Signorina Brescia," he said. "I know that," she said softly, and he asked, "would you work with him again?" Anna said she would.

He made an offer, and she accepted with the proviso that he had to negotiate directly with the Sol Hurok office represented by Grace Giordano in Milano.

"What opera do you want to do?" he asked.

"Gianni Schicchi! After all it takes place in this city, it's a perfect opera." She was enthusiastic about this opera.

There was great excitement, and Di Giacomo invited them to an evening pranzo in a posh restaurant by the canal. Santo accepted and was thrilled at the attention his Anna was getting. Yet she needed a man worthy of her to be not only her husband but her protector. In the world of predators, he did not want Anna to be single much longer. Daniele would compliment her life in every way, the more he thought about it, the better he liked it. Yes, come to think of it, D'Andrea would make her a perfect husband. He'd be working in one part of the world, and she'd be working in another, with oceans apart the great advantage would be spending as little time as possible with each other, so Anna would have a wedding ring, and the predators might not be as aggressive. He knew full well what a predator was, for he been one all his life, and his best coup had been the methodical pursuit of Gemma.

They left the theater, and returned to the hotel. Kay told Anna that she had made Santo ten years younger with this holiday.

Kay and Anna talked for a little while, and Anna inquired how Kay was faring with Santo's mother. Kay answered, "Weird." Anna laughed. "She called my mother a slut every time she saw her, and did it to her face."

"I wondered what she muttered under her breath when she saw me? You know, when I got involved with Santo, I thought for my own preservation I'd better take Italian lessons."

Anna laughed and asked if she had ever heard the Countess say anything to her, and Kay thought that she had. Kay giggled at the explanation Santo had for his mother's utterances. He told her that his mother had a nervous tic, and muttered things, but Kay figured it was Touret's syndrome, for that's what Santo led her to believe. Anna howled at his cover-up.

"Bull! Kay, she cursed all women in Poppa Santo's life. What you don't know is that the Italian mother doesn't cut the umbilical cord from a son." Kay giggled, and then Anna told Kay how often her father Maurizio became childlike when he spent time with his mother. "My mother knows it, and falls in line with it." Kay raised her eyebrow.

Without Santo, they were free to gossip, and gossip they did. Anna talked about her family, her grandmother Jenny, who dared to marry a Sicilian. Kay was fascinated by the revelation that Italians weren't prejudiced against other groups as much as they were prejudiced against each other.

"My mother thinks Grandma Jenny married beneath her. In fact, my wonderful Al, had two strikes against him. He was Sicilian and dared to be a jazz musician. Daddy and Momma think that jazz is for common people."

Anna then talked of Al and how close they had been, and Kay realized that Al had been Anna's lover. She wondered aloud at how deeply involved Anna was with Daniele, and Anna laughed.

"Besides abject hatred, spite work, and public mortification, what in God's name could transpire? His change of heart astounded me. I like it, but it knocked me for a loop." Kay was incredulous at how very naïve Anna was. She told her that when the D'Andreas dined with them that night, that Daniele devoured Anna with his eyes. Everyone saw it. Anna was surprised. She purposefully avoided looking at him.

"Darling, that was obvious. Do you know what Santo said when we got to our room that night? He said 'watch those two.' They'll be married within a year. I'll bet my life on it.' Daniele glowed; you didn't even see it."

Santo was growing tired. A whole week was more than he could take. On Thursday, he cut the vacation short and told Kay they were going home. Anna accompanied them to the airport. On Friday, she was free. She didn't let Daniele know that she was in town. There was much to think about. She went out to eat alone, and, no matter how she down played her look, she was noticed, smiled at, and a gentleman muttered, "Brava Brescia!"

In America, this would not happen. Opera stars were little-known except by the limited audience who were opera lovers. Even then, because of the visual distance between them and their audience, they would not be recognized on the street unless the fan had seen a photograph of them.

She looked forward to going home and to anonymity. Yet, she wondered at the tenuous relationship she had with Daniele. Would it happen? Perhaps she would terminate her apprehension and give the possibilities a chance.

On Friday afternoon at 3:00, when most people were indulging in their third course at dinner, Anna went into the opera house. She thought she'd take a chance and walk through the corridor to Daniele's office. No one was around, and she saw his office door ajar. She got closer and saw a light emanating from his room to the hallway. He was sketching on his pad. She watched him and loved that serious expression of his. She tiptoed behind him and put her hands on his eyes. He was startled.

"Anna?" he asked, as he pulled her hands away. She gasped. "How did you know?"

"I smelled you. I thought I was imagining it." He turned around on the tall stool, and walked to the office door, and locked it.

He touched every feature of her face with his fingers, almost as though he was sculpting a magnificent piece of art. Aroused by his skillful touching, his hands slid to her body, and she felt that he was etching her image on an inner canvas. As he led her to the couch, he began the act of love like Ravel's Bolero, adding layers of fuller orchestration in the repetitive theme of love. They arrived at the peak of their passion together, and clung to each other, as though it was the first time for each of them.

They slowly dressed, but continued to caress and touch each other. Daniele whispered huskily, "I shall never be the same."

"You are incredible," she cried.

"Let's get married before you leave," he urged.

"Daniele, I can't think about anything except what just happened. Please don't plan. Just hold me."

Anna went back to her hotel glowing in the aftermath of their intimacy. It was perfect.

That evening, Daniele came to Anna's room. He seemed self assured for there was no mistaking the intensity of her passion now. Once more, he urged her to marry him right away. She hesitated and told him that she couldn't do this to her family. Marriage had to be a special event, a glorious celebration, she was an only child.

"With an ocean between us, I'll lose you." He meant it.

"Daniele, why are you afraid? What could possibly tear us apart?"

Like a starving man who had been deprived of food for so long, he felt that each moment of love he could have with her, fed his soul. He was a changed man and everyone noticed it in the company. Franco and Franca Franceschi were the first ones to know about the engagement. They spent evenings together at their home, playing with the baby, and enjoying the sharing of their friends' domesticity.

Franco teased them about having a family and told them they'd probably have fish in a tank. Anna protested and said that she did want a family and wanted every one of them to look like their father. He moved in to her room, and they made love day and night.

* * *

After she did her concert at Ferrara--and received tremendous accolades--the time was drawing near for her to leave. Daniele and Anna went shopping for a ring, and she wanted something simple, but he urged her to wear something ostentatious so that the world would know that she was his. She was amused, but insisted that all she wanted was a solitaire diamond.

Before she left, Daniele took Anna to his mother, who was delighted that Daniele had succeeded in his romantic quest. However Donato D'Andrea's reaction was negative. He paced the corridor and muttered: "Brescia! How could this be?" Daniele sensed the growing fragile mental state of his father. Anna was puzzled, but Daniele explained that his mind was going. Yet Elena had given them her blessings. Daniele was devoted to his mother as her father to his.

The night before Anna's departure, she and Daniele retired early. It was their last night together, and with every passing moment, Daniele's mood got darker and darker. At midnight after making passionate love, he reiterated his fear that when she went home, it would be over. She tried to reassure him, but it was hopeless.

He told her to go to sleep, and he watched her for hours, memorizing her loveliness in his mind. Daniele took his sketch pad out of his briefcase, and sketched her naked form in a gentle soft sleeping position. Gainsborough, he thought as the fullness of her breasts enhanced her sensuality.

The next day, Franco came to pick them up with the limo and accompanied them to the airport. Daniele had asked him to come for he needed a diversion so as not to fall apart when Anna left.

When she was ready to get on the plane, she hugged Franco, and turned to Daniele, who fought valiantly to control his emotions. She kissed him, and felt the quivering of his lips. His fear that he'd never see her again, crept into Anna's mind. It was the saddest moment for them. When passengers were asked to board, Anna did it quickly. She blew him a last kiss and boarded the plane without looking back.

"Franco, I shall never see her again," Daniele said softly, and Franco put his arm around his friend.

"Courage, my friend," Franco said "You've survived the war, and marrying a diva could be the worst mistake of your life. Remember, she's married to the career. Let her go."

"Franco, you and Franca are happy, but your voice comes first. Franca knows it. My God! We're not ordinary people. Don't denigrate the possibility. Perhaps God will grant me my deepest wish." Franco sighed. He had never seen this side of Daniele. "Honestly, Daniele?" he said, "I like you better in this state of madness. Now you too are human like the rest of us." Daniele laughed, and they drove back to La Scala.

Chapter Twenty-Four
REALITY HITS ANNA

Gemma met Anna's plane. She had been gone for eight weeks. During the ride home, Gemma briefed her on family news. Nothing much was new, and suddenly she saw the ostentatious diamond on her daughter's ring finger. She jerked her gaze away and felt her heart racing. What had her vulnerable child, parading in the mature body of a young woman, done? How could she get engaged in so short a period of time? There was no hint of any interested suitor while they were in Milan. Had she had sex and confused it with love? What in God's name was she thinking? Gemma felt that, had she stayed behind, this couldn't have happened. She would not address this sudden turn of events.

Anna felt her mother's tension and heard her sighing frequently as she tried to regain her composure. Anna slipped off the ring, and put it in her purse. From her mother's perspective, it was irresponsible, and Anna began to learn another lesson in life: things never were exactly as they seemed. What to do about it, she didn't know, however had she attempted to explain circumstances, Gemma might have understood, but the secrecy already positioned the situation as smacking of willfulness. Still naive in worldly matters Anna had hard lessons to learn. One of them was to shut her parents out of her life, which initially protected her from censure, but aroused suspicion because she had shut down. How could Anna confess the strange circumstances of hate relationship erupting into love two days after they left. Impossible, so she kept it from them.

Meanwhile Gemma was seething. How unstable was her daughter? Did she succumb to men that easily? Was Anna beginning an unsavory life of lovers any time someone paid attention to her? What in heaven's name would Maurizio think of this? She grew more anxious with anticipation just thinking about her husband's reaction. But, the act of slipping the ring off and saving it was like a slap in the face. Nothing good could have transpired, Anna thought, if so why the secrecy. Even her break up with Al had been shrouded in a veil of secrecy, the recording, the telephone calls, and the affair on weekends, and all this shocking behavior despite a Catholic school education. She had lost her innocence willfully, and Gemma felt was that her daughter was becoming promiscuous. She broke the wall of silence with small talk.

"You have a welcoming committee at the Cascios. Carli, Chet and the baby are waiting for you there." Anna was greatful for the sound of her mother's voice, realizing that she had made a huge error in judgment, her mother's attitude had become cold. She felt guilty, and a dull thud in her stomach made her aware of her colossal faux pas.

"I'm looking forward to it, mom, I bought gorgeous clothes for my godson, and your gift mom? Wait'll you see it."

"Thank you. By the way, your grandparents are all well, and they can't wait to hear about your experience. Do you have any news you'd care to share with me?"

"Yes," Anna said, and that was the beginning of the repercussions. The unsaid and silent screams from her mother hurt so badly, I might, but I'm not ready to share yet. Well, Gemma thought, at least it was something.

They arrived home, and Gemma helped carry Anna's luggage. As they got into the building, Anna said she wanted to stop in at the Cascios first. Gemma wasn't surprised, she needed time to catch her breath with the impact of Anna's actions. "Do come upstairs as soon as you can, your grandmother is waiting for you." Anna said she'd be but a few minutes.

The elevator door opened and Anna knocked on the door. Carli flung it open and the two hugged, kissed and wept with joy. "I'm so proud of you Contessa," Carli murmured, Charlie and Maria were crying with the impact of seeing Anna again. Only twenty years old, and an international star. They were awed by such a tremendous accomplishment. Chet walked in holding the baby, who already was robust and older-looking. Anna squealed as Chet handed him to her. He opened his mouth on her face in a semblance of a kiss, and they reacted with "how cute," Charlie said, "look at him, he missed his godmother," and as the excitement toned down, Chet went to the living room, and emerged, "sorry to interrupt, but there's a mystery guest anxious to see you, Anna, come."

It was quiet except for the baby's babbling. Maria had a sneaky smile on her face, and Anna thought, Al? It couldn't be. She stood up and looked at each of them and asked, "is this a joke?" Charlie said, "Contessa, go see for yourself."

Anna walked in. There was no one in the living room. This had to be a joke. She said, "Okay, where is the welcoming committee here? hello?" and her voice went up and down like a vocalise. Suddenly the drape moved, and Al came out, with a wide grin, "Come 'ere," he said and she went to him and he said, "let me see what a diva looks like, we followed your success with the excitement of watching a baseball game. I am so proud of you." Anna gave him a side glance, "and now that I'm a diva you can't touch me any more?" his eyes glistened, and he smirked, "dare I? she got closer, and still he didn't move, suddenly he grew sober, "you took the entity to it's winning run, sweetheart you belong to the world." Anna was so filled with emotion that she burst into tears. He put his arms around her and they erupted into a passionate eruption, "this doesn't mean," he murmured between kisses, "that I have stopped loving you," he wiped her tears away with his big white handkerchief, and Anna whispered, "I needed to hear that, I'm hurting so much." Al sensed a big change in her. She had gone through some big hurdles, and he felt it. They locked in an intimate embrace again, and suddenly Charlie Cascio was coughing and clearing his throat announcing that he was in the room. "Contessa, your mother is here." Al let her go reluctantly, and he said, "my beautiful Diva, the world awaits."

She buttoned her blouse, and Charlie turned away embarrassed. "She'll be right out, Signora Brescia," he said. Anna walked in from the living room, said goodbye and joined her mother in the hallway.

Al's face was flushed, "you alright Al?" Chet asked, and Charlie glared at Al. "What the hell were you doing, making a meal of her?" Maria hit him with a towel, "Cafone!" she sneered. Al didn't respond, he said, "Sorry Charlie, lost my head, thanks Carli." he walked out and Chet left with him. Charlie Cascio exclaimed, "You should'a seen them in there. Carli, why the hell is he marrying Concetta?"

"Grandpa, you of all people should know why. His mother wants Al's wife to make broccoli rape instead of sing. Isn't that the Sicilian thing, Grandpa? You oughta know that. Love has nothing to do with it." Charlie glared at her, and Maria touched her head muttering, "Some people have their feet in America and leave their brains in Sicily. You're not the only one, Charlie." He turned on his heel, picked up the baby, and said, "you love me Adamo, right? Even though I'm Sicilian?" The baby giggled and flailed his arms hitting Charlie squarely on his nose. "Even he's got it in for me," Charlie remarked. Carli laughed, "poppa when I sleep at Anna's tonight, if Adamo fusses, just call me up and I'll be right down." Charlie said, "come on Carli, we brought up two girls, maybe we're out of practice, but we haven't forgotten how to take care of a kid." Maria glanced at him and her expression said it all, "notice how he says we? Who the hell is we, the we is me. I'm the one who takes care of the kid, okay Charlie, stop giving yourself credit," he laughed, "look Maria, without we you wouldn't even have two daughters, okay?" Carli laughed and so did the baby, and she said to her grandparents, "I used to study you two as a kid, some day I'll show you my notes." Charlie scratched his head and said, "these kids have no respect, in my day we'd listen to our parents, we didn't take notes." Carli argued, "but aren't you flattered?' he retorted, "for what? What are we some animals in a laboratory to be studied?" Carli ran over and hugged him, "Grandpa you are a comedian and you don't even know it." he smiled knowingly and muttered, "I know, your grandmother calls me a Joker."

Gemma came to the door to pick up Anna.

"Stop by my mom's first, then hurry upstairs, Grandma Anna is growing impatient." Anna walked in to the welcoming arms of Grandma Jenny. After the initial greeting she said she had to rush home. Anna invited them to dine upstairs that evening, but Grandma Jenny said, "Anna, it's better this way. Go up now, she's waiting, and when you can, we'll have our own private dinner and celebration, okay?" Anna kissed her grandmother and hugged Arcangelo who looked so awe struck, you'd think he had seen a ghost. Anna smiled, this was the look on the face of the Cascios, beautiful Carli, Chet, and everybody except Al. He was proud, loving and supportive and so warm and passionate. I don't get it, she thought, we're so great together.

"I love you both. We'll have our own celebration, with Momma, okay?" Anna felt deeply saddened by the schism in her family. When she finally walked in to her home, the elevator door opened and Grandma Anna was waiting with a bouquet of roses. Anna and her grandmother held each other. "Welcome, my Diva," Grandma Anna said.

"This place was quiet without you," Grandpa Vittorio said softly. "Even the canary stopped singing," Grandma Anna said. They came in, and Anna kicked off her shoes, ran inside and borrowed her father's shirt from the shirt closet. As she went from place to place in the apartment, enjoying seeing the familiar surroundings, it was as though she was seeing it for the first time. What joy and excitement her presence brought into the house. Maurizio basked in the light of her brilliant success in Milano. He brought the newspaper clippings in his briefcase and carried them with him to the opera house. He shared these with his musician friends who asked about Anna's La Scala debut. Grandma Anna had a spread in the dining room for the family, and Anna noticed that Grandma Anna had made all her favorite dishes. Grandma Anna made risotto balls as large as an ostrich egg. Vegetables graced the table beautifully and color-coded. Grandma Anna couldn't paint with a brush, but her table always looked as though it had been set for a king. Oranges were peeled, sliced and put in a pinwheel arrangement with sprigs of green parsley between each circular slice of orange.

Young Anna stayed for forty minutes, tasted everything Grandma Anna had prepared, then went back downstairs. She knocked on the Cascio door, and, when Grandpa Charlie opened it up, Carli screamed as did Anna, "I'm back my dearest friend," she said, and they hugged each other and jumped up and down as they did when they were little girls.

"When is the first time we did that? Quiz, Carli, quick, answer!" Anna demanded.

"When, after much thought, Your Highness, you told me that you had decided that I could be your best friend," Carli said quickly. Adam fussed, and Carli and Anna laid down on Charlie and Maria's bed, flanking the baby and whispering while he guzzled his last bottle for the night. Anna caressed his chubby arms and marveled at how perfect he was. When he fell asleep, Charlie came in and placed the baby in the crib next to his bed. Carli took her overnight bag, and the girls kissed the Cascios goodnight and went upstairs to enjoy private time.

Anna wore her father's short sleeve white shirt, and pajama bottoms, Carli wore Chet's white shirt and his boxer shorts. Anna loved the look, and said she'd ask her father for a pair of his. Now they were ready to share the news that best friends share. Carli wanted details of events Anna had covered in her letter. She was filled in on Salome's dance of the seven veils she did with thinly veiled naked breasts in front of the cast and, in particular, for Daniele. Carli's eyes opened wide in shock. Her sweet, modest, friend did this? "Why?" she asked.

"He insulted me by telling me that I acted the part of Gilda like Salome, in front of everyone on stage. I had to have the last word, and, I had a second motive. I wanted to get him so aroused that he'd want me. My weapon, sex! What perfect revenge, I thought."

"Hot stuff!" Carli exclaimed "Oh my God this is better than a dirty movie. Do you have any wine?" Carli asked. They tiptoed to the kitchen and poured two glasses of French wine. "They're both yours. I don't drink." Anna placed them on Carli's night table. Anna showed her the expensive engagement ring. Carli squealed. Anna told Carli everything about Daniele D'Andrea. She left nothing out, even the intimate moments. Carli saw such changes in Anna. Her modesty was gone, and she sounded worldly.

Anna told Carli it was her turn to talk about Al. "There's nothing to tell, really, that you couldn't just guess. His mom made a marriage match, and he and Concetta are engaged. Didn't he tell you?" Anna grew pale. "He's still in love with me, Carli." "Yes, I know." Carli drank the second glass of wine quickly not wishing to get into this sensitive topic with Anna. She could see that Al was still a sensitive issue. Carli passed out after the second glass of wine. Tonight she would have uninterrupted sleep, since Adam was not with her. Anna had time lag from the trip, so plan A was scrapped for plan B, much needed sleep.

* * *

The next morning, Gemma and Maurizio went into the formal dining room, and Gemma mentioned the ring.

"I didn't notice any young man in her life in Milano. How could she get engaged? That's insane." Maurizio asked his mother to join them for a cup of cappuccino. She dragged her feet, and Maurizio didn't like the way she looked. He insisted that she sit down. Anna Brescia told her son that she was concerned that some opportunist would marry Anna just to come to America. She warned her son to terminate this stupidity before young Anna would be caught in a web of intrigue.

Maurizio assured his mother that he'd take care of the situation soon. Meanwhile, he had a few hours before he had to report to the theater for rehearsal, so he took his bike, kissed his mother and wife, and left for a tryst with nature in Central Park.

Gemma got up to clear the dishes; usually, her mother-in-law would tell her to not touch them. This morning, her mother-in-law looked pale. Gemma suggested that her mother in law go back to bed, and Gemma would clean the kitchen. Anna Brescia did, shuffling her feet as though it was painful to walk.

Gemma was late in leaving for school, preoccupied with her mother-in-law. She looked in on her, and Anna was fast asleep. She pulled the drapes shut.

At noon, already twenty minutes late, Gemma thought she heard some noise from the kitchen, and figured her mother-in-law must have been awake by now. She called out goodbye, but Grandma Anna didn't hear her, and Gemma rushed out. Maurizio and Vittorio returned, changed, and hurried to the theater. After Carli went home, Anna left to see her two friends in the makeup department at the opera house.

Vittorio found his young granddaughter at the theater talking to her backstage buddies, showing them the ring and raving about La Scala.

Jimmy and John were curious about the differences in the way the opera houses operated, and Anna filled them in on funding, makeup, and the glorious conducting of the legendary Arturo Toscanini.

"What's he like to work with," Jimmy asked, "demanding, his purpose is to adhere strictly to the composer's intent. If a singer holds a whole note for more than four beats, he flies into a rage and accuses the artist of arrogance. Nobody feels neutral towards Toscanini, you either love him, or hate him, but no matter what, you respect him. I felt as though I was working with a holy man, does that make sense?"

Jimmy was awestruck, "before I die, I want to see that man conduct anything even the Star Spangled Banner." Anna embraced John and Jimmy and they noticed her diamond ring. "You didn't," Jimmy said as he held her hand to admire it, she giggled, "I did," Suddenly grandpa Vittorio walked in from the costume department.

"Anna, can I have a word with you?" Grandpa Vittorio asked, he seemed displeased. She followed him into the tailor shop. She was apprehensive.

"You brandish a ring to makeup men, and yet you say nothing to your family? Now that you're a diva have you decided not to answer to your family? Who is he?"

"The stage director, grandpa," Anna answered timidly.

"Then you should have shared this with us, do you know how hurt we were to see you for a fleeting moment while you invited Carli to spend the night? That was the time to talk to us, instead we were literally banished. Vergogna!" She apologized, "Mia Culpa, Grandpa," and ran out crying. Just then, Maurizio walked in and intercepted his daughter, "Anna, let's talk, now!" She cringed, because the worst was yet to come. He pulled her along as he raced down the corridor of dressing rooms, found one unoccupied, and shut the door behind them. He offered his daughter a chair, and he sat facing her. He held her left hand and looked at the diamond. "What is this?" he demanded, "an engagement ring," she said, Anna grew frightened because his face contorted with a disapproving grimace.

"And when were you going to tell us?" Maurizio asked, as he wiped his sweat,. "It was sudden, we fell in love and I was scared to tell you."

Maurizio stood up and began to pace the long, narrow dressing room with his hands held behind his back, and he called her irresponsible, dishonest and ungrateful. Anna was frightened on two levels, his harsh criticism, and his growing rage. She stopped him from pacing, "Daddy,

I know this sounds crazy, you and mom had many years together, you lived in normal times those days, when time didn't slip through your fingers as it does today. We fell in love, he's in Milano, and I in New York. We are both artists, the distance, the shortage of time, he said he loved me and asked me to marry him, I said yes," Maurizio began to calm down, "just like that, why didn't you tell us? was he a singer?" Anna gently led him to the chair again, "it wasn't the singer, it was the stage director, D'Andrea." Chills covered Maurizio's body and suddenly Maurizio grew enraged. He stood up, the chair fell, and he kicked it sending it across the long narrow dressing room.

"Infamy! Pigs! That man's father blocked me from working at La Scala!" Maurizio shouted, and Anna begged her father to lower his voice.

"Take that Goddamned ring off. How dare you? We never told you the whole horrible episode of our lives to protect your precious Poppa Santo Averso. Sit down!" Anna was frozen in fear. She was afraid that her father would get a heart attack; he was pale and shaking.

"He wanted your mother. When I auditioned, I was sure that I had gotten the position. A week later, a letter came in stating that I had not been chosen, even though I had played well. Your mother, unbeknownst to me, was pregnant and scared. I left town to recuperate from the shock of rejection. Had I been offered a contract, your mother and I would have been married. Santo Averso bribed D'Andrea to block me because he wanted your mother. I told her I was going to America, I would send for her, but she ran out on me. Averso married your mother, gave you his name and tried to destroy me. Your stage director's father is Donato D'Andrea, okay? After her marriage, she found a note from D'Andrea thanking him for the generous bribe. If you marry him, I'll disown you." Anna gasped.

"I'll send back the ring," she said as she took it off and put it in her purse.

"Don't send it back you probably earned it." He sneered. She walked out of the dressing room like a sleep walker. Stunned beyond anything she had ever experienced, her father clearly implied that she had had an affair. She could not deny it.

Anna ran out to the street. She was having some strange physical reactions to the confrontation. She wanted to die. Everyone in her life wanted what she couldn't give. She felt as though she was the object in a tug of war. After walking forty blocks to her home, she wanted to collapse in Grandmother Anna's arms. There she would find an oasis.

Her mother wasn't home, but Grandma Anna was, and Anna took the elevator to her floor, rang the doorbell, no one answered so she used her key. The apartment was dark, because the drapes were drawn in the living room, as they always were on a sunny day so that the furniture wouldn't fade. Anna put her jacket in the closet, went to her room, kicked off her shoes, and put on slippers. She went to the kitchen, her grandmother wasn't there. Perhaps she had stepped out.

Anna got herself a glass of water. It seemed strange not to see Grandma Anna in the kitchen, washing greens or preparing for the evening meal. Anna went to her music room and practiced vocalises. The phone rang, and, to her surprise, it was Daniele. Anna wanted to cry. He told her how much he loved her. He was coming to America to formally ask her parents for her hand in marriage according to proper Italian protocol. He asked if her parents knew that they were engaged.

"Daniele, I've changed my mind," he screamed, "what are you saying?" She shouted, "No marriage, Daniele."

He shouted back, "Why?" The connection was noisy, and they could hear the sound of water. "I'll write you a letter," she said. She went to her desk and wrote him the exact tale her father had told her about his father's bribe, and Santo's diabolical scheme. The letter was brief but to the point. She sealed it.

Meanwhile, she wondered where Grandma Anna was. Perhaps she was at the store. On occasion she went shopping. Normally she loved staying home. Anna went out, mailed the letter, and returned home. Her grandmother should have been home, but wasn't. She called Charlie Cascio, who came up right up. He opened the bedroom door, and saw Grandma Anna in bed, sleeping. He opened the drapes and let the sunlight into the room. His eyes focused on Anna Brescia, he felt for a pulse. There was none. She wasn't breathing. "Anna, brace yourself, your grandmother is dead." Anna began to whimper, and Charlie said, "come downstairs, Maria'll make you a cup of tea. Come." Charlie called Gemma and Maurizio and gave them the sad news. Young Anna took to bed, and didn't get up for days. Inertia overcame her, and the loss of her grandmother had been a very deep one.

* * *

Anna Brescia had died in her sleep. She had been having strong headaches; the day of Anna's arrival, she had not felt well. The wake and funeral was attended by operatic personalities. A show of deep respect for the Brescia family was exhibited as many members of the Metropolitan Opera company came to pay their respects, orchestra members, singers, backstage tailors, seamstresses, make up men, stage hands, conductors, and the administration. Everyone loved the Brescias; the artists in particular loved Vittorio. After a two-day wake, Anna Brescia was laid to rest in Woodlawn cemetary in the Bronx. Within a month after his wife died, Vittorio quit his job and moved back to Milano to be near his brother. Maurizio was devastated at his mother's untimely death and deeply disturbed over his father's move to Milan. He felt abandoned. The family began to disintegrate, Vittorio left, the Diva did not accept the tragedy easily. Maurizio suffered the most. He lost sleep over his nightmares.

The young diva terminated her relationship with Poppa Santo. She broke off with Daniele, and received a gracious letter of closure from him. She kept that letter for the nobility of its tone and the acceptance of the inevitable outcome:

"My dearest diva: I received your letter and I am in shock. The revelations about my father were a horror. You shall never be subjected to my attentions again, I promise you. If you decide to return professionally to La Scala, I shall work with you as I would a stranger. Do not avoid engagements here because of me. This opera house and its mystique have built many careers, as it will build yours. It was an honor working with you. My best wishes, Daniele."

Chapter Twenty-Five
BOTH SIDES OF THE OCEAN.

Milano:

Vittorio Brescia had ambivalent feelings over his wife's death. He was sad that she had died, but relieved that it hadn't come to separation and divorce. He called his brother in Milano. He requested two things: to find an apartment near La Scala, and find out if the costume department had a vacancy.

When Vittorio arrived, his brother had the apartment ready, and Vittorio moved in. The next day he went to La Scala and visited the costume department inquiring about a position. The tailors directed him to personnel, who told him that there were no openings, but told him to leave his resume'. Franco Franceschi in for a costume fitting, overheard Vittorio Brescia's inquiry, and overheard the Brescia name. His ears perked up and he asked the gentleman if he was a relative of the diva Anna Brescia.

"My granddaughter, sir," Vittorio answered. Franco got excited. He took down his telephone number and told him that he would call him. Though Vittorio was disappointed that there was no opening, he was delighted to meet the leading tenor of the company. Already, that was a plus.

Franco lost no time. His fitting completed, he went quickly to Daniele's office, where he found him working on the sketches for his next opera.

"Daniele, do you have a moment?"

"Come in, Franco." Daniele wore his serious face when he was involved in a new production. Franco told him that Vittorio Brescia inquired about a position in the Costume Department. "Without a recommendation, who's going to hire him?" Franco asked. Daniele put on his jacket, took off his glasses, and went directly to personnel.

He inquired about Brescia and they told him that there was a need but other applications had to be considered. Daniele grew incensed, "Surely the name Brescia hasn't been forgotten here--what the hell is going on?" Surely they could make room for someone that talented. Brescia's designs were written up in American opera magazines. They told him they would reconsider. Daniele recalled how Anna had bragged about her grandfather's talent. Armed with that information, he listed a number of innovative ideas Brescia had originated with the Metropolitan Opera House in New York. Brescia had not been fired, he argued. He had chosen to come back to his homeland after the war. Persistent, convincing and slightly overbearing, Daniele D'Andrea won his point. "We'll ask him to come in for an interview." Was the best they could do. "You won't regret it," Daniele said.

Within a month, Brescia was called and hired. He had no idea how or why, but he was hired. He wrote to his son in New York and told him of the happy news.

* * *

New York:

Maurizio's sadness over his mother's death warranted counseling. He was so devastated by his father's quick emigration to Milano that he couldn't even go to any part of the apartment especially the kitchen. Gemma purchased a small refrigerator to put in their bedroom.

Anna Brescia was busy as ever. She attended Al's wedding at the Immaculate Conception Church on Gun Hill road, and agreed to sing Ave Maria.

Al called her up the night before the wedding, and they talked for two hours. It was a warm and honest conversation. She was flattered that Al still cared for her, and that he held her in high esteem as much as he did.

"You sure you won't come to the reception?" he asked.

"Al, if it were me, would you?" She lay on her bed, sipping her room temperature water, and she knew that this was the end of the line for them. The Crossroads where each one left to follow his destiny. "Hell no, baby. I just wanted you to come so that I could show you off to my parents."

She laughed. "As though it would make a difference. Al, she's not wrong. I'd never cook for you." He laughed and they bantered back and forth, as though it was their wedding they were talking about. They flirted outrageously and said some intimate things to each other, but it was goodbye. Al didn't say it; she did. He wanted to be able to walk out the door of their lives, but not a regular door, a revolving one, and he said so. If they had to be together because life was difficult, he'd want her to see him, and conversely the same with her. She couldn't be firm, not now. Part of him didn't want this marriage, and she wasn't about to hurt him further than he had hurt himself by choosing this Sicilian tradition to find a mate. When they hung up, Anna was emotionally spent. It had been so difficult to part with this uplifting beautiful man who dared to treat her casually, instead of with deference. She'd miss him.

* * *

Milano:

Franco invited Daniele for dinner, and Vittorio Brescia to celebrate his being hired at La Scala. Vittorio was flattered. He was alone, all of his familiar neighbors were gone, and the opera house employees became his new friends.

Vittorio felt special. Italy still operated under the caste system. Lower and upper classes of people still didn't interact in Italy. Franco was a tenor, Daniele D'Andrea was a stage director and designer, and he was in the Wardrobe Department. He was low man on the ruler of this particular caste system, so he was apprehensive about this invitation.

Franco had told him of his "compare," D'Andrea, and Vittorio, though uneasy about having to meet his granddaughter's ex fiancee', decided to be civil. He had no other choice.

The dinner party included two other couples from the company, singers, of course. Brescia was delighted, for though he was without a female companion, the women flanked him and asked questions about America. There was such a hunger to know about these shores. It turned out to Brescia's delight that he was the center of attention at the party.

Anna's name came up, and Vittorio shot D'Andrea a look. D'Andrea looked down at his napkin and he shut his eyes. Brescia said that she was busy with such a growing career and that she occasionally appeared as a guest on radio shows in New York.

"Is she going with anyone?" Dolores Sangella, the contralto, asked.

"Always. There is no shortage of suitors in her life."

"From one moment to another, one doesn't know," Vittorio added. "In fact the family is the last to find out about her affairs of the heart." Vittorio added.

Daniele felt that the last remark was directed to him. Of course, she wouldn't be without suitors. If only they could have married when he'd asked, none of this would have happened. It was all too late, the act of infamy, bribery, and willful destruction of a man's life was the highest form of mortification to Daniele. Daniele suffered every day of his life over this and felt that he didn't deserve any modicum of happiness in his life. He buried himself in his work, keeping himself busy with that, and protected himself by shunning emotional intimacy. He had come full circle, from life to death, from death to life, from life to death again. He was lost. This was beyond forgiveness. This had to be one of the lowest rungs in the levels of Dante's Inferno.

Daniele helped Vittorio Brescia with every fiber of energy and influence he had. He owed the Brescias something. He had to help Vittorio, but no one must ever know about it. He swore Franco to secrecy.

Daniele spoke privately to Brescia and asked him about his opinion on costumes. In fact, he asked if he would be so kind as to meet with him an hour earlier the next day to give his opinion on cumbersome costumes and how they affected the movement of a singer. Brescia immediately lit up. This was his forte. He had re-designed certain clumsy costumes at the Met, and they were adapting the new design for certain roles. No mention of Anna ever came out of Daniele's lips.

It took months, but Vittorio Brescia enjoyed the time he spent with Daniele. They became friends slowly, and the thread that bound them together was their creativity in different segments of the production.

In September of 1948, when Daniele inquired about the next season, which the company was excited about and speculating about ad infinitum, he found out, to his delight that Anna Brescia was hired for four performances of Bellini's La Sonnambula. He was asked to stage it. He grew anxious about the anticipation of working with her again. She dominated his thoughts, since he learned he was going to see her and work with her again. However, he had enough time now to figure out how he would act with her. It had to be an "act," for he had vowed to keep his distance, and avoid familiarity. She would be known as Signorina Brescia. A lump of anguish almost choked him. He needed the discipline he knew intimately during the war. Control of his emotions had to be tantamount to anything else.

The sin of his father's duplicity against Maurizio was tantamount to a heinous crime for Daniele. It had fractured an already fragile relationship between them. Daniele withdrew almost all contact with his father after learning about it. He shared the revelation with his mother, and the family dynamic was never the same. Yet retribution came quickly. Donato became more and more distant; he left the world of reality and had to be put in a sanitarium. Like Judas, he self-destructed.

Franco was thrilled with the dinner party at his house. He couldn't understand why Daniele distanced himself from Brescia, and Daniele wouldn't reveal the details of the intrigue.

"Daniele, got a moment?" Franco asked as he walked into the office.

"Come in. Nice party, Franco. It was the best. I'm glad you invited him."

"Excuse me, Compare, why aren't you connecting with him? It's like war, you know? You could be making points. She's coming for La Sonnambula, and you're directing. I mean, come on, Daniele. DO something." Franco was sweating. He never saw such a lack of strategy.

"Franco, butt out. There's an insurmountable wall here. It's private business. Don't mention her name to me again."

"Well, okay, but whatever the hell happened, you just got him a job. Does he know that?"

"NO! No one is to know that. Promise me! I need to put this away if I'm to function. Don't mention her again to me!" he grimaced and Franco backed off.

* * *

In New York:

On the other side of the ocean, Anna was learning new roles, and checking out future jobs for which she had to study. She talked to Aldo about coaching her, and he made time for her in the evening after supper. He was heavily booked with other coaching jobs in New York.

The next few months were intense for Anna. Suddenly she began to incur severe headaches. Her parents were terrified. They took her to a neurologist from New York Hospital, the youngest graduating doctor from Cornell Medical school.

Gemma and Anna walked in to the office of Dr. Antonio Cipolla. Anna smiled for the first time in months. Her former school buddy who used to slip her his art work in lieu of love letters when she was in the second grade, was her doctor. When they saw him, Gemma exclaimed, "Oh, my God, Rosa Cipolla's son Antonio!" They embraced warmly.

Antonio brought Anna into his examining room and quickly expedited her intensive examination. He ordered X-Rays to rule out tumors of the brain, and he did some external examinations to see that all of her vital functions were working. They were. He asked her about her life, and Anna exploded. She told of the losses of both Brescia grandparents, the loss of a man she loved, the loss of an Italian love, due to ugly intrigue. "Everyone I love left me. I have my parents now, and I'm so scared that something is going to happen to them. He buzzed the nurse and told her not to send the next patient in. Anna needed him.

"I was so in love with you, I still am. I'd never leave you," Antonio said. Before he let her go, he asked to take her out to dinner. She agreed.

"I still have that sketch you sent me with Grandma Jenny when she visited your mom in South Beach. I love it." He told her he'd call her with the results of the test, but he didn't think that anything was wrong.

He felt she had been through a tumultuous stressful time and that will trigger off these migraine headaches. Anna felt better already, and was thrilled to connect with Antonio again.

Gemma and Maurizio were terrified. Grandma Anna who had never complained, had begun to incur major headaches. Weeks later, she'd suffered in silence, and then died in her sleep. Gemma was frightened.

The results came within a few days, and Antonio called Anna, telling her that she did not have a brain tumor, and that all of her headaches were due to stress. However, he asked her to come in for a complete work up and physical.

"You're thorough, aren't you?" she said.

"Yes, I have to be. I still hear my mother's voice, 'you gotta be the best'. Remember?"

* * *

Milano:

Vittorio got a raise. He had become, in a short period of time, someone who was respected for his own talent rather than his granddaughter's. It was flattering to him how often Daniele deferred to his opinion and expertise. He even asked him about staging at times, since he was so knowledgeable about performances. One day, Vittorio got the courage to bring up the forbidden name.

"I have a question." Vittorio asked Daniele, "I read the next season's offerings, and I adore Bellini's work. By the way, Anna was a good choice. I understand you're directing it. How do you propose to do this when she sleep walks?"

"Good question," Daniele said, "I haven't begun to think about it yet, but I'd appreciate some suggestions. I want her to be in this dream state, and it's usually played by the extension of her arms as though she's afraid to bump into props. But someone who is sleepwalking doesn't do it that way. They walk in a dream state. The arms could be loose. I picture the hands going up in a groping searching movement, I think. When she arrives, I'll ask her opinion." Daniele didn't want to say as much as he had, and his face was flushed with self-recrimination.

"I dare say, Maestro, you have thought about it. My opinion? Why? Your appraisal is brilliant. No wonder your fame precedes you. Bravo Maestro!"

When he went home that night, he thought about Daniele D'Andrea, and for the first time since his employment six months ago, he let go of the built in wall of distrust of this man. He was formidable, totally professional, and damned attractive. He could see how easily Anna could have fallen in love with him. What a tragedy that travesty created. He would have been the perfect husband. Brilliant, talented, passionate and a great asset to Anna's career and life. He was saddened at the loss for both of them.

Gemma wrote to Vittorio telling him of Anna's headaches--and that she was experiencing some life-threatening medical problem.

The next day, Vittorio attempted to bring up Anna's name again. He walked in to Daniele's office and Daniele welcomed him. Putting his pencil down, he faced Vittorio.

"Ah, Signor Brescia. Nice to see you. What's on your mind?" he asked.

"I don't think I should bring this up, but in case she doesn't make it, I thought you ought to know," Vittorio said sadly. Jesus! Daniele thought. Something was wrong. "Anna?" he asked, turning away not wishing to be seen.

"Yes. Gemma writes of intense headaches, just like my wife's. In the event of a turn for the worst, I think you'd want to know, correct?' Daniele gripped his desk as he sat down again. His legs buckled under him, and he almost fell. He grimaced with pain, physical as well as emotional.

"What's being done?"

"She's going to a neurologist. I'll keep you informed." Daniele got up, limped to the window. Brescia walked out. Poor soul, he thought. He could see that the man was visibly moved. What a tragedy! What a double tragedy if Anna died!

Milano to New York telephone call:

Daniele could not bear it. He placed an overseas call to New York. The phone rang and was picked up in one ring. The overseas operator connected them; then, after identifying herself as long distance operator, she connected Daniele.

"Hello? Papa?" Gemma thought it would be Vittorio Brescia.

"Pronto! Signora Brescia, son io, Daniele D'Andrea." Gemma gave a big sigh. He must know about Anna, she thought.

"Yes." She answered in English, "how can I help you?" she said in a formal, staccato voice.

"Brescia told me about Anna's illness, how is she?" his heart was beating out of his chest, he put his fist against it to quiet down the thumping.

"Fine, no tumor. Don't tell Vittorio, I'll call him tonight."

"Certainly and would you please tell Signorina Brescia that I called?"

"Yes, Goodnight."

Gemma was upset. She didn't know what was going on in Milano between Vittorio and Daniele. It angered Gemma that Vittorio would befriend the son of the man who blocked Maurizio from La Scala. Gemma's respect had sunken to a new low. She had no use for a womanizer, and she found out that for years he'd had someone on the side.

Anna walked in. She'd had a wonderful time with Antonio, and Gemma asked her about the date. Dinner was wonderful! Antonio was wonderful, and he proposed marriage. Perfect marriage, Gemma thought.

"What did you say?" she asked excitedly.

"I thanked him for making me feel desirable, Momma, but I turned him down." Gemma was disappointed.

"Did he kiss you?" Anna nodded yes, "and did you like it?"

"It was okay, Mom, but no Fourth of July rockets."

"Too bad, what's his name called from Milano, and asked if you were alright. Grandpa must have told him. They seem to have grown close. So much for loyalty."

"Oh my God, what did he say, Momma?"

"Nothing much. He asked about you." Gemma hated the intrusion of the telephone, especially when it was from an undesirable caller. "Don't even entertain the thought of this man!" she admonished.

"Momma, I love him," Anna said as she shut her eyes.

"Your father would keel over," Gemma argued.

"I'll never hurt my father." Anna held back her anguish as Gemma walked out, adding emphatically, "I hope not!"

$$\text{\textbf{ႦᲚᲮ}}$$

Chapter Twenty-Six
ANNA AND DANIELE MEET AGAIN

The months passed, and, with time, came new layers of discovery and change. Anna grew closer to her mother. Her father struggled with depression and overwhelming sadness over the loss of both parents. Maurizio had discovered that his father had renewed his passport months before his mother died. Had his father been planning to leave his mother, or merely to visit his family?

Anna spent the summer performing opera in concert form in Tanglewood. It was more casual than the operatic stage--and easier, therefore more fun. However, in the back of her mind was the return to La Scala. She could shut her eyes and see Daniele at his desk, with that serious pensive expression as he sketched, took notes, and created new concepts in staging.

At the end of the season, Anna came home and resumed coaching with Aldo Di Tullio. He became a godfather figure in her life; always easy to talk to, and offering suggestions filled with the wisdom of his years. She confided in him the dilemma over her forbidden love in Milan. Aldo shared with her how hard he had to work to achieve his own success fraught with obstacles all along the way.

"Anna, without the fight, you don't appreciate what you get. It's just the human condition. Your father is very traumatized about this. We had a coffee one night and he talked. Madonna mia, what a situation it was for him. I suggest that you pursue your dreams, both personal and artistic, but don't turn your back on your family, Anna. They are the constant in a turbulent world, they are your rock."

Inevitably Anna's time to leave came. She was excited over the prospect of seeing Grandpa Vittorio again, performing at La Scala and seeing Daniele. Not sure of herself in the affairs of her heart, she grew more confident in everything else. She was well-prepared for her role, and, thanks to her coach, she felt ready. She knew that the staging would be interesting, with innovations tucked here and there to give the scenes credibility.

She arrived in Milano on a Friday morning, and Grace Giordano was there to meet her with the limo and take her to her former hotel. She even had the same double room suite and was delighted. Home away from home, with the same paintings on the wall, and the familiar. She unpacked, showered, and wore a navy blue slack suit with her father's white shirt, and a long red scarf. Her hair had been straightened out in an expensive New York salon because she didn't like being "cutesy" any more.

She went to the theater in excited anticipation of seeing her grandfather at work. He had a vague idea of when she was coming and knew that she would come to the wardrobe department. She breezed in and saw that familiar head bowed in work with his pincer glasses on the edge of his nose. She wiped a tear from her eye. She walked quietly to his table, and he looked up and saw her, pulled her into his arms, and wept.

"My darling diva," he said, and it was a healing between them. He showed her what he was doing and discussed the innovative changes in costuming he worked out with Daniele. She heard her grandfather refer to Daniele in a manner which intimated that they had been working together. She was pleased.

"Go to him--he's in his office." Grandpa said. "We'll go out to dinner at 1:00. I asked him to join us but he said he didn't want to intrude on our time."

She recalled how incensed Poppa Santo had been over Daniele's unexpected appearance in Florence. And now her beloved Poppa Santo was out of her life for good. It had left a gaping hole in her life. Her grandfather was happy to see her, and at least that relationship wasn't severed. But Daniele? It was impossible to eradicate him from her mind, and trying made it worst. After climbing Mt. Everest, the little hill in the back yard was nothing.

She had to see him privately, this way there would be no masks between them. She went to his office on the next level, and saw people milling about the corridor, everyone going in and out, activity so intense that no one noticed her. For this, she was grateful. The door was ajar. She peered inside. He was working at his desk with sketches spread out before him. His wavy hair fell on his forehead as he studied and sketched away. He had lost weight. She stepped into his office and quietly shut the door behind her. He did not know that she was there. Sensing the presence of someone in his office, he put his pencil down, and turned around and faced her. For a moment, they were frozen, lost in each other's gaze. He stood up, and bowed, then looked into her eyes.

"Dio mio!" he exclaimed.

"You said you'd treat me like any stranger," she said softly.

"Did I? It was what you had to hear at the time. I didn't want you to avoid La Scala because of me." Encouraged by what he didn't say, she retorted, "are you really able to do that?"

"I gave my word, Anna. You know what I feel. Nothing is changed. There are no answers. Come here, I'm working on staging. Would you like to see the sketches?" She approached the desk, and leaned close to him. He slid off the tall stool and offered it to her. He bent over her and pointed to the set on paper. She slid her hand over his hand, brought it to her mouth, and kissed the palm of his hand. He cupped his mouth, trying to stifle his outburst of emotion. Without turning around, Anna said, "and how long are you going to torture us because of the sins of your father?" He wrapped his arms around her, and buried his face in her hair. "I won't have you turn your back on your parents. Dante's Inferno is filled with tortured souls who did. However, tell me what to do to become acceptable to them and I'll do it." Anna arose and faced him. "Daniele, my grandfather is the key. Have lunch with us today and we'll talk about it. I cannot go on like this. Headaches, nightmares, panic! Who said you can't die of heartbreak? I almost did."

He said he would meet with them, but he did not wish to infringe on them right now. Infused with hope for a life together, Daniele assured Anna that he would do anything to win over Maurizio and Gemma Brescia.

Anna and Grandpa Vittorio needed private time to catch up on family news. Daniele was right not to accept the invitation.

Grandpa Vittorio waited in the lobby for Anna, and out they went to lunch. Much was discussed, and Anna filled him in on her father's fragile nature, and how he was improving. She told him about the apartment and the expense of changing everything including furnishings. Her mother felt that a complete redecorating job would help Maurizio's state of mind. The kitchen where his mother used to be had to be changed: cabinets, floor and window treatment. Too many memories of their presence had to methodically be put to rest. Vittorio was not surprised. "He was always too attached to his mother, and I knew that if and when she died, he'd be on the precipice of a breakdown."

Anna then asked him about the quick emigration right after grandma's death. She told him that her father had been stunned by the fact that his passport had been issued long before Grandma's death. She asked for an explanation. What she heard surprised her greatly. People live in the same house, share meals, time and space together, and most of the time have no idea what's going on inside of each other's minds.

"Your grandmother and I lived apart."

Anna was puzzled. "She didn't want our son to stop needing her. She was a mother, not a wife. I was invisible to her. I sat at my desk in the living room like a statue, and escaped mentally through my work. She dusted me once as I sat on the chair. She didn't realize it was me." Anna started to laugh, yet stifled it when she realized how horrible that statement was.

"We shared a bed, only to sleep in. You're a big girl, I can tell you, I had someone on the side for years. She was a fellow worker at the Met. Unhappy with her husband, and I with my wife, we took a flat together, and met sometimes after work for our mutual needs. It went on for over ten years. I got in at 3:00 in the morning, always coming home, and like the time she dusted me as a statue, she never asked about why I was coming home that late. Our apartment was very large in the city, and your parents never knew. Maybe Maurizio suspected something, but we never spoke about it. Yes, I was planning to leave her. She wouldn't have missed me." Anna was wide eyed as the impact of his narrative shattered her childhood illusions. "My son is fragile because of her. She rendered him helpless, and no woman in the whole world could have put up with her like your mother did. Your mother is special, Anna. She is the kind of wife I would have worshipped. She never said word one against her mother-in-law.

You know, your grandmother held a grudge for a lifetime. She hated Jenny Liguori. When my son and your mother were having difficulty right before he left for America, she called the Liguori home and Jenny was rude to her. You know? She never forgave her for that rudeness. No one mattered except her son. I paid the bills therefore, I was necessary, otherwise, I was quite expendable." He caressed her hands, concerned that Anna was uncomfortable with the reality of his marriage.

"My son is like his mother. You notice he can't forgive? Why the hell do you have to put your life's choice of a mate in the garbage pail? Daniele did nothing to him. He loves you, and I can see how he has suffered for the crime of falling in love with you. Anna, listen to me. Save yourself from this emotional blackmail, assert yourself, your father can be swayed. You're no longer a child, so don't bend to his will." Her lip quivered. "Grandpa, we need your help. He won't marry me without my parents' approval. Can you believe that?"

Vittorio said that it didn't surprise him, and that he'd work on his son. He told Anna that Daniele was a prince among men. When he arrived and inquired about a position in the wardrobe department, he couldn't get it without a recommendation, "Daniele went to bat for me, I was hired. Yet, he never told me what he had done, and this is the Daniele D'Andrea I know. Now I head the department of improvements in costume design. Franceschi, Daniele's compare, included me in their dinners, it was democratic because people converged there from different classes in society. Daniele was in a class of his own. I didn't want to like him, but I did. He treated me with respect, and often asked my opinion. He kept his word to you to end the relationship. I've never seen such strength of character. Don't discount him." Anna was thrilled at her grandfather's appraisal.

"Anna, I didn't ask you to come stay with me because I've made an alliance. Once more with a woman in my own department. How else do we meet someone, if not through our work? I want you to meet her. She's forty years old, widowed, and her name is Gina. We enjoy everything together. Everything."

"No, I won't meet my grandmother's replacement. I won't be disloyal to her memory. I loved her too much. I don't censure you for your point of view, but it isn't mine. May I ask you to help me bring my father around? How do we deal with him?"

"Directly. Ask them to come to Milano early. Set up a private dinner with the four of you, and announce your marriage."

"Me? Or Daniele?" She truly needed to orchestrate the protocol of this momentous important occasion.

"We're Italian. Let Daniele start. I'd begin rehearsal as soon as possible." he was thrilled that his granddaughter had turned to him for help. Vittorio's sense of self grew, because of Daniele D'Andrea's attention, and now Anna's request for help. "Grandpa, I never knew who you were." He sighed with resignation "Neither did I. I had to find myself, but once a long time ago, I fell madly in love with your grandmother, and then she forgot her role as wife, and was absorbed totally in her role as a mother. Don't allow this to happen in your marriage, put Daniele first before your children if you want him to stay in your life." They parted, and the truth melted the walls of uncertainty between them.

Anna called her parents. It was midnight in New York. She didn't wake them up because her parents were nocturnal anyway. She spoke to her mother then her father.

"Daddy, all is well. Your father has a beautiful life here. I want you and Momma to come before I do my first performance. We have a lot to discuss." Immediately Maurizio knew. "I'll make arrangements, I'm anxious to see my father, and you, are you alright?"

"NOW I am," she said meaningfully. His eyebrows arched up.

"Take care of yourself. I love you, Anna."

"Daddy, I love you, too. Is the kitchen finished?"

"I've been cooking. Does that tell you anything? Your mother is my angel, the best!" he added. "Daddy, change is good, that's how we grow."

"Yes, see you soon." He felt a sense of resignation as he hung up.

"Gemma, we have to face the inevitable," he said.

"Maurizio, they love each other, how can we deny our only child?"

"Gemma, it's so damned hard, but I'll need your help, okay?" She put her arms around him, "all I want you to do is to try."

* * *

Daniele and Anna met at 7:00. They were so light-hearted, one would never know the dark cloud under which they had been living. They went to a trattoria in a narrow street. Of course, as the handsome couple walked in, all eyes turned to look. They were a striking contrast, she dark-skinned with jet black hair, and he light, with electric blue eyes, and wavy blonde hair sprinkled with increasing whiteness. They sat at a table by the window, ordered a light dinner, and Anna filled him in on her talk with her grandfather.

After dinner, they went back to the hotel. Anna fell asleep, and Daniele lay in bed pondering the wondrous events of the past few weeks. What amazed him was that all the forces of destiny were racing to one end, to give him the miracle he had asked for. Vittorio's move to Milano had been a tremendous catalyst for Anna's return. Another great miracle was Anna's life threatening headaches which finally stopped, proof that she had suffered greatly over the breakup. With Vittorio Brescia in his corner, Daniele's sense of anticipation for a positive outcome grew stronger. In the morning, Daniele watched her sleep and extricated himself from her body to shower. She felt the place next to hers and he was gone. She slid out of bed, and went to the bathroom.

"Daniele?" she called gently, and he shut off the water. "I thought you left me." "My darling, it is you who leave me." Anna giggled, "Daniele isn't what we're doing a bit rushed? We don't even know each other." Daniele suddenly frowned and thought, "a man and a woman marry, they think they know each other, but the man doesn't even know himself, and the woman, caught up in the euphoric state of romance, doesn't know herself either. Last year you left with a ring on your finger, large, for the world to see that you belonged to me. You left, and I bet once you got home, you had forgotten me already."

She seemed not to have heard him, and he decided not to repeat himself. As Anna went to bed, she pondered on love, and knew that it was a difficult union for two strangers to sign their lives away with promises they knew they could never keep.

Chapter Twenty-Seven
THE FINAL CADENCE

Maurizio and Gemma left New York with a mindset of nothingness. Gemma tried to engage her husband in speculation over what the situation would be like, and he asked her to be quiet. He had too much to sort out, and he lay back, held her hand, his lifeline, and delved into the past. His childhood in Milano as a son to an Italian family had had no fault. Whatever he needed or wanted, his mother had anticipated even before he articulated it. Music had been in the home. Vittorio had adored the opera, and recordings and arias were going on all the time. His occasional perfunctory remarks were forever recorded by his son. "God visits this earth now and then, and he chooses those who create, a Verdi, a Mascagni, a Bellini and like Him, they make this earthly existence just a little better." At ten years old, Maurizio's birthday gift had been an oboe with private lessons. He'd studied faithfully, and learned about all those who "were chosen to create." He'd adored his father.

His mother had lived for her family. She'd made her daily treks to the market to buy fresh fruit and vegetables daily. Vittorio had been the king of the home, she, the doting queen. Contention had not cropped up often, and when it had, the voices never grew to unbearable crescendos.

Since Italian boys did not experience the difficult teen age years syndrome by tearing away from parents and authority, Daniele had never quite left the cocoon of his nest. His relationship with the two people who were closest to God, his parents, had grown only closer.

The La Scala trauma in his later years had been treated intelligently by his mother in particular. It was she who had suggested emigrating to America to try there for a career in an operatic orchestra. His father had applauded the move, for more than the musical reason. Vittorio had been devastated over the breakup of Gemma and Maurizio, and he believed that his wife's insensitivity to Gemma had given Maurizio the false belief that Gemma would always be there for him. The stage had been set for the breakup of a loving eight year relationship between the lovers.

In America, after Vittorio and Anna had emigrated, they'd watched young women one after another break up with their handsome, successful son. "A momma's boy" was the prevailing criticism.

Maurizio had known his father's feelings, for when his mother hadn't been around, Vittorio would verbalize them, carefully, easily placing his comments in passing, "soto voce"—softly.

Then, as though there was divine intervention, Gemma had popped up in New York with their grandchild. Life had been good and beautiful for the Brescias after Gemma moved in with their baby and her mother.

What followed had been the reminder of the crossroad of Maurizio's life: Santo Averso! A quirk of fate had played yet another cruel joke on Maurizio. His beautiful only daughter had fallen in love with the son of the "snake," Donato D'Andrea.

Maurizio mulled it all in his mind. After his mother died, he had been dealt yet another blow: the revelation that his father had in recent years, not been present in the marriage to his mother. This was up there with the Averso betrayal. Anguish and pain had then followed when, after Anna complied with his wishes to break up with D'Andrea, she'd been beset by horrific headaches. The fear of losing her had been very real indeed for it had been similar to his mother's symptoms.

Now he sat on a plane to Milano with his beloved Gemma. He had to bend and give them permission to join in a life together. He knew nothing about Daniele. It was time to find out. It was time to take a good look. It wasn't going to be easy given his self-indulgence all his life. Now he had to put Maurizio Brescia aside and help his child in the most meaningful way, which was to bless her choice of a life's companion. Often, Maurizio talked to his mother's spirit, and he was comforted by hearing her voice in his mind. She was definitely telling him to change his heart. Without Gemma by his side, none of this could have been possible. There was no training in his whole life. Everything centered on him. The ball of decision was in his hand, and he had to step up to the plate and play.

They arrived in Milano, and Anna, Daniele and his father met the airplane. Maurizio tensed up, "Corragio, amore mio," Gemma whispered.

Anna anticipated resistance, Daniele was very apprehensive, and Vittorio: resolve. After they drove through the roads to the hotel near La Scala in a room on the same floor as their daughter's, they rested, and made a date to meet that night. The plan was for Maurizio and Daniele to meet in Anna's two room suite and talk privately. However, Vittorio had to speak to his son first. Vittorio minced no words as he spoke in great detail over the noble elegant soul of Daniele D'Andrea.

Maurizio listened and softened his preconceived notion of D'Andrea, as his father's portrait of a man he disdained, was painted through his father's verbal palate.

"Soften your heart, son. When I joined the company, I resisted all contact with D'Andrea, but I've gotten to know Daniele. He is a noble soul. After he found out his father's duplicity, he honored Anna's decision to break up. He never mentioned her again. He lost weight, and grew quiet, a shadow of what he used to be. He kept his word to stay away from her even though it was killing him. There, my son is a nobility of spirit not common these days. I speak objectively. He's perfect for Anna, heaven forbid if her choice had been another singer, but Daniele is a stage director, and not in competition with her career. It's perfect. Don't condemn him for his father's sins."

"Why didn't you tell me?" Maurizio asked.

"I couldn't. The timing wasn't right. They were apart, I could not intervene in your daughter's life, but when she came back their love was rekindled. That's when I decided to step in. Remember your struggles over Gemma? Put yourself in Daniele's shoes." Maurizio was softening up, his father's testimonial was very persuasive on every level, particularly Anna's operatic career. Rather than interference, there'd be support, and with her safely married, it might discourage some predators in the operatic world.

"He's a stranger whom I know only through your eyes."

"Let's go." Vittorio said anxiously, "I can imagine how nervous the young man is."

Vittorio and Maurizio walked in. Maurizio was uncomfortable, as though if there were any where else he'd want to be, it wouldn't be here. On the other hand, Vittorio was resolute, and felt quite confident about a favorable outcome. His input was the only barometer Maurizio had, putting Vittorio in a position of power.

As they joined the women, Maurizio approached Daniele.

"Signor D'Andrea, we need to talk." They went upstairs to the hotel room, Maurizio unlocked the door. In front of the windows facing the piazza was a small round table with a bottle of acqua minerale, and two glasses, and a small bouquet of flowers. Vittorio, had skillfully set the stage for an intimate talk.

"Signor Brescia," Daniele began. "I'm honored that you came to Milano."

"I came for a different kind of performance." Maurizio said, and Daniele smarted at the caustic comment. His task was difficult. He had to disarm Maurizio's antagonism.

"Sir, I am not my father. What happened was impromptu, none of it was staged. Even before I met her, I fell in love with her and I fought it. From our first encounter, we became adversaries. I was unrelenting, and unnecessarily critical, but the Diva in her did not back down. She gave me the best performance of her life. I grew to love her. I pursued her. Our courtship lasted only a few days, and then she had to leave, I proposed, she accepted and I bought her an ostentatious ring to let the world know that she was spoken for. I want your blessing." Maurizio chuckled, "not my permission?" Daniele looked at him straight in the eyes, "your blessing, sir."

Daniele stood up. He extended his hand for Maurizio, who took it and gripped it, sealing his approval. Together, they had one mind, which was to go to the bathroom, as they turned, Maurizio bumped into Daniele who got off balance and almost fell, Maurizio caught him, and they laughed. Suddenly the tension dissipated. "Sir," Daniele said stepping back, "seniority first" and Maurizio, said, "is your need greater than mine?" Daniele shrugged, "I just wanted to wash the sweat off my face." The encounter relieved the tensions.

Maurizio had more to say, about his daughter Anna. Daniele listened intently and realized what a close family they were. Talented, beautiful, and loving. He smiled warmly and said "I'd be honored to be part of your spectacular family," Maurizio noticed Daniele's apprehension, "I think that's possible." he said as they left the hotel room to join the rest of the family.

* * *

As they stepped into the elevator, Maurizio said that a wedding could be planned for next year, but Daniele said, "no sir, with all due respect, I don't trust fate. My preference sir, is that we marry before she leaves Milano."

"And? If my daughter needs more time?" Maurizio could feel Daniele's anxiety return.

"But I won't like it," Daniele said.

"I understand that," Maurizio said and he smiled at the tenacity of this young man. He had to have been a good colonel during the war, persistent. Had Maurizio had such fervor with Gemma, none of his anguish would have happened.

"One more thing, Daniele, drop the sir and call me Maurizio."

As they came out of the elevator, Anna was pleased, her father seemed sanguine enough.. She ran to her father and put her arms around him.

"Thank you Daddy. He loves me AND he's a genius. You'll see. You'll grow to love him as Grandpa has." Gemma kissed the future bride and groom, and blessed them.

Maurizio found out about Daniele's genius when Anna appeared at La Scala in La Sonnambula. Daniele had worked diligently to make the sleep-walking scene natural. He always felt that the sleep-walker extending her hands made her look as though she was afraid to bump into the stage sets and he wanted more "verismo" in the part.

He worked with Anna, and they rehearsed it, and it was never quite right, but when she saw his frustration, she made an extreme effort to give him exactly what he wanted. It had to be realistic.

The night of the performance, Daniele sat in the box with her parents. The difficult scene began, and as she walked, in her white flowing nightgown, her hair cascading around her face, she moved so that she would bump into the props rather than avoid them. The audience was mesmerized. It was brilliant. As she did, a sharp object ripped her arm, and it bled. Anna didn't react. She remained in the "sleep state" as blood oozed on her arm, and her nightgown. The audience gasped audibly, and watched the blood stained figure eerily moving across the stage. Daniele was terrified. How badly was she hurt? He wanted to run backstage, but he would be blocked. Suddenly he realized that she was okay and that she'd taken the accident skillfully and made it work FOR her. He stood up in the back of the box and watched. What a consummate actress she was! At the end of the opera, the audience went crazy. Standing ovation, tears, screams of mixed calls, "Brava la Diva" "Brava l'Americana!" shouted down by "Brava La Milanese."

There was a definite hysteria in the theater that night. The Brescias were frightened as they saw blood literally pour down her nightgown, but because she didn't react, they weren't sure if this was part of the act. They turned to look at Daniele face and saw his obvious distress. Gemma whispered to her husband, and he put his hand over his mouth, to stifle his emotions. He stood up, and grabbed Daniele, "what is going on?" Daniele said, "an accident, Maurizio, there's a doctor backstage, calm down." Maurizio reassured his wife that it was all under control.

After the performance, the family went backstage, where they were deeply moved by Anna's triumphant success and courage. Maurizio and Gemma were shaking with concern and awe of their daughter.

Maurizio recalled to Daniele, "at five years old, she told me she was an opera singer, and I laughed, she meant it." Daniele was filled with powerful emotions.

"You two are a pair," Maurizio said quietly to Daniele.

"Thank you, Signor Brescia. She is superb. She makes me look good." Maurizio impulsively put his arms around Daniele, and said, "That's because you ARE good." Daniele was pleased at the affirmation, especially from a man who had given him a qualified acceptance into the family.

Gemma looked deeply concerned over the wound which was still oozing blood through the bandage. The doctor rushed in and told them that the ambulance had arrived. Anna needed stitches. They waited in the corridor, while the dressers helped get her out of costume. As they left the theater, avid fans waited outside and applauded as she was carried out to the ambulance. Daniele's driver, Roccio, who had also been summoned, waited to transport the family to the hospital. Anna had 12 stitches in her arm, and though it pained her, she managed to smile at her family who looked as though they were ready to pass out.

"Are you alright, Anna?" Maurizio asked.

"Yes Daddy, take care of Momma. Get her some juice before she passes out." Daniele kissed her forehead and whispered, "I've never seen anything like it in my life, this was a first." She whispered back, "and so you got the verisma you wanted, if I wasn't hurting so, I might have laughed at the irony." Daniele whispered "mia culpa, my love, I'll never ask for a realistic scene from you again."

"What did my parents do?" she asked.

"They thought I staged it, but when they looked at me, I was biting my hand in horror; your mother crumbled in your father's arms. It was, a moment in theater. I, for one, shall never forget it."

After the hospital, Anna returned to the hotel by limo. People were still milling in the piazza, discussing that opera history was made that evening, and that La Diva gave the performance of her life.

Finally they went back upstairs to Anna's suite. Gemma motioned her husband and father in law to come into the bedroom so that Anna and Daniele could be alone. Vittorio sat at the foot of the bed as Maurizio stood before him.

"So, my son, what do you think now?" Vittorio asked.

"My God, they compliment each other. I saw how upset he was," Maurizio said, "that accident, she didn't even react. Her hands were bloody, and yet she walked as though she felt nothing. She was superb! I shall never forget it." Maurizio marveled at the scene which caught the attention of the international operatic world.

"Neither shall Milano!" Vittorio chuckled, "and that's what makes a diva!" he said proudly.

The next day, the newspapers equated Anna Brescia's bravery to a soldier in action. The incident made headlines. It also dredged up other accidents and mishaps on stage which had occurred in the past, and in which singers utilized the mishaps as part of their act. La Scala's critical audience was on its knees to the Diva. It would not be forgotten.

Chapter Twenty-Eight
FINALI

After the first performance, Maurizio had to get back to New York. Daniele ingratiated himself to Maurizio, imploring the Brescias to reconsider giving him permission to marry Anna as soon as possible. After Gemma and Maurizio talked, they agreed to an early wedding. Since Maurizio couldn't stay because of his commitments in New York, Gemma remained for the next three performances and the wedding.

The brief ceremony at the church where Gemma used to attend Mass was attended by Franco and Francescha, as maid of honor and best man, and other members of their close musical circle.

Anna wore an ivory lace dress, and her black hair was swept back in a chignon. She wore a mushroom hat on her head, and all of her accessories, including flowers, were in lavender. She looked incredible. Grandpa Vittorio gave her away.

Dinner was at Santo's former restaurant at the piazza La Scala.

Friends, ecstatic over having been included in this rushed wedding, were enthralled that finally Daniele married his "Juliet." The music was provided by a string quartet from the orchestra, the restaurant was closed off, and festivities continued in music, song, arias, operatic spoofs, and stories at the microphone, which sent everyone into gales of laughter. The wine flowed, and the so called impromptu wedding reception lasted for 8 hours.

Newspapers covered the romantic event with stories of their romance, continuing the saga of the operatic couple's Cinderella story. Anna and Daniele promised to pose for photographs, and after the reception, they were allowed in the restaurant for the shoot. The human interest story was a source of delight to the Italian populace, whose love of romantic news was insatiable.

The next day, the happy bride and groom were driven to Lugano by Daniele's driver, Roccio. There they began their new life as husband and wife. They were recognized all over, and treated like Italian royalty by restauranteurs. Certainly many photographs had appeared in the past few months. Anna enjoyed the attention and explained to her husband that adulation of operatic personalities was indigent only to Italy. Daniele was proud of his beautiful wife. Every moment was precious to them, for the road to this marriage had certainly been fraught with incredible obstacles.

Anna filled her husband in on her parents' love story, after which he remarked, "it was destiny. My God tesoro, our struggles were parallel." That commonality was the impetus which touched Maurizio and Gemma, giving the young couple permission for an early marriage.

* * *

Anna kept something from her parents. She confided in Daniele that they would go nuts if they knew about their plans for a family.

"Why? We're both single children, and when our families die we'll be alone. If we hadn't married, it would be a lonely life."

"Daniele, I'm a diva, yet I have desired a family for a long time, but honestly I thought that I was not entitled to the life of ordinary people." He reassured her that there were other female singers who had families.

"Daniele, remember after our engagement? I asked you how many children you wanted, and you held up five fingers. Do you seriously feel like that?" She sat up and looked into his blue eyes, and he nodded yes.

"Can you imagine life without children? My godson Michael Angelo would be the only baby in my life, and you? Adamo! No, I defer to you as to how many, but I guarantee you that we shall have all the help you need. You need not lift a finger. You'll have baby nurses, cook, housekeeper, and all you have to do is to be their mother, and to sing to them."

She told him that she couldn't cook at all, and had no clue as to when to put the pasta in the pot, AND had no desire to learn—and didn't know one lullaby, "except Brahms, when I practiced piano." Then added, "after all what queen gives up her queendom?" He laughed at her exaggerated appraisal.

Daniele assured her highness that he was a good chef. His mother had always welcomed him into her kitchen.When Anna and Daniele returned to the states, she was to remain in New York to meet her contractual obligations, and he had to leave in two weeks for his in Milan. Maurizio asked them to live with them in the large apartment and Daniele had no quarrel at all, because he knew that when he wasn't at home with her, she'd have family around her. It was a comfort to him. In an Italian family ethic, this happened more than not. The apartment had a separate three-room wing to the left of the kitchen and the right wing was the Brescias.

A week before Daniele returned to Milano, Kay called Anna and Gemma. She told them that Santo was terminal, and that he'd be dead in a few days, though it was sheer will power that kept him alive. He begged for Kay to call them to his bedside so that he could make his peace.

Maurizio, whose singular bombastic fuse could blow up at the mention of Santo Averso, hit a couple of high notes with his answer. Shouldn't he be grateful to the God who has permitted them to live full, fabulous and productive lives? He could not say no to his wife. She had never asked him to change his mind before, but this time she was adamant.

The two couples went. It was terrible to see how black and emaciated the body of Santo Averso had become. He was unrecognizable. He spoke briefly to Maurizio, asking for his forgiveness and telling him that he was a great oboe player. He begged Gemma for her forgiveness, "for my greatest sin was to love you," and she wept and held his bony cold hand. Anna evoked more tears in his eyes, but he said, "and you? never was a child loved as much as I loved you, even though my blood did not flow in your veins. I am leaving you half my fortune. You will need it, and Anna, I beg you, don't have one child. I hated being an only child. Surround yourself with children and enjoy the greatest role in the world, that of motherhood." She wept and held up her five fingers. Santo looked at Daniele, questioning her projected family, and Daniele smiled and said, "yes, with the grace of God."

Each made his peace, and as they filed out of the bedroom, Santo beckoned to Kay to call back Daniele. With difficulty, Santo spoke:

"I wanted to kill you in Firenze, but I knew that you would make my queen the best companion in life. I prayed for that. Forgive me for wanting to kill you." His prayer was almost child-like and Daniele had mixed emotion. "I knew that, Santo. Go in peace!" He made the sign of the cross on his forehead and heard him expire. Daniele was the last one to see Santo alive. He shut his visionless eyelids, and took his pulse--which was gone.

The wake was one day long and the funeral occurred the following day. After the burial, Kay gave up her apartment at the Ansonia. She sold everything, and moved back to Tarrytown New York, to resume her life as a teacher in the Ossining schools.

The Brescias kept in touch with Kay because she had become an extended family for them, particularly for Anna. They had grown close over the years, and no one wanted her out of their lives.

Two days before Daniele left, Anna invited the Mulligans, their offspring, the Simons, Chet, Carli, Chet's parents, the Cascios and Adamo to eat out. They went to Moon's restaurant. There they had their American wedding reception, and Moon made sure that he hired a classical trio. The surprise for Anna was Chet, Al and George. The classical Bridge. She screeched with delight when she saw Al and George. Chet was acting nonchalant until Moon made the announcement.

Daniele sensed immediately that something still flowed between his bride and the jazz musician. He resented it when Al kissed her on the mouth, held her and wouldn't let her go until Moon gave the high sign to get ready to play.

It was a wonderful wedding reception, unusual, though, because the bride and groom resided 3000 miles away from each other.

The years were kind to this next generation of immigrants and their offspring. Daniele continued to cross the ocean for his work, and finally he was able to get more work stateside, and he came to live with his family and his mother. Anna insisted that Elena come live with them.

There was a mutual like and love between the women, and Elena felt as though she had been reborn, for the life of her son and daughter-in-law was like nothing she'd ever known. Music, joy, activities, endless activities especially with the boys and their sports world. Elena D'Andrea loved being on the merry-go-round of their lives. She wouldn't come to America until her husband had passed away. When she did come, she was sad to say goodbye to a life which she had deemed a good life with a good man. A dissipated life all because of one act of infamy. She wept some times with the memories of the happy beginnings they once had. Daniele was her whole life, and now, with Anna and the boys, she was always laughing and sharing something with one or the other.

The babies came, and with each one, came an additional nurse. Daniele had promised Anna she would always be the Diva, the Queen and the only wife in the world who couldn't boil water. She was, after all, so proud of that. She mentioned it frequently in magazine interviews. Nobody believed it of course, because she was Italian. This amused Anna, for she contended that people believed what they wanted.

When Santo Averso's will was probated, Anna came into several hundred thousand dollars. Since Charlie Cascio became a favorite with the Brescias, he offered Daniele some advice. "Real estate! Everything you could buy." He took Daniele and Anna to Staten Island, and they saw a mansion, which had close to 20 rooms in it, overlooking the greater part of Staten Island in Todt Hill. She loved it. The expanse of land was stunning, and Daniele, used to crowded city living, felt he needed space with the growing family. He bought it, and then together with his father-in-law continued to buy homes, refurbish them, rent them, sell them, and soon he became a real estate pro.

After the house was ready, the family took the trip to Todt Hill with two rented limousines. The Brescias, the Cascios and the D'Andrea's lined up the children in their expensive suits and marched to the elevator for the trip to their new home. Vittorio was 7 years old; Luigi was 6 years old, Maurizio was 5 years old, Franco, 4 years old, and baby Donato was 2 years old. Ironically, he was Maurizio's favorite grandson, because he was the only one who loved to hear him play the oboe. The other boys held their hands to their ears. They hated the sound.

The house was marvelous. It had marble floors in the dining room, and a huge kitchen. Charlie and Maria had given them a gift of a

24-foot marble table, which had to be assembled in the dining room. The house had eight bedrooms plus two guest rooms for family and friends. Five bathrooms sometimes were not even enough, and Charlie suggested they put up an outhouse as an alternative. Of course, Anna screamed with delight when he suggested it. There was a wonderful dynamic among them. They LIKED each other. They truly CARED about who and what the other person was about.

To be invited to the D'Andreas was to be admitted into their family.

The families gathered at Todt Hill for every Christian holiday, including Kay Semenci Averso, or as, Anna referred to her, "The Countess." Elena D'Andrea always sat at the head of the table because of her wheelchair. The Mulligans, Senator Tom Porter, and his wife Katy Cascio Porter, the O'Leary's were included at every holiday gathering. Daniele enjoyed the company of Brian Mulligan as well as the gentle Senator Tom Porter. These three men came from different worlds and traditions, but their bond was a deep abiding love and respect for the women they had married. Coupled with that, was the closeness they enjoyed with their in-laws. In fact, Charlie Cascio teased Maurizio about loving Daniele as a son, and Maurizio retorted, "I swear to you, Charlie, I didn't want to love this man, but how can one find fault with such a good soul?"

Daniele had found gold in every department of his life. His sons were magnificent. Though he had wished for a daughter, Anna put her hand up and said, "Basta!"—Enough--"My body is tired." Especially when Donato ended up being a boy.

The boys were tall and slender. The older four's total proclivity was to sports. Eventually they worked professionally in sports, especially basketball. The baby, Donato, fair haired, blue eyes and cherubic mouth, loved music, and at age 4, learned how to play two instruments, the recorder and the piano. Both Gemma and Maurizio doted on this one.

Daniele gave free reign to his sons in terms of choices. Always though, he taught them that with freedom came responsibility. He taught them without lecturing how to love and respect a woman. His motto: "if you love your children, then love their mother." This philosophy stood them well, for indeed they grew up to be wonderful sons and husbands to the women who were blessed to be in their lives.

One holiday, Anna called Al and asked him to bring his twin daughters and wife to an Easter Sunday dinner. He immediately accepted, but Concetta refused the invitation. She told him to go by himself, and he did. They had a wonderful holiday, and Anna and Al talked incessantly, laughed and enjoyed each other's company. Daniele wasn't pleased, but he would never stand in the way of anything she wanted, for then, he would create a climate for intrigue and lies. At least the flirting took place right before his eyes. Maurizio and Gemma were also very uncomfortable with Al's obvious affection for Anna.

He'd rather feel the twinge of jealousy, rather than not allow her to embrace her old friends and lovers.

"So, here you are," Al said as they walked in the garden after dinner, arms around each other's waist, "acting like the dowager Queen surrounded by your loved ones, and being waited on hand and foot. Damn, Anna! The guy even gets up to pour your juice. You know if you were married to me, you wouldn't have gotten away with that shit!" She burst out laughing at how glib his use of vulgarity was.

"Anna, seriously" he nuzzled her neck and kissed her, "is the entity still king?" he asked. She squirmed away, concerned that they might be seen, "not queen?" she teased.

"Is my friggin Sicilian blood showing?" She laughed. "In answer to your question, yes. My husband and I both bow to the muse of music and the opera. It's the way it is." She gave him a side glance to see his reaction, and, of course, once again, his answer was outrageous:

"Damn! I wish you had regrets. I miss the smell of you. He kissed her on the cheek then whispered, "You know, you were a lousy dancer." Anna giggled--he always had a turn with a phrase.

"I tried to tell you. Why did you ask me to dance at Carli's wedding?"

"I wanted you and I still do," he said seriously as they faced each other in the apple grove.

"We were beautiful, Al," she said softly.

"Too bad I couldn't live with your entity. I think about it every day. I got this wonderful Sicilian wife, so why the hell do I still think of you?" She pushed him away in her best stage manner, and responded, "because I'm a diva, and you can't get me out of your mind."...He grabbed her and pulled her behind the fig tree, and kissed her, she kissed him back--then pushed him away, "Oh God, Al, we'd better not. This is wrong." She found it difficult to push him away.

"Is it? You're the best thing that ever happened to me. I can't turn it off like a faucet," he said with child-like candor.

"I know," she whispered.

She thought of endings, lots of them, and this one in particular. They walked back to the house, not touching each other for they'd been aroused by the contact. The dinner party was over, and Al was the first to leave with his girls. He thanked Daniele for his graciousness. He liked the guy a lot. The man was a class act. "I loved Anna," Al said as he shook Daniele's hand. "I know that," Daniele answered.

"Glad we met. You're perfect for her." Al said, "I know," Daniele answered.

Later, as Daniele kissed Anna goodnight, he asked, "Did you enjoy your friend?"

"Mm," she murmured. As the years went by, there were so many endings. One day her ability to sing would end and she wouldn't be a diva. She thought of who she would be, and then she felt her husband's hand on her thigh, "My beautiful wife," he whispered, and she knew.

Printed in the United States
48730LVS00004B/19